THE LOST DEPOSITION OF GLYNNIS SMITH McLEAN

Second-Class Survivor
of the RMS *Titanic*

THE LOST DEPOSITION OF GLYNNIS SMITH McLEAN

Second-Class Survivor of the RMS *Titanic*

A Historical Novel

Scott Stevens

iUniverse

THE LOST DEPOSITION OF GLYNNIS SMITH McLEAN
SECOND-CLASS SURVIVOR OF THE RMS *TITANIC*
A HISTORICAL NOVEL

iUniverse books may be ordered through booksellers or by contacting:

iUniverse
1663 Liberty Drive
Bloomington, IN 47403
www.iuniverse.com
1-800-Authors (1-800-288-4677)

ISBN: 978-1-4917-8256-9 (sc)
ISBN: 978-1-4917-8255-2 (e)

Library of Congress Control Number: 2015919836

Print information available on the last page.

iUniverse rev. date: 01/30/2016

To my family—Valerie, Alyssa, and Amy—and to the Valiant Cate (Vanessa) who got me started.

INTRODUCTION

From March 31, 1909—the day the keel was laid down for the construction of what would be the largest, most opulent ship to steam across the North Atlantic between Great Britain and North America until April 15, 1912, the day when those frigid waters closed over the spot where that ship disappeared on her maiden voyage—many lives were on a collision course with the iceberg calved months earlier from a glacier in Greenland and set to strike a glancing blow to that ship. So many lives—more than 1,500—foundered with the ship that night.

Hopes and dreams torn asunder.

No plans were kept.

And no life was ever the same again.

Sunday, April 15, 1962. Fifty years to the day from when the frigid North Atlantic waters closed over the stern plates of the White Star Line RMS *Titanic*. A good many survivors of the sinking had been tracked down and interviewed for the fiftieth-anniversary commemorative editions of the numerous magazines and newspapers being made ready for publication and focusing on this day. All were asked their stories—their recollections—of this night in 1912 when their worlds came apart.

Many recalled (again, for many had previously been interviewed by author and historian Walter Lord before 1955 for his book *A Night to Remember*) what it felt like when the ship first brushed the iceberg:

"Barely felt it."

"Grinding jar."

"Like rolling over a thousand marbles."

As well as what they were doing at the moment of impact:

"Sleeping."

"Reading."

"Smoking."

And their reactions to the first call to the lifeboats:

"Didn't believe the ship could sink."

"Didn't want to leave the ship and take to the sea in an open lifeboat."

"Didn't want to leave husband."

"Father."

"Son."

Their responses to the news of the sinking:

Initial calm at the news—and denial.

Then as time went on, there came a realization of the seriousness of the situation:

Confusion, then panic.

Tales were told of heroism and of shame.

Of gallantry and of cowardice.

Some of the stories were exciting. For instance, Ruth Blanchard (Becker) told of how she'd almost been left behind without the rest of her family; her mother and two younger siblings had boarded Boat 11, and twelve-year-old Ruth had been fortunate enough to get into Boat 13 just a few seconds later. Her mother didn't know she was alive until they were reunited on the rescue ship almost nine hours after the sinking.

Second wireless operator Harold Bride, aged twenty-two, spoke of how he'd been briefly trapped under overturned Collapsible B and how he'd later stood on the keel of that boat with more than twenty other men under the charge of thirty-eight-year-old Second Officer Charles Lightoller, senior surviving officer from the ship, for an hour and a half until they were taken off by Boats 12 and 4 with the rockets from the rescue ship just in sight.

Baker (Chief) Charles Joughin recalled how he'd thrown at least fifty deck chairs from the doomed liner into the water and then walked on the *side* of the dangerously listing ship as her stern rose high preparatory to taking her fateful plunge. His amazing equilibrium was in spite of inebriation caused by the brandy he had consumed in the brief time between the collision and the sinking, preventing him from stumbling and falling overboard. He'd then stood on the very stern plates of the ship as it went down and treaded water for over an hour alongside Collapsible B, never once getting his hair wet or even seeming to be affected by the freezing water.

The British film *A Night to Remember* (based on Mr. Lord's extraordinary book) had come out in 1958, four years before the publications of these commemorative Sunday editions. Although altered for the sake of cinematic drama, it was a fairly accurate representation of the last hours of the legendary passenger liner and the events leading up to the disaster. Surviving Fourth Officer Joseph Boxhall, now a retired commodore, was hired as technical advisor for the film to aid in accurately portraying the events of the voyage and its climax.

And the interest escalated from there. Throughout the years since the liner's sinking off the Grand Banks of Newfoundland, many stories, articles, and books were written. One of the earliest was by first-class passenger Colonel Archibald Gracie.

He published an article in the *Outlook* magazine on April 27, 1912. His book, *The Truth about the* Titanic, was written that summer, submitted for publication shortly before his death in November 1912, and published the following year.

Even fifty years later, interest hadn't slackened; if anything, it was increasing. Obituaries worldwide would make note of the passing of any survivor of the sinking; on occasion, this would be front-page news.

Grand schemes to raise the liner were considered almost from the moment her bow touched bottom more than two miles down. Legends were heard of treasure in the cargo holds, staterooms, and purser's safes waiting to be salvaged. Eyewitnesses offered conflicting reports regarding the ship's condition as it went down. Had it gone down intact? Did it break up—or *blow* up—when the water reached her boilers? Or did it split in half as some survivors adamantly insisted they'd witnessed?

Despite the technical questions, the plans for salvage, and the few mementos, and brushing the what-ifs and educated guesses aside, the stories of the disaster and its human tragedy always stirred the heart. Of the 705 people saved, a large percentage were first-class passengers—and too many of the total were men and crew members. Lifeboats were not filled to capacity; one of them lowered with only twelve people in it though it had a capacity of forty.

Even more startling, while the *Titanic* carried more than enough boats to satisfy the British Board of Trade regulations, she still could not carry even half the ship's rated passenger and crew load. There was room for fewer than 1,200 people in the twenty boats (four boats more than regulations of the time called for), yet the *Titanic* could have carried nearly three thousand persons—passengers and crew combined.

There were better than 2,200 on board when the *Titanic* departed Queenstown (now Cobh), Ireland, sailing out of sight and into history. The stated claim was that the *Titanic* was intended to be its own lifeboat. Fifteen "watertight" bulkheads lay transverse from port to starboard (left to right) and gave the ship sixteen "watertight" compartments that would, in theory, allow the ship, sinking though it *may* be, enough time afloat with a negligible list to either side and/or bow to stern to enable rescue by all nearby responders. This claim gave rise to the illusion that *Titanic* was "unsinkable."

The loss of loved ones. Families parted forever. Many of the third-class passengers unable (for whatever reason) to reach the boat deck until *after* all the boats were lowered. Many women and children lost (most of them those same third-class souls).

Lives changed forever.

The April 10, 1962, edition of the *Los Angeles Evening Herald-Examiner* mentioned an exclusive new piece of information that would be published five days hence: the discovery of testimony intended for—*but not found among*—the transcripts of the Senate inquiry, given by a passenger whose name appeared only on the first, incomplete, list sent by wireless from the rescue ship, RMS *Carpathia*, and relayed to New York with help from the more powerful set on the RMS *Olympic* (the nearly identical older sister ship to the *Titanic*) on April 16 and not repeated anywhere.

Within hours of the moment the rescue ship docked on the night of April 18, the inquiry had begun in New York. It later moved to Washington, DC—with some statements taken wherever the witnesses could be found and others as sworn affidavits—and concluded just days before being presented to the full Senate on May 28, 1912.

Transcripts of the inquiry would become publically available after 1918.

This testimony had been given near the end of May (on the twenty-fourth), the day before the chairman of the inquiry boarded the RMS *Olympic* to question her captain and her wireless officer and to reinterview one of the firemen who'd survived the disaster and was now assigned a berth on the older sister ship. That would also be the last day testimony was gathered prior to compiling and submitting the final report to the Senate. It consisted of its chairman (Michigan senator William Alden Smith), his longtime stenographer (Mrs. Mary Altford), and the aforementioned passenger, and was given in her hotel suite in New York rather than in Washington, DC, before the full board. This testimony was never added to the records of the inquiry, and there was no mention of its existence in the extensive catalog of notes and evidence. There was just a cryptic entry in the senator's personal journal regarding his final intentions before returning to Washington from New York near the end of May. For years, it had been taken by historians to be in reference to the aforementioned visit to *Olympic*.

The testimony belatedly presented to the world through the *Herald*'s publication on this golden anniversary was more of an interview than a deposition, though the senator asked many of the same questions throughout the narrative as he had during the official inquiries held over the course of the previous five weeks. This informal atmosphere resulted in a more relaxed environment than that for the testimonies given by earlier witnesses.

As the senator was nearing completion of the inquiry, and as the preparation of the final report at this stage was best left to his staff, the senator was at ease and under no pressures for time. He decided to devote an entire day to speaking with this final witness and thereby obtained the longest, most descriptive narrative taken than any other in the entire investigation. The interview began right after breakfast and took place at the Plaza Hotel in New York, where the young widow had been staying since the *Carpathia* docked in the late night hours of April 18.

The senator seemed captivated by the calm directness of the young lady. Instead of merely focusing on obtaining her testimony in the same fashion as he had with all the other witnesses he had faced, the two of them also swapped information on his recently acquired knowledge behind the history of the Olympic class vessels of the White Star Line and she the story of growing up in Ireland and meeting and marrying her young husband only to lose him in the early-morning hours of April 15.

Following the interview, she informed Senator Smith that she had a ticket to return to England on the *Olympic* when the ship was resupplied and ready to sail later the next day. After the five-day voyage, they would dock in Southampton, England. Her family would bring her back to the home she'd thought she'd left forever when she and her groom had boarded the *Titanic* at Queenstown, Cork County, Ireland, on April 11, bound for their new lives in America. The senator and his aide, upon the conclusion of their deposition with the young widow, would be touring the *Olympic* the next morning (prior to her departure) and returning to Washington on a specially chartered train to finalize the report and submit it to the US Senate.

The granddaughter of Mrs. Altford had discovered this "lost" interview among her personal belongings when *her* parents passed away a few months before. Through contacts, she offered it exclusively for publication to the *Los Angeles Herald-Examiner* and its star special features reporter, Samuel

Bellingham, for a special Sunday edition. The *Herald* eagerly accepted this offer—provided that the facts and the details of the deposition were cross-checked, the identity of this previously unknown "survivor" was verified, and the authenticity of the stenographer's papers was proven true.

It was the real deal.

After careful transcribing, fact-checking, and organizing of the information was completed, Mrs. Altford's original notes were returned to the family. They were being besieged with offers from, and were resisting, all temptations to sell them to memorabilia collectors. A decision to donate to the National Archives, where it might eventually be included in the files of the inquiry, was still pending at the time of the article's original publication.

However, that was just the beginning. Though she was a ticketed second-class passenger and was known to have boarded the ship—except for the initial wireless-transmitted list from the *Carpathia* via the *Olympic* and several shore stations—this passenger's name did not appear on any of the recognized lists of survivors. A search was launched immediately to locate and learn the fate of the previously unknown survivor. It was obvious that Senator Smith had worked from *all* available survivor lists since he did interview her, but since no mention of the interview, let alone the transcript itself, had been included among the vast volume of papers, notes, and evidence generated as a result of the inquiry, she was allowed to slip into obscurity. Was she dead? Alive? If alive, where was she? Who was she? What was her history? Nothing was known; she was a mystery.

Walter Lord had painstakingly sought out what survivors he could find to interview for his groundbreaking biography of the tragedy (he'd talked to sixty-three for the book), and *he* had no knowledge of her. Granted, there were many he couldn't find who had either chosen to remain in obscurity after the sinking for reasons of their own or had vanished into their changed lives, leaving no clues about their eventual fates. This usually applied mainly to the women (who would marry and thus have changed their last names), but men too "vanished" into time. Others died in the time between the sinking and his search for them. Many who were still alive, but whom he'd missed in his initial sweep for witnesses, he'd later found and come to know and love well.

However, Glynnis Smith-McLean was not one of them.

Through careful and meticulous research (using Mrs. Altford's notes for background information), Mr. Bellingham was finally able to find her. Still living in her town of birth fifty miles southwest of Belfast, she'd remarried, raised several children, and was now enjoying retirement with her husband of nearly fifty years. She was quite surprised at her sudden celebrity. Of course, she'd read the book and seen the movie (up to a point—she left the theater shaking when the scenes on the boat deck were shown and refused to ever see the film again), but she'd never attempted to "cash in" on the tragedy. Her story remained untold; only her family and friends of the time knew of her experience. She'd not even told her children. It was an event she'd lived through in her past and moved on from; the activities of her later years consumed all her time and attention.

She saw herself as a farmer's wife and mother of three who'd survived a tragedy that so many others didn't, and she could not understand the attention she was getting so many years later. She had put the tragedy behind her and had no wish to recall it after all these years. She would not allow her picture to be taken or any real details of her past fifty years revealed. It was too late to insist her name be kept secret; news of the "lost" deposition had already spread globally, but she pleaded to be left in peace.

Mr. Bellingham was one of very few persons who managed to impress Mrs. Branigan (no fool was she; in spite of being a "simple" country girl, she was highly self-educated, well-read, and inherited her sharp intuition from her parents). His gentle and sympathetic manner struck her as sincere and deep. Because of this, she opened up to him and told her story, eventually allowing—also exclusive to the *Herald-Examiner*—the publication of diary excerpts from before, during, and immediately after the tragedy to accompany the deposition and her subsequent conversation with Senator Smith. She had not opened the diary since the date of the last entry several months after the event, and she had kept it securely packed away in a trunk that had been stored in the back room of the home she'd lived in since her second marriage. By allowing this to accompany the publication of her deposition, she could illustrate the life she'd had prior to the tragedy and pay tribute to the young man who was her first love and who had remained anonymous for all those years. His body had never been recovered; it was either lost at sea, was buried at sea without identification, or was one of the many unidentified victims who were interred in a special cemetery in Halifax, Nova Scotia, with a number in lieu of a name on the headstone.

Mrs. Branigan and her family graciously entertained Mr. Bellingham while they pored over a copy of her deposition and paged through the volumes that comprised her diary. At the end of the visit, she impulsively allowed him to reference their chats as needed to illuminate portions of the diary, her testimony, and her narrative—and to touch *briefly* on her life since the sinking.

The reader will note that there are several contradictions between the three versions of the events that are recorded here. This is normal and to be expected.

First, the diary entries, written at the time or very soon thereafter, would probably be the most accurate—followed closely by her recollections to Senator Smith after the recording of her deposition and narrated as she viewed the events on the "movie screen" of her mind a few weeks after they occurred. The least accurate, but more in the chronology and detail than in any singular fact, would be the deposition itself. It is difficult to pull selected items out of context and clarify them without the events immediately prior and following that item to help place them in proper perspective. While it may seem, for example, that Mrs. Branigan and her late husband retrieved their valuables after both had visited the boat deck to ascertain what was happening—as her diary entry of April 16 (written aboard the rescue ship *Carpathia* since there was no entry for April 15) indicates—her recollection to Senator Smith a month later places it as before, when only her husband had gone to investigate, and she had yet to leave their cabin. Considering the harrowing ordeal she'd just undergone and the fact that the experience was still so fresh in her mind (she was still in shock and perhaps a bit confused), her diary entry might be suspected, her later recollection could be more accurate. Likewise, with a month's reflection between the event and the interview, she perhaps tried to order the events in a logical way that would make sense to her. As she admitted to the senator, she'd not opened the diary since the rescue. It could be that the earlier diary is accurate and the recollection, mentally framed to allow her to understand what had happened in a way she could begin to accept, would be suspect.

In either case, the *event* is the truth, and its placement on one side or the other of half an hour's time passage is irrelevant. She *did* board *Carpathia* wearing her husband's greatcoat, and in the pockets were her 1912 diaries and all the money they'd brought with them. Those facts, regardless of when they occurred, hadn't changed.

Taken in context with previously published and currently available information given by other survivors and those who were involved with the events, the reader was asked only to accept that Glynnis Smith-McLean-Branigan had a story to tell.

The story was hers.

She was a *Titanic* survivor.

So the discovery of the "lost" deposition—accompanied by a uniquely rare and incomparable candid narrative recorded without embellishment by a highly trained and detail-oriented court stenographer immediately after the deposition were at long last presented to the world as historically valuable documents that would aid tremendously in understanding the events of the night that the RMS *Titanic* sank, taking more than 1,500 lives to the bottom of the North Atlantic. In addition, the inclusion of a selection of diary entries chronicling the relationship, the romance, and the loss of the young Irish bride's dreams lend a sense of pathos, giving the story a life that the deposition alone could never convey.

What follows now is a republication of the entire feature from the Sunday supplement to the *Los Angeles Evening and Sunday Herald-Examiner* from April 15, 1962—the fiftieth anniversary of the sinking of the RMS *Titanic*. It is reproduced verbatim, along with editorial notes published within the same article to inform the reader about the source and the circumstance, thus justifying the inclusion of the piece in the context of the entire publication. It was an extremely long piece; indeed it was the sole article in the supplement that week, but it was distributed at no extra cost to the readers of the paper due to its extraordinary historical significance.

The Lost Deposition of Glynnis Smith McLean
Second-Class Survivor of the RMS *Titanic*
Exclusive to the *Los Angeles Evening
and Sunday Herald-Examiner*
Sunday Supplement of April 15, 1962
In Commemoration of the Fiftieth Anniversary of the Tragedy
Samuel Bellingham, Special Features Reporter

It was at 2:20 a.m. from the vantage point of the lifeboats when the water closed over the ship's fantail and the world's largest and most luxurious liner vanished from sight forever. More than 1,500 lives were lost fifty years ago this morning when the White Star Line's brand-new luxury liner, RMS *Titanic*, struck an iceberg on her maiden voyage and foundered approximately six hundred miles east of Halifax, Nova Scotia, Canada, while en route to New York. Approximately four hours later, 705 people were rescued by the Cunard liner RMS *Carpathia* and rushed to New York where they arrived late in the evening of April 18 as a stunned and increasingly angered world awaited their stories and demanded changes.

The stories *were* told. To newspapers, in magazine articles, and as novels. Dramatizations in motion picture houses. Testimonies of the survivors, saviors, and those on the periphery of the tragedy. Those involved in the design and construction of the ill-fated liner were questioned in regard to the materials used and safety features incorporated. Fingers were pointed and blame assigned and either accepted or rejected, lawsuits were filed; most were settled. Broken lives were patched together and resumed, though not unchanged. Careers were made and ruined; fortunes won and lost.

The changes *were* made. Lifeboats for all. Twenty-four-hour wireless communication. In response to demand for ice patrols to aid in safer navigation, the US Coast Guard International Ice Patrol was established by the first "Safety of Life at Sea" convention in 1914, with funding provided by signatory nations for its maintenance and upkeep.

Then came "The War to End All Wars," and with it the end of the Edwardian Era and the "innocence" lost (if it had ever *been* innocent). Technological advances brought by the age of steam. Airplanes, dirigibles, and bigger and fiercer battleships. Scientific advancement. Atomic energy. The "Race for Space" and the shrinking of the world through global communication with satellites such as Telstar.

And the world would never again be the same.

Some say the innocence ended when the water closed over the rudder of the *Titanic* on that cold April night fifty years ago. Trust in man's innovations was shattered when the "unsinkable" *Titanic* actually sank. All else was a logical extension of this one event.

So it has been said.

In truth, too much faith *had* been put in the increasing advancement of human technology. Vast leaps forward in innovations meant to make life easier and more leisurely had been accepted blindly, in spite of facts proving contrary. Life was still rough for those not fortunate enough to be among the "aristocrats" whose lives of leisure were about to be expanded by the new technology and (soon) automation. Those in the lower classes would still have to work and sweat for their gains, but they'd finally reap *some* reward for their labors. This had been the case for generations uncountable before them, and there was no sign that their situations would change in the future.

Emigration to America was increasing steadily as technology allowed for the development and construction of larger, faster, and "safer" ships to carry them. The United States was the promised land for many of those who set their dreams of prosperity and success as their goals. Emigration numbers were up, and the steamships of the world were made bigger to accommodate those numbers. Indeed, many of the larger steamship companies built new ships specifically to entice those people to spend their meager savings to cross and made the passenger appointments more comfortable to attract them. More space, better meals, and a comfort they'd never before known. Of course, this didn't mean that the first- or second-cabin passengers didn't gain an increase in *their* luxurious appointments: indoor swimming pools (*Titanic* boasted one of the first), squash courts, spacious promenade decks—*Titanic* even sported a Parisian café to lend a Continental air to dining pleasure (for first-class use only, of course, and not part of the ship's service; one paid extra and out of pocket to dine there, a discount on their passage was offered to compensate). As a result of the improvements in comfort, steerage class (so called because their berths were located in areas that also accommodated a ship's steering mechanisms) was now referred to as "third," and was nearly as comfortable as the old "second class," which was upgraded to closely approximate the previous "first-class" cabins.

In the *new* "first class", a person was treated like a "king."

Those few emigrants who could afford it traveled second class on many of the outbound liners from the European Continent. They were few; second class on the older ships was still more than the average laborer could afford. By comparison, second class on *Titanic* cost as much—if not more—than first class on many of the older ships. *Definitely* out of reach of all but the most well-to-do of the middle class (as defined by American standards of the time), and first class on *Titanic* was out of reach of almost everyone. These upper class berths were "Exclusive" (capital letter intended), reserved for the idle rich. Millionaires and those with successful business ventures or family fortunes that society in that time period demanded be put on display. The "elite" were to be fawned over and worshiped by the lesser masses whose labors supported lifestyles of the carefree gentry—the likes of the Astors (real estate), the Guggenheims (mining), and the Strauses (politics and retail), whose fortunes were either inherited or were the result of shrewd investments (or, in the view of socialists and like-minded unionists, exploitation of the working class).

Second class saw many who were upwardly mobile (authors, teachers, and clergy) and those whose success in business or other ventures was not as providential as those in first—the Beckers (missionaries), the Browns (hotelier), the Wares (carpentry)—but who had disposable income nonetheless.

Third class, formerly though in some instances still referred to as "steerage," contained mostly emigrants. There were some travelers who, due to minimal finances, were resigned to traveling in this lowest community who weren't emigrating but were visiting America with the intent to return to Europe. However, by and large, these were people—from many countries and many cultures—who intended to cross one-way, setting up new homes and new lives on the frontiers of America. These families included the Anderssons (laborers), Asplunds (laborers, students), Fords (farmers, laborers, students), and Goodwins (engineering, students).

Throughout the early months of 1912, a major coal strike had ravaged transatlantic shipping between England and America. Many ships were idled, and much coal had to be imported from America on board those vessels capable of transporting it. Such was the case at the time of *Titanic*'s maiden voyage. Originally planned to take place in March, it was rescheduled for early April. The strike had ended the week prior, but coal was still scarce and would remain so for weeks to come. *Titanic*, in order to be able to sail on her maiden voyage as advertised, used coal from other ships owned by her parent (the White Star Line) or purchased from other lines, leaving those vessels stranded and her passengers to accept accommodations either on *Titanic* (reduced accommodations, yet still more opulent than those on board the initial transports now idled) or change schedules for a later date. *Titanic's* sister ship, the RMS *Olympic,* had brought back nearly five thousand tons of coal from America to aid in the new liner's voyage.

Two of the passengers whose itinerary was changed in this manner were newlyweds. Ian and Glynnis McLean were immigrating from near Belfast, Ireland, to San Francisco. Mr. McLean had a position as an apprentice engineer awaiting him upon arrival. They were slated to depart as first-class passengers on the American-owned SS *City of New York* on April 10 from Southampton, England, until that voyage was canceled due to the strike.

Ian and Glynnis McLean were both born in the same village south of Belfast. They'd grown up together. Ian was the son of a prominent local banker (who, among other things, helped finance the construction of small oceangoing vessels and thus had contacts at Harland and Wolff), and Glynnis was the only daughter of an equally prominent farmer and landholder. Friends as children, they fell in love as they grew older and married in a rush as Ian learned of his acceptance to the apprenticeship in San Francisco. Not wanting to leave Glynnis behind (and she not wanting to stay without Ian), they convinced their families to allow them to marry young (he was eighteen and she sixteen) and immigrate to America. The job had come through a contact via Thomas Andrews, managing director in charge of design (architect) at Harland and Wolff Shipyards, the builders of *Titanic*, who'd met Ian several times while *Titanic* was under construction. He had impressed them with his intuitiveness, and the cost of the first-class tickets on board the SS *City of New York*, as well as monies to allow them to travel by rail across America, was a wedding present from extended family members. Mr. Andrews enabled the McLeans to trade in their tickets for second-class accommodations aboard *Titanic* when their original fare was idled due to the coal strike.

In all the recollections and testimonies following the disaster of *Titanic*'s foundering fifty years ago this day, those of Mrs. McLean had not been known. Her testimony was taken but never entered into the record. The only clue within the voluminous transcripts and notes of the Senate inquiry was a journal entry made by Senator William Alden Smith, the Republican senator from Michigan and chairman of the inquiry. It stated, "Meeting with final survivor morning 24 May, inspecting *Olympic* 25, meeting with Captain Haddock and wireless operator before returning to Washington 26."

While the notes and transcripts of the inspection of the ship and the meeting with the captain and wireless operator, and a reinterview with a surviving *Titanic* fireman, *are* part of the record, there is no further information at all about the meeting with a survivor a day earlier. It could be argued that the fireman interviewed on the twenty-fifth *could* have been the survivor scheduled for the twenty-fourth, but as the senator's interview made clear, the third person talked to on board the *Olympic* was an advantageous opportunity. He could not have been the survivor talked to a day earlier.

That survivor was Mrs. McLean.

A few years ago, the descendants of Mary Altford, Senator Smith's loyal and long-serving stenographer, were going through a trunk belonging to their grandmother, which had been stored in the back shed of the family home. They sat down to read through bundles of papers—journals, notes, and transcripts—and stumbled across some pages missing from history. What they'd discovered was revealed to be authentic testimony of a passenger saved from the sinking of *Titanic* but never included with the published records of the Senate inquiry at the senator's request. He felt that the information was redundant and added nothing new to the information he'd already gathered.

The journals were the personal thoughts and recollections of Mrs. Altford (pretty much *her* diary) and contained many off-the-record observations, anecdotes, and views both personal and professional. Found in the pages of one volume was a recollection of an informal after-lunch conversation between Senator Smith and Mrs. McLean in *exquisite* detail. This was unique in that no other witness involved in the tragedy had such candid contact with the senator or with any other investigator during the course of the investigation, allowing the members of the committee to maintain impartiality during the course of the inquiry.

Mrs. McLean's comments about her experiences aboard *Titanic* were unlike any other that the senator had heard up to that point. All the information he'd gathered to that point was technical, biased, or bluntly stated. Mrs. McLean spoke from the heart and with complete openness and eloquence, something that no prior witness had been capable of doing previously. The senator's later comment was preserved for posterity in Mrs. Altford's journal. He said, "It would make a marvelous story."

Exclusive to the *Los Angeles Evening and Sunday Herald-Examiner* is that story. Told by Mrs. McLean in her own words, from contemporary diary excerpts written from her early childhood, and by the informal conversation with the senator after giving her deposition. A story of a love that grew from friendship to the wedding and honeymoon sailing—appropriately on the maiden voyage of the world's most luxuriously appointed ocean liner—to the tragedy, her heartbreak, and just a little bit beyond.

After months of research, I, assisted by the editorial staff of the *Los Angeles Evening and Sunday Herald-Examiner*, had been fortunate enough to locate and gain the trust of Mrs. Glynnis McLean (now "Branigan") and obtain her blessing and cooperation in telling *her* story of that night in April 1912.

From *her* perspective.

Alongside and in support of the newly discovered documentation.

The history of life begun, dreams dreamt, and a nightmare lived.

Her deposition—the centerpiece of the story—pales in the light of the story told around it.

To paraphrase the conclusion of *The Adventures of Tom Sawyer* by Mark Twain (who passed away two years before the tragedy): "It being strictly a history of *an event*, it must stop here; the story could not go much further without becoming the history of *an era*." The italics are mine and reflect the change in the quote. There was a history as to how, and why, the McLeans found themselves on board *Titanic,* and that story needs to be told.

The world already knows what came next.

Let us begin.

THE DIARY—GROWING UP IN ULSTER

While the diary of Mrs. Glynnis Smith-McLean-Branigan was written almost entirely prior to her tragic voyage on *Titanic*; several entries were written during the voyage. It begins on her eighth birthday with the receipt of the first of what would become nearly one hundred books of various sizes, thicknesses, types, and designs. Almost every day of her life from that point until two months after the tragedy, when she made a conscious decision to put down her pen and store the books, was documented—some days in detail and some just a few sentences. It provides an extremely rare glimpse into the life of a young Irish farm girl in the first decade of the twentieth century, an intelligent, observant, and reasonably well-educated girl, considering her class, her background, and the social mores of the period.

The excerpts published here were chosen by Mrs. Branigan to give more than a glimpse into the loss she suffered when her beloved first husband perished in the cold North Atlantic waters on that April morning. It was her desire that, as well as giving an insight into her upbringing and how she found herself as a second-class passenger on the most luxurious ship ever built at that time, honor should be given to the memory of her first husband, Ian McLean. This honor was long overdue in his recognition as the most gallant and courageous man she'd ever met. She grew up with him; he was one of her playmates as a child and eventually became her husband. And had fate been otherwise, they'd both be here in America, celebrating their golden anniversary (fifty years ago on April 9), and we'd probably never know of them.

Her intent in allowing the publication of the several excerpts is to display how their friendship grew into courtship, and then into marriage. She wished to honor his memory in a way better than the publication of the deposition alone would ever allow.

Mrs. Branigan was never without her diary in those dim, hazy days just after the turn of the twentieth century. If she were traveling, she'd take with her only the diary she was currently recording her experiences. However, as she was on board *Titanic* as an immigrant with no intention of returning to her native land, she'd packed the more recent of her 1912 volumes with her (from February onward). Her parents would send the others; they had offered to pack her belongings and send them to her once she was settled in her new home. At least, that was the original intent before tragedy struck.

These diaries were the only things she'd saved when she abandoned the luxury liner on that cold moonless night, carrying them in the pockets of the immense gray overcoat her husband insisted she wear out on deck. She made only one entry while on board the *Carpathia*, and just one other following her conversation with Senator Smith. Her final entry was penned when she arrived back at her family's farm two weeks later, after which all the books were placed carefully in a locked trunk, and they remained untouched until recently when she agreed to allow them to be read and excerpted in today's publication. Neither her second husband (of forty-eight

years now) nor any of her children had seen them; they'd long
wondered what was in that locked trunk in the back of the
storeroom, but their curiosity never overcame their respect for
her privacy.

Here, then, are the chosen excerpts from the diaries of
Glynnis Smith-McLean, in honor of her husband, Ian.

SB.

Diary Entry—July 17, 1903

Hello, diary! It is my eighth birthday and you are my grandist
gift! I can write down my thots and my dreems and things that
happin to me in my poor littel life in my cozy littel home. I will
also practis my spelling grammar and dikshun in you. Also my
punctuashun, sentins strukure and vocabulary. Within your
pagis I can try to better myself without fear of being laft at by
my playmats. Or induldged by the grown-ups. You shall keep
my secrits and my histree—all at the same time!

First I shall introdus myself.

My name is Glynnis Smith. Not a very glameuris name I
say but it suits me fine. I am proud to be a Smith for I love my
family and they love me. It is a comun name and we are comun
people. And Glynnis has sound to it, dont you think so? *I* do. It
sounds like a contradicshun (I just learned that word and this is
the first time Ive had a chance to use it, did I spell it right?) with
a grunt to start and a soft hiss to end with a sharp turn in the
middle to separate them. Thats how it sounds to me ennyway.

I am eight today. Eight isnt old but it means Im a littel
closer to being a grown-up. Im small for my age. Im only 102
centimetrs in height. I guess thats almost three and a half feet
tall in Amercan mesuremints. You see I want to go to Amerca
someday. Im learning all about it from visiters who come to

Ireland and from the Irish who have been there and have come back home. They say it is a land of plenty and oh that sounds so grand! Someday Id like to go and live there. It sounds beautiful what Ive heard of it.

Im a bit over three and a half stones (thats fifty pounds, isnt it?) and I have the red hair and blue eyes we Irish are famus for. But my hair isnt red as a carot oh no! Thats more of an oringe. Mine is a darker red like the sun through the smoke of a forrist fire. I know that color has a name but I dont know what it is. But I think it is a lovely color and so it suits me. If only I could be rid of my freckles. It makes me look as if Im with the meesils or the pox all spotted and not in a pretty way. My skin is fair and Ive been lucky that I dont burn when Im in the sun but I turn a nice tan—a very light shade but noticeibel from my wintry whiteness. My hair as I said is a dark red but not too dark. And strait with just a littel bit of wave. Im thin but Im starting to build up like the yung womin which I am beginning to be. I am stronger than I look because I do many chores that the boys also do. I run and play when my chores are thru.

Right now it is summer in my littel villige between Belfast and Lissburn in County Antrim, Provins of Ulster and chores and play is what I do this time of year. I have three brothers two are older than me and no sisters. We have other children near my age in the villige and we all meet in the after noons after chores and play games. We hide from each other and chase each other through the fields and climb trees and have a wunderflee grand time. I fear the day my Momma and Poppa tell me Im too old to play with the boys and so I enjoy my play while I can.

I wonder why we cant play together when we get older? Maybe one day I can look back at this page and know the answer. I hope it makes sense then because it surely duznt now!

Addendum—February 10, 1911

It's because of *propriety*. Once boys and girls become men and women, it's not considered proper for the two to mix and mingle and play as children, for we're not anymore, though we're not yet adults either. We're in between; we're in our teens. Maturity of one's bodies when the minds are still so young supposedly leads to temptations that the church surely warns us against all the days of our youth—and beyond!

Ian laughed at this when I finally let him read it—for he's one of the boys with whom I played back then. And now, he's nearly a man! And such a fine, strong man at that. To think: We've loved each other all this time, and we still promise to be wed someday. Once a childish fantasy and now—oh, how I pray!

Diary Entry—March 30, 1904

Winter was over last week, and it's suppost to be spring. But there's still a bit of snow on the ground, and the winds are oh so cold! But the afternoons are a bit warmer each day and the sun is rising sooner and staying out longer. But it is light enough now that I can stay outside after my lessons and chores to write in my diary and watch my father and brothers as they begin cleering the fields for the next planting of crops. Our farm is small, but it supplies us with the food we need for the year and plenty left to sell at market or trade for things we need. But the ground is still hard from the freezing winter so the men (Men? My brothers aren't but twelve and fourteen—they've a long time to go!) can't do much more than decide what to plant where and mark off the boundrees with sticks and string until the ground is soft enough to dig and plow and plant.

I help with the planting because I like to get my hands in the dirt. Poppa says that's the way of our people. We're farmers, and we have been since the beginning of time, so we're born to it. I don't know if he's right, but I'm sure he is because Poppa's never been wrong before. I just know I feel calm and at peace when I'm in the field and helping to raise our crops.

Momma's been teeching me to sew and cook and keep house and to make pottery and baskets that we can sell later at the market. My projects are clumsy, but she says I'll find my way soon enough. I'm young yet and my fingers aren't as skilled as they will be with practiss. I try hard and I know I'm getting better. I saved my first one from last spring just so I can see how far I've come in learning, and I can tell the difference. I hope to get as good as Momma. Her weaving is so tight and snug and her flowers are placed in them so pretty!

Momma's so good and patient with me and I want to please her so much, so I'd best put this down and go back inside and work with her some more.

Oh, theres the neybor boy. He's Ian McLean. His family's from Scotland back over one hundred years ago. They live in the village his father's a manager with one of the banks (there are three). Ian is ten and great friends with my brother Peter. He's twelve. John is fourteen. My younger brother is William—he's five. Ian likes to come help in the field, its great fun for him, and he likes it better than his books and numbers which he likes a lot themselves. He wants to be like his father—maybe even become a bank president someday. He also dreams of being an engineer—not on the railroad but as a builder of machines. He's always studying how things work, how the parts are made in such a way that they fit together to work so perfectly—he's absolutely amazed by these things. He tells my father he comes here to clear his head because he says his head hurts from so much studying.

And he's so nice to me. Different than the other boys. They all like me, but Ian treats me nicer. I feel strange when he's around. But it's a good strange. I like him.

Diary Entry—April 3, 1904

We're just back from Easter Mass. We're Protestants, which is the Church of England. Most of our county is, but there is a scattering of Catholics here and there. Sometimes theres troubles between our two religns, but Poppa says that under all the different religns that there are in the world people are still people and we should all love and respect each other. I agree because the church says to love one another and the church is right because it's God. And Protestants and Catholics both believe in God and Jesus so I don't know why they argue. Maybe when I'm older I'll understand. But I'll still think it's silly.

I saw Ian and his mother and father go to their church. They are Presbyterian (I think I spelled that right, I tried to remember the word from the sign when we passed by this afternoon), which is similar to us but different enough that they have their own church. Poppa says that's the main description of the Church of Scotland where Ian and his family came from. Church of England is Protestant. That's us. Poppa says the Church of Scotland is all right with most people. Nobody says anything bad about them. It's different with the Catholics. Some people around our village call Catholics "Fish Eaters," and they sound so hateful when they say it. I don't know why, I eat fish too. But Poppa says that's not the same. And to not pay attention to people who talk like that. He says we're *all* Christians except for the Jews. I don't know anything about them. I've only seen a few I think.

Because it's Easter Sunday, we had a special church service that lasted more than two hours. I love going to church and learning about God and Jesus and Mary, but it's so hard to pay attention for so long! I get restless and wish I could go outside and play in the grass (which is starting to grow after the cold winter), and then I get tired and try to stay awake. I know it's important to learn about our Savior and how he died so we might be saved and go to live in heaven with God, and I try to listen and learn about the Parables and the Gospels and the Cross and the Resurrection (that's another word I tried to remember how to spell) but my! I saw I was not the only one who wished to be someplace else even the adults (even Poppa!) was restless but church is our duty and our honor, so I behaved as best I could until it was over.

I do love God and Jesus and I do want to go to heaven someday. I just wish there was an easier way to do it. I'll be glad next week when we only have to go for an hour. It's easier to keep the Sunday holy when you don't have to work at it.

Diary Entry—August 22, 1905

All day in the fields. Pulling weeds, watering, checking for damage. It's been so hot this summer it's hard to keep the crops alive. We're lucky we have our own well. So many people don't, and we've been helping our neighbors by letting them take water from us for their own crops. Our well is a good one. It's been on our land for hundreds of years, and Poppa says it's never gone dry so there's plenty to share with others who need it. The water's fresh and pure, not like so many others in the village, which taste sandy and sour. Our neighbors are very thankful and call us good Christians. Poppa just bows his head and says that he's glad to help. He remembers times long ago when he needed help and these same people were there for him. He told my brothers and me that this is what neighbors do for each other and we should never forget it. Everything we have is by the grace of God, and nothing is truly ours unless it's earned. I guess since we didn't earn the water then it's not ours—it belongs to anybody who needs it. This makes sense.

Ian has been here most of the summer helping us. School is out, and he's too young to work for money and he hasn't any brothers or sisters or many chores to do at home so he comes here. His father and Poppa are friends, I guess, though I never see Mr. McLean come here and I don't think Poppa goes there. And we don't go to his bank. But Peter and Ian are friends, though they're two years apart in school, and Poppa likes Ian so he lets him come and help—and gives him a few pence now and then for helping.

And we feed him. Can he eat? I'll say he can! He works so hard, and it makes him hungry. It makes Momma proud to see a boy eat so! Poppa can't think where he puts it—he's so thin! John says it goes to his muscles, and I can hear envy because John's arms are as thin as straw no matter how hard he works. John doesn't realize that he's much stronger than Ian—it just doesn't show. Poppa says that muscles show on some men (boys, I say!) and not on others.

Ian McLean. Why am I writing so much today about him? Is it because he's spent more time working with me than with my brothers? That he talks to me more than to them? That he listens when I talk and the others don't? I've known him all my life, and he's never paid so much attention to me before today. And he sat next to me at dinner and supper, and we had our tea and biscuits together between. My brothers were there too, but it seemed like they weren't.

Ian is nice to look at. For a boy. He's got red hair like me, but not as dark. His skin—that's dark. I heard Poppa tell Momma once that the McLeans had some Roman blood in them. Maybe that's why. Romans are Italians, and they're a dark people. I've seen a couple of them before. Two boys in my school. Their father works in the marketplace.

Ian's tall, almost as tall as John, and they've four years between them. And he's strong—the muscles on his arms show when he's working. He's got eyes as green as emeralds, and his smile is open and friendly. And perfect white teeth! I've never seen the like! I brush and brush, and mine aren't as pure white as his.

He's very smart too. Poppa asked him after school let out for summer, "How is your report?"

And he said, "I am near the top of my class, especially in numbers."

Poppa asked him, "Do you still want to clerk when you finish school?"

Ian said, "I do, but I am also thinking about engineering."

Poppa asked, "What kind?"

I said, "Building things, like ships and trains, or those automobiles that are starting to be seen more and more in Ulster Province, especially around Belfast."

Bloody noisy things—oops! Forgive me for cursing, but the *travesty* of those contraptions! Ian and I have talked of this many times while working in the field together. He'd gone to Belfast with his father in May—over to the Harland and Wolff shipyards—and was amazed what went on in building a ship! A customer of his father's bank was looking for money to build a ship and his father wanted to see the plans, to see if the loan was a good one, and he took Ian with him. Ian saw the drawings and all the thinking that went into making them—the sizes, the materials, and the numbers—and he saw something much better than counting shillings and pound notes into a book.

My, but his eyes sparked! I saw the man in the boy that day. My heart fluttered so; he was *beautiful*!

If you could call a boy that.

Diary Entry—December 25, 1905 (Morning)

Christmas Day! This is the happiest time of the year for me for as long as I can remember! I just love the joy and the festival, and I don't even mind going to church because the story of the Baby Jesus and the manger and Holy Bethlehem are all reminders of God's gift of eternal life to his children.

In our church, we have a play where people act out what went on when Jesus was born. We have Mother Mary on an ass, we have Joseph walking by her side, we have an inn where they're turned away, we have a manger where the Baby Jesus is born, we have sheep and goats and lambs and cows, we have a bright star in the sky (Poppa said it was probably a planet, but how perfect for the play!), and Three Wise Men—just the whole thing like the Bible says it happened!

The Mass was at midnight, when the eve becomes the new Holy Day and all is dark except by candlelight and the pastor says his Mass from the Gospels and it lasts until dawn—and I never got tired or bored or restless. I was so excited! I get that way every Christmas because of the Holy Gift that God gave us in his Son our Lord Jesus and my life feels so much freer and my burdens (I'm only ten, but I have them, like school and chores) seem so much lighter and I know I'll be saved someday. And they usually have a rag doll to play the Baby Jesus, but this year, Mrs. O'Hannihan's new little baby boy—one month old—got to be the Baby Jesus and wasn't he just perfectly beautiful for that? He looked just like the picture in the Bible, so calm and watchful over everything that went on around him, almost like he understood, but babies can't understand at that age, can they? But he must have, because he didn't even whimper, not even with all those big scary people and animals around him. I almost believed it was real—it felt so that it was!

Ian and his parents were there, even though they don't belong to our church. On Christmas, because the story of Jesus's birth is so important for everyone, and most of the people here are Christians of some form or another, and we all honor the birth of the Savior, our church invites everybody from everywhere to attend this festivity. Even nonbelievers, like Jews and Moslems and heathens are invited. I guess the hope is that they will be so struck by the wonder and beauty and holiness that they too will believe and we can all be Christians together and love each other and there will be no more wars and fighting. They mostly all come and they say how nice the play is and they thank everybody and they go away. I don't know if they believe now or not, but I hope they do.

Ian looked so manly all dressed up—even though he's only twelve. He's taller than his mother and almost as tall as his father, and he was solem throughout the Mass after the play. I could see his lips move during the prayers, and I could almost hear his voice during the hymns. I'm sure it was him singing in a strong, sweet voice that sounded as pure as a songbird, but I couldn't have, could I? There were so many people between us and all of them singing, but I want to believe I heard him. I should ask him to sing for me, if he's not shy about it. Then I'll know.

I've been home now half an hour and I should be napping like the others before Momma gets up and prepares breakfast, but I'm too excited to sleep! When breakfast is done, we have presents to open from friends and family, and we have relations coming for dinner tonight. I'm glad I'm the only girl in this large family of mine because all my uncles and aunts and cousins spoil me so! And little William is the youngest of all of us, so he gets his share too!

I'll write more tonight. Merry Christmas, my little Diary!

Diary Entry—December 25, 1905 (Evening)

Aunts and uncles and cousins—the house was so full of people that I chose to eat my Christmas dinner outside where I could breathe!

It was all so delicious, and I could burst with all I ate! How could somebody as small as I eat so much even I can't begin to imagine, but eat I did! Roast quail, yams, potatoes (what we're famous for in Ireland, but after the famine which I learned about from Poppa when I was old enough to help with the crops, not much is grown in our country anymore), Indian corn from seeds brought from America, and ham from our largest sow smoked and cured since September, and cranberry muffins and squash and turnips and onions that we got at market or traded with our neighbors and apple cider, and it was a feast! I'm so tired, but I wanted to write what I could while I was still awake.

There were presents for all of us children, mostly clothes for the older ones, but little William got a toy boat and a whistle. I got books (my favorite, Elsie Dinsmore!) and pencils. Uncle Thomas told us of the meaning of Christmas—not just the birth of the Baby Jesus, like we saw last night (this morning!) at the church, but what the meaning should mean to us today. That it should mean loving our neighbor and helping each other in need and forgiveness to those who hurt us. And that we should always keep God in our hearts and Jesus as our example and the Spirit as our beacon. And to never let temptation or evil enter our lives.

Just before I came into my cubby to write in this diary, Momma took me aside where nobody else could see and gave me a small wrapped present in secret. She said that as we were leaving church this morning, Ian McLean had handed it to her to give to me. Momma had a quiet little smile on her face as I turned red when she said this and I bowed my head to hide, but I was smiling too. Ian giving me a present?

Momma told me to open it and when I did, I was so happy! It was very small redheaded doll, with blue eyes like mine and the sweetest little smile in her face! And Ian had even written a little note, which I will copy down here even though I will put it in my keepsake box and keep it forever. It said:

> Please don't be silly and throw this doll away. This pretty little doll looks exactly like you do. I so much enjoy looking at you and watching you laugh and smile that I thought you might like something that will let you see yourself like I see you. Then you will see why I like to be with you and talk to you. You make me happy. I wish I had a sister like you, but I have no sisters or brothers. So can I have you instead?
>
> Your friend,
> Ian McLean

I went even redder when I read this, and Momma smiled sweetly when she read it and gave it back. She told me I had a special friend in Ian and that she and Poppa liked him very much. She was glad Ian likes me, but she said to be careful, because we were growing up and some of the playing we do now would not be proper for when we become young ladies and gentlemen. I told her we mostly talk and work in the field together, that when I play, he usually just watches, because he's so serious and his mind is always working so hard that he's too tired for him to do much playing. Momma nodded her head and said that was okay then, but remember to be careful as I grow up and always be a proper lady. She was sure that Ian was a proper gentleman, and she and Poppa had no fear that he would change. But they would be watching us to keep us safe and clean.

I can't figure this out. Maybe when I'm older. We stay as clean as we can when working in the fields, and we always wash afterward. Why wouldn't we be clean?

Ah, my diary, I'm too tired to think about what Momma said. But she only means to keep me from getting hurt and to help me grow up strong and smart. Maybe this is more of her way of helping me to become a grown-up someday.

Addendum—February 10, 1911

Now it's Ian's turn to blush. He remembered the doll, and I told him I still have it. It's in a place where I see it last thing at night and first thing in the morning. It really does look as I did when I was little and when he first gave it to me!

I gave him back his note to read, and was he flustered? My! I've kept that note in my keepsake box all these years, and I'll keep it forever still. It's the first note he'd ever given me (and he's given me hundreds since; I've saved them all!), and it holds the most special place in my heart, because *I* like to mark it as the beginning of our love.

I'll put the note back when he's done threatening to "tear it up" (I know he won't, but he must have his dignity restored—ha!) and we'll talk for a bit longer before I must go in for the night and send him home. My escapades (*our* escapades, for we're always together when time is free) are waiting to be written in their proper place in the continuity of this diary (should I start calling you a "journal" now? No, I think not. "Diary" you began; "Diary" you shall remain), and I don't want to misplace it here.

What that I would have planned to leave an empty place after each entry so that I can put in a later comment on my life as it was, from the vantage point of what it is now? This was not foresight, I assure you, dear little diary. However, I'm glad for it, because I can answer my childish (youthful?—better!) questions with the maturity I've gained as I near adulthood.

Or, as I read in a book last week: "If I knew then what I know now."

Apt in this case for I sensed it; surely I did. Ian was in my life then, and I kept him near instead of turning him away as a "pesky boy"—and he's here now, and I'm ever so glad for it!

It is time. He must go to his home, and I must retire for the night. We'll see each other in the morrow. 'Twixt then and now, I've today's histories to record and the nightly sight of my graven image as Ian saw me six years past.

And sweet dreams to cherish!

Good night!

Note: Mrs. Branigan still has the note, but the doll was lost when *Titanic* foundered. The keepsake box was left with her family when she married and embarked on the trip to America, the hope was that it would either be sent to her once they'd settled down in their new home, or she'd retrieve it on a return visit in the future. As it was, the doll was all she took. The romantic in us can but wish that it remains nestled within the vest pocket of Ian McLean on *Titanic's* boat deck.

SB.

Diary Entry—May 12, 1906

I'm nearly eleven now, and I notice my body is changing. I've begun to develop bosoms, and they're so tender and sore! And my waist, hips, and legs are taking a more womanly shape; I'm no longer a thin little girl now but an awkward, clumsy thing who's growing crookedly and roundly and not in balance or evenness. I'm three inches taller than I was in February, which is the last time I was measured. My clothes are getting too small, and I've taken to wearing my older brother's shirts around the house; I feel so obvious! Of course, Poppa and the boys don't notice anything different, except I won't look them in the eye—but Momma guessed right away! She's so smart and sensitive to my feelings and moods; since she was a young colleen herself once, she remembers and she's quick to reassure me that my confidence in my growth will come quickly enough, once I'm used to it.

I'm avoiding Ian best I can. I can tell he's hurt when I merely peer around the door at him and tell him I can't come outside and talk with him, but what can I say? He's a boy! It's so embarrassing!

I have to make this short, because I'll depress myself if I go on. Until tomorrow?

Diary Entry—July 17, 1906

It's my eleventh birthday, and you've been with me for three years; how time flies!

You're eighteen separate books now, all called "My Diary," and I don't distinguish between any of you. I keep you all together in a box, my "keepsake box," which is where I place those things I treasure most. Ian's notes and letters are with you.

I've just finished the sixth level in my school this year, and I've learned so much! I love school, and I love learning. I went back through you and saw how my grammar, vocabulary, and diction have improved, especially over this past year. I've come to realize that because so many girls are forced to leave school by the time they reach ten or eleven, the teachers try to give them as much knowledge as they can in the last year, and especially the last half, to help them through life. So many girls in Ireland aren't able to go to school at all. So many of them are poor and are needed to help out at home with projects or looking after the younger children and helping to keep house. I'm fortunate that my family is well-off (we're not rich, but we want for little and need nothing), and an education is important. Momma is very much in force about this; she left school at eight to work in the fields until she met and married Poppa. Since then Poppa, John, Peter, and I have been teaching her daily—Poppa through life and we children through our daily lessons. She's gained so much from what we've helped give her! And why shouldn't she? She's given us life and love, what we return is such a small thing in comparison! She now says that she's a more suitable partner for Poppa; she can support him and help strengthen his ideas and projects much better that she now knows and understands what he has to say to her. He's been patient with her and her gratitude for that is shown in any number of ways, but mostly by being his life's true assistant in all he says and does. So when he asks her what her opinions are, how proud she is to be able to speak with thought and clarity—and how serious he is when he listens and considers and often agrees and accepts the advice he sought from her!

I don't know anything about the "women's suffrage movement" that's being spoken of in America, but here in *this* household (and quite a few others I've been invited to) women are equal to their men. They have to be. We're *farmers*. Every one of us is part of the force that feeds us, clothes us, and keeps us sheltered. Poppa may be the head of the house by tradition, but Momma has an equal say in the decisions that are made. And Poppa listens when she speaks for she is not without a voice and will be heard!

Momma gave me a couple of glorious outfits for my birthday today and all the trimmings—corsets, pantaloons, stockings—everything. Now, it's not like I haven't had dresses before; after all, I *am* a girl. However, nothing as fine as these! I feel grown up in my new clothes, and now my older ones only make me feel silly and inferior. However, I'm growing up now; Poppa calls me his "young lady," and my brothers bow and refer to me as "The Queen." It is all in fun, I know that, but I feel self-conscious at the same time that I laugh.

I also feel different. Inside. Like I'm me, but not me. A different me—one who's about to see the sun like the petals on a rose when they first open from the bud. Is it my womanhood? My maturity? I feel it might be so. I act differently, and I talk differently. My mind is in a spin because I feel like I'm still a child, but at the same time, I feel like I'm too old now for many of the things I still like to do.

I *think* different. It's like I consider things that never used to bother me before with a seriousness I'd never *had* before.

Like life. And purpose. Who am I? What am I? What is my reason for being? Where will I go? What will I do? How will I turn out?

I never used to care, never used to think beyond the here and now.

That's changed in me. I don't know if it's a good thing or a bad thing, but it's a new thing. It scares me somewhat. I spend more and more time with Momma, trying to study her and see if I can find a clue in her manner that can help me see where I am bound, who I will become, and how I might turn out.

I see myself in her. This is normal I suppose, since I am her daughter, but I see the girl she used to be, and that girl is a lot like I suppose I still am. She is strong and quiet most times, but when her troubles are few and her work for the day is done, she can laugh longer, louder, and easier than anybody else in our home! Poppa told me once he met Momma when she was a little girl, younger than I am now, and he remembers well how she was then. And that I am indeed my mother's daughter, for he sees the girl she once was in me. Ever since then (and it's been the past year since he said this), I've been watching and seeing myself in her.

I'm glad I'm so much like her, because I dearly love Momma. She's been so good to me and so patient with me when I've become headstrong and troublesome—especially since I started growing lately. I know I'm moody and short-tempered these days, and I try so hard to contain my emotions. Momma says this is normal for a girl, part of what we go through when we start maturing, but I know I hurt her sometimes when I snap at her. The fire in her eyes that she used to only direct to my brothers is now turned on me, and it terrifies me to think my mother could be mad at me for anything! I only want to please her, and she says I do, and I only hope that's true. Yet sometimes at night, after I've entered my thoughts and activities in you, I lay awake and think about the day—thoughts too complicated to write because I can't sort them out properly even yet. And I go over things I've done and things I've said and the reactions they've gotten.

And I sometimes cry over them, because I know I've caused hurt even though I'm not aware of it at the time, and the victim brushes the insult or injury aside as if it was nothing.

I cry over it because I feel so mean and despicable when I am that way. And I vow to be a better person—not tomorrow, but right away—and I beg forgiveness at the first chance that presents itself to me. I'm always told that I caused no pain, but if I beg forgiveness, then I am gladly presented it, and I feel better for a while.

Until the next time I weaken and repeat my sin.

I pray to God and the Blessed Virgin for the strength to fight my demons, and to give patience and tolerance to those against whom I trespass. This is my constant plea. And my salvation through this confusing period I'm experiencing. Momma says this will pass. Please, God. May it be soon?

And lest I do not forget! Ian came by briefly to wish me a happy birthday on his way back from town—he had chores at home and wouldn't be able to stay long.

I was dressed in one of my new outfits, and Momma was checking the fit to see where she might take in a seam here or let one out there when his knock came at the door.

I was the closest, and was thus the one who answered.

His eyes widened when he saw me, he whistled in stunned admiration (that's how I believe it to be, I'll not be swayed otherwise), and he took a step back to take in my full height.

"I'm going to marry you someday," he said clearly, and then he stammered that he hoped I had a very happy birthday, and he wished he could stay but he had to be off.

I blushed to the roots of my hair, but I was so happy when he said that.

And surprised! Even if he could have stayed; I couldn't have spoken. I was too unable to think of something to say, except, "Thank you."

Then he was gone.

I turned to Momma, and she was smiling dreamily and looking very strangely at me.

Diary Entry — September 1, 1906

Summer is weighing heavily upon us; this is the hottest time of year in Ulster Province. It's the time that we worry the most about crop failure because the hot sun and dry air are so harmful to the plants we've worked so hard to nurture up to this point.

I'll be going back to school soon, but in the meantime, I'm working as hard as anybody twice my age to fertilize the plant roots and keep pests and animals away from the almost mature growth. The food we've stored since the last harvest is just about gone; we've enough to last until harvest time and not much longer. We're fortunate to have our own fresh well with its seemingly unending supply of life-sustaining water. We share this with our neighbors, so all of us are doing well— much better than some in the country who aren't as blessed as we and are losing too many crops to the heat and "critters" (that's a word they use in the American West, I read it in a book).

At anytime between four and eight weeks from now, we'll start our harvest (school is dismissed so the children can help bring it in), store what we need, and then make the rest available to sell at market. Momma and I have already finished our crafting to sell alongside the produce from the farm. The extra money we bring in can help sustain the household for goods we can't supply ourselves. We also trade with those who may have things we need, so everybody benefits. It's an efficient system, and I sat with Momma and Poppa late several nights this summer to learn about it so I can be more of a part of it and see where our labors go each year.

Today is also Ian McLean's birthday. He turns thirteen, and he's already quite the man! I can't help myself to see him and follow him with my eyes whenever he's within view. I know people notice me watching him, and I don't care! He's so handsome! He's taller than his father now, and he's quite filled out. He's very rugged—but graceful. When we're together in the field, he sometimes will take my hands and swing me around, then put his strong hands upon my waist and raise me in the air, up so high! And he holds me there it seems like forever; he's so strong! Then he puts me down gently and takes a step back, blushing as he says it's the boy in him and to please forgive him. And I always do, because he is so harmless, and I do like him so! His face is clear; not pocked and pimpled like so many other boys his age, and I'm pleased to say that mine is the same. We then go back to work and resume our mindless chatter for we both love to talk, and we love to hear the sound of each other's voices. It never matters what we say—as long as we are always saying something to the other.

I made him a special gift of my best straw broom, which Momma said would bring in several pence at the market, and she did not object to my making it a gift to Ian, though she could not think of what a boy would do with a broom!

I couldn't tell her without feeling foolish, so I simply said that I'm sure he'd find a use for it. I told Ian that it was to sweep his cares away should he ever find he has any—and that he would always think of me when he did so. I blushed as I said it, but since I'd practiced this little speech many times over the past few days, I was able to recite it with but a few trips and stammers.

He smiled and then swept the few dead leaves from between us until he stood inches away from me. Then he rested the handle in the crook of his left elbow, took my right hand in his, bowed, and then kissed the top of my hand! Gallantry! I nearly fainted with joy!

I quickly recovered and looked about to see if any might have seen. We were fortunate that we were unobserved. I quickly curtsied to him and then backed away before somebody should see us and misconstrue our actions.

Am I too young to feel all aflutter when I think of this afternoon? I would talk with Momma, but I'm afraid she'd misunderstand. Ian is my friend. A special friend. He's always been my favorite person to be with, to talk to, and to work with. We're best friends! Surely, nothing could come of that? Could there?

Addendum—February 10, 1911

Oh, if I knew then what I know now! Propriety. *That* word again! We knew it instinctively, though we didn't know it consciously. Surely, something *did* come of that, for here we are. We are not betrothed, actually—but not far from it. We've never seen another of the opposite sex to us; it's been *only* us. Schoolmates have long said we were an inseparable pair, and we are proud to be so! I'm fifteen years old now, and he's seventeen—and we're already old and comfortable mates. He sits here with me as I write this and smiles, yet he's never moved to compromise me nor have I ever encouraged him to. We are *best friends*—and more. *Much* more. My parents' early warnings have long faded into the past, for they know us and trust us together. Ian is and has always been and will always be welcome among my family—and I have been and continue to be in his as well. All say we will be the perfect married couple someday, and we're fairly certain of it ourselves, but we're too young. We both freely state this, and we will see what the future holds for us before we decide we are ready.

If it *is* to be us. Neither of us has nor will commit as yet. We're too young and not prepared to settle. We know this; we try to be wise, and this seems to be based on wisdom. We're not prepared; it would be foolish and dangerous to begin life without a foundation.

But from tiny acorns, it is said. My birthday that year was the start. His birthday later the same year was the anchor. As we read further, I'll remember (and he'll be reminded) of others.

Diary Entry—January 1, 1907

'Tis New Year's, and all is quiet now. It's just before dawn, when the world is hovering on the brink of sleep and wake. The sun's not up yet, but there's a brightening band to the southeast of where I sit on the back patio of our proud little farmhouse.

Listen to me! I'm talking like one of the books I love to read so dearly! And yet the description is apt. It's unseasonably warm right now, at a time where the air should be crisp and frosty. By warm, I mean it's about ten degrees outside (in America, that's 50° Fahrenheit—I found the formula in one of my school books) and that's good spring weather, not winter. It's peaceful, not a sound in the world. Not a breath of wind, lowing of a cow, nor bleat of a lamb. Calm and serene.

Quite a contrast from just a few short hours ago when we were all up—the entire village—welcoming in the New Year! Such clamor—one would have thought it to be the end of the world!

1907!

Poppa says we're the first in the world to celebrate its coming, that a new day begins along an invisible but worldly recognized line called the "Zero Meridian," which runs from pole to pole through Great Britain (of which Ireland owes fealty to and is our neighbor to the east, with Scotland on the northern portion and England on the southern) and heralds the start of a new day.

That is odd because our schoolmaster just recently educated us with the fact that the international date line, which separates one day from the next, runs jaggedly from pole to pole down the western Pacific Ocean. Meaning, if it's Monday in the Sandwich Islands, it's already *Tuesday* in the Orient! That the crossing of that line in a westerly direction causes one to "lose" a day, as it were.

So wouldn't that mean that the New Year actually begins in the Orient, twelve or so hours *ahead* of us? I know they're both right: Poppa and my schoolmaster. Poppa showed me on a map he keeps in his office the Zero Meridian, and our schoolmaster showed us on *his* map the international date line. Both are right, yet both are opposite. So where does the New Year *really* begin? So confusing!

Ian and his family were here with us last night at my request and my parent's invitation. Mr. McLean had a bit much of the whiskey last night and was feeling quite at ease. He spoke to my father and a number of the older "boys" who were present about the improvements being done at the Harland and Wolff Shipyards in Belfast. It appears that Lord Pirrie, the chairman of the yard (I guess that's the same as being the "owner"), was in the midst of constructing two huge platforms where ships larger than any before imagined would be built—ships larger even than the *Mauritania* and *Lusitania*, both of which are nearing completion and would sail later in the year—and *already* being hailed as the marvels of the seas!

He went on to say that this would require the hiring of hundreds of laborers to build the platforms and cages that will surround and support the ships being built and build the ships themselves. Anybody present would be well advised to stake their fortunes on the shipyard's future; it was sure to be bright.

Ian's eyes were wide and aflame with excitement as he listened to his father speak. He'd never forgotten his earlier visit—was it last year? I just checked back within your pages, and I see that it was August 1905. So it's a year and a third that he went with his father to the same shipyard and marveled over the vast room of drafters and designers all concentrating on creating the newest ship to sail upon the seas! If he was older than his thirteen years, I'm sure he'd have led the procession to ask Lord Pirrie for a position with his company, but it was well that he wasn't for he'd need a lot more schooling yet to be ready for the kind of work he dreamt of.

And yet, one has to wonder. What type of ship would Harland and Wolff be constructing that would be larger than the two I've just mentioned? And for *whom?* And surely, something that large can't possibly float! But Ian says, "Why not?" The *Lusitania* can. Any vessel can provided that the water displacement is less than the weight of the ship—or something like that. I've not got a mind disposed to grasp and conquer the type of complicated thinking such as what he spoke of, and I probably have gotten it wrong in my memory and thus rendered into posterity within your pages improperly. Regardless, Ian says it can be done. The calculations have all been worked out; why else make the preparations? I could see him putting his mind to it even as we spoke, so I prepared to sit quietly by and let him think.

That was when the clamor of the New Year struck us. I could see him reluctantly put this task aside, and we celebrated with the rest of the gathering.

At about two o'clock, our guests bid us farewell with thanks, and they made their way to their own homes while we ensured ours was safely secured and turned in.

That is, all except myself. I came out here to be alone for a while, at least until I should feel tired enough to sleep. But after a while, I chose to retrieve *you*, my diary, and enter the past day's events and my view in regards while they were still fresh. Ordinarily I'd have waited until morning, but now I can see morning is come—the sky is brightened and color is entering the world. Soon, the sun's first rays will burst upon this glorious scene before me, and the life of a new day's dawning will bestir.

Ah, again I sound like my books. I must learn to find my own mind.

Diary Entry—August 4, 1907

Another hot, dreary summer, yet I love it!

We rose with the dawn, and Momma prepared the most *scrumptious* breakfast for us. It was not heavy as we had hard work to do—but full of what we would need to give us the energy and stamina (I always wanted to use that word since first I learned it last spring) to last until the noon dinner.

Ian came by to help as he usually does, though lately not as much as before. He's been begging and borrowing copies of technical (is that right?) journals to study, and so he's not here as often as he used to be.

But when he *is* here, nobody seems to work harder.

We talked during our dinner break about his reading. It seems that the large slips that Harland and Wolff built are being planned for use by the White Star Line of Liverpool. Word is getting out from some of our neighbors who have relations working at the shipyard that White Star is going to build a fleet of liners to compete with the Cunard ships. Nobody knows this for sure yet, but the rumors are growing more and more toward the truth. Everybody knows White Star needs to do something; they've been losing business to Cunard since it was announced that *Lusitania* would sail on her maiden voyage early next month.

And *Mauritania* soon after that!

This would mean more work for our Irish shipbuilders who build the best ships in the world! The Cunard ships were built in Scotland, and while they know what they're doing (I suppose), we Irish know better!

And White Star *never* orders a ship from any yard but Harland and Wolff.

A Belfast shipyard.

An *Irish* shipyard!

My heart swelled with pride and patriotism—even though the news was not yet official. The new ships would be *White Star Line* ships!

Which means that they would be *the best!*

This year the results of our planting have been abundant, more so than in any other year. Poppa says that we'll actually have to lower our prices at market because we won't be able to sell everything we anticipate as surplus otherwise.

We'll still make a profit, however. Momma and Poppa and I stayed up late the past few nights determining exactly what we may expect to reap from the fields—not just for our yearly sustenance but for sale or trade at market. Poppa estimates that—barring any unforeseen happenstance that would reduce our yield—we should have about 40 percent more to sell than we did last year.

Ian was with us tonight as Poppa needed his smartness, and it was he who came up with the numbers.

Ian said, "If you have five bushels left over after taking *your* requirements out of your product, that's your profit. If that's what you have every year, that's your normal expectation. To have 40 percent more is to have two more than normal or seven total. That's your profit increase over the previous year. And you can normally expect to sell those extra two for the same price as you did before, and have that extra money—if you sold them for, say, a pound each you'd have five pounds normally, and two pounds in addition with the extra two bushels."

Seven pounds!

Poppa smiled, but Ian held up his hand.

"However, sir. You don't have five normally. You have five *hundred* normally. And you sell them for a pound each. Add the 40 percent above that—and you'd have seven hundred to sell. You'd expect to get seven hundred pounds."

Poppa nodded eagerly, but he was puzzled at what Ian seemed to be telling him.

"People here have only so much money. They come to spend ten pounds, and they expect to buy ten bushels. They won't buy the rest. You profit nothing if you can't sell the other four bushels profit over ten basic.

"What you need to do is sell them *eleven* bushels for ten pounds. Lower your bushel price by 10 percent. People will think they've gotten a bargain, and you won't have two hundred bushels unsold and rotting in your cellar. Also, people will buy from you rather than from the next seller, because your price is lower. So you have more customers. And you sell to more people. You sell everything you have and gain a *30* percent profit. Not the 40 percent you'd hoped. You lose nothing but the 10 percent that you forfeit as a *marketing* strategy. So you see where I'm leading, sir?"

Poppa nodded his head slowly. "You say, Ian, that if I lower my price 10 percent, then I make 30 percent by selling everything—but if I don't lower at all, then I make nothing?"

Ian shook his head. "Not quite. You would probably sell what you always sell because your product is good and people know you. You may sell some of your extra. Maybe 10 percent profit is earned. But you have the rest that didn't sell, and you make no profit on unsold product—product that will go to waste and be hogs' feed in six months.

"But if you risk a 10 percent loss per bushel, and take a chance that lower prices will mean more customers, you stand a very good chance to sell everything. You'd have no unsold product, and you'd gain 30 percent, which is 20 percent more than you would have if you left your prices high."

Poppa nodded; he was smiling at Ian's words. "Supply and demand, is that right, son?"

Ian nodded and said, "Yes and no. You have plenty of supply. You have to create the demand. If you and others with the same product had little supply, people would pay more because it's hard to get anywhere. And they wouldn't care where they got it, so long as they could get it. A few pence difference won't matter then. But if you and your competition all have too much supply, you have to lower your prices to get people to buy from *you*. You have to undersell your competition so people will buy from you instead of them. You create the demand by lowering the prices when the customer has options to choose from. You want them to choose you.

"That's supply and demand in a time of plenty. Everybody's got the supply. You have to create the demand by making your supply more attractive and the better value. And instead of staying at the same price and setting your goal on gaining the entire 40 percent profit, you lower your price, attract more customers, and settle for the 30 percent. Otherwise, you have nothing to offer that can't be obtained elsewhere—and you might not sell your surplus. You won't gain the forty you wanted; you might only gain twenty. Or ten. Or none. Which is why you allow a little loss to gain a bigger profit. That's what is meant by less is more."

I could see by the gleam in Poppa's eye that he understood perfectly now. I'm sure he was thinking back on the times where he had surplus and wasn't able to sell for what he wanted; in some instances, he couldn't sell *any* of the surplus at all, and it *did* wind up as hog's feed! We produced extra but hadn't *gained* extra. In fact, I recall where we made no profit at all and took a *loss* after the expenses were considered, even when we had surplus.

Poppa nodded and jotted this all down. "Son, I'm grateful. I'd have never thought of this myself—sure as I'm born. If this works out as you've said it, ten of that thirty is yours; put it toward your schooling."

"But—"

He looked up at Ian's protest. "I reward value with value. If you still refuse, I'll speak with your father, and he'll accept on your behalf. But I do ask, out of consideration for your friendship with me and mine," and he cast a side look at me as he bent back down over his writing, "that you not share your thoughts with my *competition*. As generous and as neighborly as I am, I've a family to support."

Ian stood and extended his hand to my father to shake; a deal had been made "man to man." Neither of them saw me blush at my father's implication.

"Sir, I have the utmost consideration for the friendship you and yours have extended to *me*. Consider ourselves in agreement."

This was an hour ago. Ian and my father talked for a short while then Ian accepted the invitation to stay the night in the spare loft as it was too late for him to walk home. I've retired to my cubby to write before I sleep.

My father called Ian a "man." A boy not quite fourteen? A *man*.

I thank God that John and Peter weren't here with us. Poppa's never referred to *them* as such—not that *I've* heard anyway.

My heart swells at the thought. Is this *pride* I feel for Ian right now?

Diary Entry—March 17, 1908

It's St. Paddy's Day! It's a national holiday for us Irish; St. Patrick is one of our patron saints. He's a Catholic saint, granted, but he is a symbol of all that is Irish throughout the world.

It's a religious occasion primarily for the Catholics, but it is also a symbol to all who call themselves Irish—a symbol of our people. It is said that St. Patrick drove the "snakes" from Ireland, which is actually a symbolism for driving paganism from our land and converting our ancestors all to Christians (since Ireland *never* had any snakes—not the reptile version at any rate). So I guess, in a way, he's everybody's saint—Catholic and Protestant alike.

And he's not even Irish by birth!

St. Patrick was the son of a deacon and the grandson of a priest. He was born in northern England, near Scotland, and was captured (I think by the Romans), brought to Ireland (to County Antrim—not far from here, actually!) and made a slave, but escaped after six years when a voice told him he could go home—a *spiritual* voice, for his faith in God grew steadily while he was a captive and he always prayed.

Another vision told him to return, and he came and preached to the Irish Christians, became a bishop, and lived as one with the people.

There are a lot of legends and myths surrounding him—like the snakes I mentioned, which we've never had in Ireland until people brought them over from other lands—and the shamrock! It's said he compared the shamrock and its three leaves as representing God, Jesus, and the Holy Ghost—the Holy Trinity of the Catholic Church, and ours too.

But *I* like St. Patrick's Day because it's a celebration of all that is Irish! The wearing of green. The shamrocks we all wear to show our pride in our nation and honor our religious beliefs. The fact that it falls on a *Tuesday* this year, so it's a holiday from school! (I like school, but I like holidays better!)

We give greetings, shout out our national motto "Erin Go Brae!" ('Ireland the Beautiful!'), wave our country's flag, and celebrate who we are and what we are.

We're Irish! And we're proud!

P.S. Didn't see Ian today. Perhaps he's not well.

Diary Entry—July 17, 1909

Today's my birthday, and I'm fourteen years old!

That makes you, my dear diary, six.

I've been looking back through you all day today as Momma and Poppa let me have this day as a day of leisure, and I spent it all in bed with you.

It's raining outside, which is unusual for July, but it happens once in a while and is welcome when it comes. The land's been rather dusty, and the rain helps to settle it and clear the air.

And it could use it!

The winds have been blowing a lot of dirty air from Belfast, to the north of us. Work began late last year on the new ships that White Star has commissioned from Harland and Wolff. Quite a number of men from our village have gone to Belfast to seek work in the yard, and many of them have come back to tell of the grand ships that are being built there.

Two of them, with a third one possible. Larger than *Lusitania* in every way. They'll be called *Olympic* and *Titanic*—two names from Greek mythology. Both intended, I guess, to symbolize power and strength.

And supremacy.

The work on these ships is going faster than on any other ships built there before because the goal is to steal the North Atlantic trade away from Cunard—and away from the Germans, who have been trying to become "masters of the sea" and take away the British supremacy that has been theirs since—well, since forever! And while it is patriotic to want Britain to retain that claim, White Star wants to be the company that does it.

Ian's been absorbing all the information about these two gigantic steamships ever since the construction was announced. He wants to learn all there is to know about them since they are to have the latest engineering technology and the absolute final word in luxury and safety. His head is practically exploding with all the knowledge he is getting, which worries his father somewhat, because he fears that Ian's health will suffer if he doesn't eat properly and get some exercise.

I try as I can and manage to get him to run with me in the fields when we aren't working, though he's not over as often as he used to be, but he makes an absolute point of spending all his time with me—whatever I may be doing—when he *is* here.

Ian has grown into such a handsome, strong, and graceful man. And he's but fifteen! He's intelligent—more so than anybody I've known who's more than twice his age—and so courteous and polite. He has a smile for everybody he meets, and he's gallant and gentlemanly.

One would swear he was raised a royal!

That's why I went back through you, my diary. Not so much as to see how *I've* grown in the six years since you were begun, but to see how *Ian* has grown—and my feelings for him as well.

I think I'm falling in love with him. Not the kind of love a girl would have for a neighbor boy she's known all her life, been close to, and has been fond of and shown concern for.

I mean *love*. The kind where your heart flutters when you think of him. The kind where the sound of his voice causes you to shiver with delight. And the smell of his skin when he's near you, how it makes you feel … I can't describe that. It's too … personal.

Where your thoughts always come back to him. Your dreams—he's a part of them too.

You miss him if you haven't seen him that day. Or that hour.

Or that moment.

And you're not truly happy until you've seen his smile. Felt the touch of his finger as he brushes a lock of your hair from your eye.

Or your shoulder.

Or your cheek.

Brrrrrr. (That's as close as I can come to describing a shiver that isn't caused by the cold.)

All he talks about is those two ships being built in Belfast.

And I don't mind it at all.

Just so I can hear his voice.

And hear him talking to me.

And sharing with me his interests.

Because he is *my* interest.

Am I in love?

Yes. I think I am.

I really, really do.

I remember reading, just a short time ago, my words to you, dear diary, written on my eleventh birthday—three years ago! When Momma bought me some new dresses to help me begin to appear as the woman I was becoming (and am becoming still!). When Ian came to the door and his reaction when I opened it while wearing one of them.

He said he was going to marry me someday.

I hope he does, dear diary.

Because I think he's in love with me.

I think he always has been.

I think I always have been too.

With him.

Diary Entry—April 7, 1910

Ian and I had a very nice discussion today regarding his future.

His father took him again to the Harland and Wolff Shipyard in Belfast last week, again for another customer who requested financing for a fleet of tugs to replace those that were beyond their usefulness. Of course the customer had excellent credit with Ian's father's banking firm, but Mr. McLean still had to review the plans and the specifications for the fleet, and that meant a trip to Harland and Wolff. Ian persuaded his father to allow him to accompany him and thus was spent four days in Belfast—days in the drafting building at the shipyard and evenings in meetings with the designers and builders of the proposed fleet.

While there, they met with a Mr. Carlisle and a Mr. Andrews, the chief design engineers for the new liners being built for White Star, and were given a tour of the immense ships under construction.

Ian raved about them! What marvels they were, and how they were bigger and destined to be more luxurious that the two Cunard liners—the *Mauritania* and the *Lusitania*. They were invited to go inside the *Olympic*, which was framed and enclosed, and was having the decks installed. They stood on the unfinished boat deck, about the middle of the ship, and looked across to where the *Titanic* was being built just meters away. *Titanic* was still just a steel frame, and the hull plating was beginning to be installed. Ian could see the girders and supports that held everything together—from side to side, front to back, and top to bottom—and all the decks and holds and engine spaces in between.

He filled my head so with all his technical talk, and I could barely understand a word of it—but I think I got it down all right.

All this was fine. I know how he's yearning to be an engineer someday, and I know he has to study hard and work his way up into the profession. And I, hoping to be his mate, will learn what I can and thus be a support to him and a sounding board for whatever ideas he may have.

We have long heard about the two ships being built, but Ian is the only one who has come and described them in such detail to us in our town—yet Belfast is only fifty miles away! Many of the lads of our village have seen the ships from afar—and more than a few actually work at the yard—but not on those two grand ladies in their slips. Those two are reserved only for the best craftsmen within the company who have earned the honor to help construct. Ian is thus the only one from our home to not only see them from the gantries but to actually stand on the deck of one of them! Yet, he treated this grand achievement with his customary modesty. He spoke of them with such reverence and awe, yet one could see the pride in his eyes as he did so. They were British ships to be certain, but they were built by our skilled Irish workers and designed from bottom up by Irish engineers.

Even in their current status, with *Titanic*'s beams not yet sheathed in her steel garment, the ships were beautiful to behold! Such majesty and grandeur! They were long—nearly nine hundred feet! And slender—just ninety feet in width. Ian said to me that this ratio would resemble the sleekness of a greyhound and allow the ships to knife through the ocean swells without the slightest roll or rocking motion evident to the passengers who would expect a grand ocean liner to be as stable as a luxury hotel anchored to solid bedrock.

And the finished height of the ships—nearly two hundred feet tall, from the very bottom to the top of the two masts—one in the front and one in the back, with the four funnels between.

Of course, the ships weren't that far along yet; this would happen after the launch, when they'd be towed to what Ian calls the "fitting dock" where the engines, boilers, lifeboat davits, and funnels, and all the other paraphernalia that comprises a completed ship would be installed—"fitted in." Right now, it would be just the finished hull and nothing above the railings save for the upper decks would be done to the ships on the slips where construction began.

Ian told me that at this stage of construction an observer could only surmise what the finished ships would look like, but he said that he had a unique opportunity to look at the artist's drawings of how the ships would appear when finished and how grand and majestic they would be! Each company had its own color schemes, mostly in the funnels, which would give an idea of the finished state of the new ships and gave them their own special beauty. Also, in their physical appearance, they'd be one hundred feet longer and slimmer in design (only five feet wider!) than the two Cunard Ships (the *Lusitania* and *Mauritania*) and their upper decks would be huskier. They wouldn't be quite as fast; that's not what the owners wanted. They wanted style, luxury, and class. Comfort was the key and even the steerage passengers would enjoy a pleasure and leisure they'd never in their lives before known.

I hope that someday he'll take me to see them. Perhaps even step aboard one of them.

Oh, wouldn't that be grand!

Diary Entry—February 20, 1911

Oh, my head, it spins so! A day that started out so good suddenly turns devastatingly bad—and then ends up turning out so perfect!

Ian proposed to me!

I'm to be *married*!

Oh, how can I describe this wonderfully mixed-up day? My mind is in such a tizzy, and no amount of pinching is able to help me come to grips and sort out the sequence or even the proper starting point of a day that was both my worst and best in my oh-so-short life!

All that is still clear to me is that I awoke as usual to go to school, as today's a Monday. So far, a normal winter day for me. I was accompanied by Peter, who was still a student. John finished his schooling last year, and William is three years behind me.

Normal.

All was as to be expected during the morning session. Our midmorning break was spent out in the yard, for the sun had come out for the first time since late last month, and the warmth of the rays was longed for by all.

I sat as usual with Ian, and we talked about nothing particularly important. He wasn't coming to our farm as often as he used to because he was working afternoons as a junior clerk in his father's bank and spending evenings poring over any and all technical journals by lamplight to gain whatever knowledge he could to enable him to pass an entry examination at some undetermined future date for admittance to an engineering academy. He was still awestruck by the *Olympic*, which he'd seen during a recent visit to the shipyard with his father. It was, from outward appearances, finished—some detail painting to do on the superstructure and obviously more work being done internally, but majestically beautiful to the uneducated eye.

Ian said that she would be ready to sail on her maiden voyage by the end of May—and that it would be timed such that the dignitaries present at the launch of *Titanic* would board *Olympic* and sail with her from Belfast to Liverpool and then on to Southampton, from where her first voyage would begin.

Quite the extravaganza!

But that's not what we talked about. We talked about how much we missed the time we used to spend together working in the fields, and the talking we did, and the fun we always had together. We had only a few moments before class resumed, so we parted company and returned to our assigned seats and returned to our lessons until the noon meal break arrived.

That time seemed to take forever, for in parting, Ian mentioned he had something very important to tell me, and I was anxiously wondering what it might be. His face was so serious, and his speech was a broken stammer. Whatever it was, just the thought of it made him nervous and I hoped it was nothing threatening to him or to his family. Was somebody ill? Perhaps *dying*? I found it nearly impossible to concentrate on my lessons as I anticipated what he might have to say to me when we met at noon.

I was not prepared for what awaited me.

We retrieved our pails from the shelves in the cloakroom and strolled across the yard to our "special" tree. We sat beneath the branches bare from the winter still embracing our land. We barely spoke a word on our way there.

Once settled, we set our dinner aside and faced each other. I will try to relate the conversation as best I can, but it is such a jumble still so, diary. Please forgive me my chaotic recollections.

Ian looked directly into my eyes and reached out to take my hand. "I've been thinking these past few days, ever since you let me read your diaries. About us." He was blushing and stammering as he spoke.

I blushed too, and I looked at him hopefully. He knew my secrets—my dreams and my passions from reading your pages—and I believed I knew what he was about to say.

I was wrong!

"I feel that you've put me on a pedestal, and I'm not worthy of that. I'm a simple Irish lad of Scottish blood, and I hope someday to make a success for myself, but I also know realistically how dim that future really is for me.

"I'm not the man you think I am. I'm a simple banker's son, gifted with a mind for numbers and a talent for building things. My goals are only hopes. I may never realize my dreams, though I'll not give up trying yet."

I was silent while he spoke, and I dared not form an opinion of what he might be trying to tell me. He wasn't finished yet, but my fear was rising within my breast.

"I can't be the man you want me to be. I read of myself through your eyes when you opened your books to me, and I could not recognize myself within those pages! That wasn't me you wrote about—the man you described with your pen was a total stranger to me. And to you, though you think differently."

I know he could see the stunned look in my eyes, and he reached out to close my mouth, which had dropped open in shock and dismay.

"I don't want to hurt you," he went on. "But I'm not the man you imagine me to be, and I won't see you deceived by a misconception. You are entranced by someone who doesn't exist. I'm not the Ian you describe in your diaries; I never was and may never be. Please forgive me for shattering that illusion you've created of me."

I remember gasping for air and running from him at that moment, leaving everything of mine behind. I could hear him call after me, and I'm certain he gave chase, but I eluded him. I wanted to be alone; I *had* to be alone! My heart was broken, and I was all misery. I wanted nobody to see me, especially not *him*!

I was hurt, confused, and desperate. If I were Catholic, a convent would be an excellent place for me to escape to, but I'm not. I put that thought aside and wandered alone throughout the cold afternoon in despair. The sun was in hiding, and dark clouds were making the world as gloomy as I felt the rest of my life would be.

And I thought. I thought about Ian—from my earliest recollections until today—and how he had always been a part of my life. I trusted him; I believed in him. I shared his hopes, his dreams, and his desires. I always believed he'd be no more and no less the man that I knew him to be. Granted, I enlarged him in my diary—that's what you're for! To write down my fantasies and my longings *as well as* my realities and events that I am part of. *I* know Ian was portrayed as "larger than life" in your pages. I know the "real" Ian McLean is what he believes himself to be. The man he describes himself as being is the very same man I love!

Or thought I did.

I thought I knew him.

And I thought he knew me.

Perhaps we really can't ever know one another the way we need to, and we're meant only to accept one another for what we reveal ourselves to be over time and build our relationships with one another on the average balance of those revelations.

That would be fine. I could accept that of him and expect him to accept no less and no more of that from me.

We do that every day of our lives in every aspect of our lives—from dealing with people to dealing with nature.

We learn to deal. Provided the "average" is a strong and secure foundation for growth for we grow *together*, not separately.

That's a partnership.

That's what I had hoped to have with Ian someday.

A partnership.

A relationship.

Companionship.

For life.

It had become pretty obvious to me by this time, and it was now late afternoon, that I had not only fooled myself but allowed myself to be fooled by Ian. His gallantry and his courtesy. His "gentlemanly ways" toward me—were they for my benefit? Or his self-esteem. Had I been patronized all these years? Just because I'm two years his junior doesn't make me a little child to be coddled and cooed to! I was beginning to think that's what had been happening! Because although the version of Ian McLean I'd set down in your pages *was* idealized, it didn't mean that they weren't based on the *real* Ian! The real Ian was there! And any buildup I may have done to him was based on my interpretation of his dreams, ambitions, and goals—the fully formed Ian—as *I* saw him, based on all the available evidence he presented to me!

I was so very angry by now; I was absolutely *furious*! He was taking me for a fool, and I'd done nothing to deserve that! I'd grown to love him as time went on. He *was* the Ian I'd envisioned and preserved within your pages. I knew him, and I saw him with wide-open eyes; were we not friends in the beginning? We had no secrets from each other; we'd shared all our experiences growing up together, and there was nothing hidden.

Or so I thought, and as I believed I'd found out differently earlier on.

I gradually made my way home. My family was anxiously awaiting some indication that I'd not met with a cruel fate after having run off from school. I was met with looks of genuine concern, but words were withheld as I came in with fire in my eyes and color in my cheeks. I stopped before my parents, who clearly knew from Peter what had transpired regarding my departure (though he couldn't have known why without talking with Ian). I stood humbly before them and apologized, begging them for forgiveness while requesting they not ask me to explain myself at this particular time. I could not have done so if they had. Bless them; they granted my wish (for the time being, as all present knew I'd be called to account eventually for my actions), and I proceeded to my cubby and withdrew you first off.

But before I could put pen to paper, Poppa knocked softly and entered.

"Ian is here to see you," he said quietly. "He saw you as you arrived and hurried over here. He's frantic. I don't know what happened between you, and if you decide to send him away, I'll support you. You're nearly an adult, though you appear to have done a very immature action today. Nonetheless, initially, this is yours to deal with."

I put you down and nodded to Poppa, and he stood aside to let me pass. He stayed back by my cubby door as I approached the front step where Ian nervously awaited me.

"We must talk, Glynnis. I'm afraid you misunderstood my intent in what I said at lunch, and I beg you to allow me to finish and explain."

I stared daggers at him and tipped my head in the direction of the well.

"We can talk there. But be forewarned, Ian McLean. There's not much you can say to me that will smooth *this*!"

I marched to the well and quickly spun to face him. My intention was not to sit before him where he would have the implied benefit of height to look down on me—but to meet him as near to eye level as my own limited elevation would allow.

"You've said your piece to me, I shall speak mine. We shall decide if there's anything more to be said by either of us!"

He opened his mouth to speak, but I stopped him before he could utter a sound.

"I am not a fool, Ian McLean, nor am I a naive child who doesn't know her own mind. I know who I am, and I know what I want. I am aware of the differences in persons, personalities, and characters. I consider myself a fair judge of character, and I am rarely wrong. Apparently, I was wrong about *you*. The 'Ian' I wrote about in the diary was not overly idealized as you so bluntly and callously called him. Have I not listened to your dreams and desires? Have I not been thrilled with you in the things you've learned—either with me or separately from me? I have written of you in a positive light as the 'Ian' who cannot fail to succeed because his strength and desire would keep him moving toward the goal he'd set for himself.

"You are correct. I have placed you on a pedestal, and I've built you up into someone far grander than you really must be. My mistake. I can't *possibly* explain what had made me think so highly of you.

"I only believed in you—in what you said and in what you did. I believed you'd given me your trust, and my tribute to that blessing was to honor you as a man without ego, one who would calmly and steadfastly progress through life, reaching one goal after another until he'd reached the top of his chosen profession—then share the knowledge that he'd gained with those who were to come after.

"More the fool am I for this. And I've only myself to blame. I can't honestly say that you led me on for I have no indication that my feelings of love for you were anything but my own.

"Love and admiration that until this afternoon was pure, unblemished, and holy; now it's tattered and torn and mildewed with tears.

"Yes, truly, I've only myself to blame. For the feelings were mine and apparently based on a falsehood, as the 'Ian' they were for and about was revealed to me to be in error by the 'Ian' that is through his own words." I said this calmly but rapidly, though my anger and hurt caused my voice to rise as I reached the conclusion. My final words to him were: "So depart from my heart, my home, and my life for there is no 'Ian' if the one I've thought to have known all my life is but an imaginary figment. Begone!"

I got that from a book and was honestly surprised that I'd used it. I knew it at the time and shook my head in puzzlement even as I repeated it. "Begone!" My eyes were full of tears, and my heart was beating rapidly. I felt faint and regretted that I chose to stand.

But stand I did, and I made my stand. I looked at Ian, my eyes had never actually left him throughout my tirade. He did not flinch even as my pitch became higher and my tone became louder and my words fairly rushed as I neared my conclusion. Had I thought of it, I'd have been certain to have realized that I could be heard within the house, yet the well was a good fifty meters behind it.

Ian never said a word. Nor did he attempt to quiet me and stop me from my speech. His eyes were locked onto mine, and he remained solemn and reserved. He waited silently as I gasped and glared at him, and my frustration with him at last broke free.

"So you're just going to stand there? You'll not offer me a defense or an explanation for your critical judgments of my written opinion of you? Even though that opinion has, up until now, been nothing but the most flattering, the most optimistic, in regard to your talents, abilities, and intelligence that any one person would give the world to have spoken on their behalf and in their regard? Are you just going to allow your cruelty of this afternoon stand as delivered? Are you?"

He just looked up at me and smiled, and with that smile, my heart melted. It was as if the first warm ray of sunshine had come to peer behind winter clouds full of thunder and rain and to make the earth begin to awaken from its slumber and yearn with happiness for the springtime that was promised to follow. I can't explain it even now, when I've had time to recall it and review it and study it. My anger vanished in an instant. No! Faster than *that*!

When he spoke he was quiet, calm, and reassuring. "If you had allowed me to finish, we would have saved the both of us so much grief, my darling," he began. "But I blame myself, for I don't know how to say these things that I feel other than to speak and let the words fall where they may with the *hope* they fall correctly. I obviously failed. Please let me begin again."

I mutely nodded in assent.

"I meant to say that I am not the 'Ian' you so lovingly portrayed in your writings, but I want to be because that's how you see me and thus that's how I *must* be—though I don't see myself that way. I guess that's what is meant when people say that one cannot accurately judge oneself.

"But I know your feelings for me are real, though the 'Ian' you love is not—not as I see myself. But that *must* be me for you said that you are a wise judge of character. I must demur. You are an *excellent* judge of character. If what you wrote of me is how you see me, then that must be how I am. And I need to accept that, but I must not try to see it for myself, for that will change me—and then I'll not be as you see me. I must remain deaf to the praises you give me and trust in you to know they are true.

"My fear is that I will disappoint you as I've so unfortunately done today. I've crushed you. I've caused you pain and anguish, and I'll pay for that for the rest of my life. My lifelong desire has been to bring you nothing but happiness and joy—for that is all you've ever given to me.

"What I wanted to tell you was that I was honored and humbled by your admiration and opinion of me. Your feelings for me cause me to ponder what I did to deserve them and how I can retain and preserve them.

"I came up with only one answer, but I clumsily approached it in a manner that caused you to become angry and run from me. I don't deserve a response from you or the answer to the question that I need to ask, and I have absolutely no right to make another attempt to try to approach this subject again though I feel I need to, or we'll both wonder what we might have lost from this misunderstanding. Yet it's the only thing I can do."

We both had been standing this whole time—from the time we stopped at the well until this instant. Suddenly, he reached out, grasped both of my hands in his, brought them to his breast, and then dropped quickly to one knee. It was so quick I couldn't react. I remained silently stunned as he looked up at me with unshed tears glistening in his eyes.

"Glynnis Smith, I beg of you. Please be my wife! Marry me and allow me the honor of being the Ian McLean of your dreams. This is all I've ever wanted in life, more than my career, more than life itself. And allow *me* to put *you* on the same pedestal you've placed me on, so we can both do justice to each other as equals!"

Of course, I said yes. It took me a few minutes to find my voice, but I said it. I said, "Yes!"

I'm crying again. I have to go before my tears erase your pages. Oh, dear diary, I'm *so* happy! And I was *so* wrong about him this day! Ian, I'm so sorry!

Thank you for your forgiveness!

Diary Entry—May 4, 1911

Ian's been spending quite a bit of his free time (weekends, mostly) at the Harland and Wolff shipyards. He's made quite an impression of Mr. Thomas Andrews, who has now become the chief architect involved in the construction of those two White Star Line ships (and the third very soon to begin in the space where *Olympic* once rose) since Mr. Carlisle retired last year. Ian has an open invitation to stop by and see him anytime his father should bring him to the yard, and it's an invitation that Ian never hesitates to take advantage of. He accompanies Mr. Andrews on all his rounds, which take up most of every day since the yard is rarely idle. The *Olympic* is due to begin sea trials before the end of the month, after which she will begin service for White Star. And *Titanic* is being made ready for her launch, which will occur at the same time. So obviously the yard is extremely active in preparation for these two events.

Evenings, Mr. Andrews and Ian are together at Mr. Andrews's home, dining and drinking (Ian!) and discussing Ian's future. It's plain that Mr. Andrews is impressed with my Ian (and my heart fills with such pride!) and is bringing Ian along in understanding terminology and formulas. Stress points, load factors, the difference between gross tonnage and displacement, and the benefits of a flat bottom, the advantage of a long narrow hull over that which came previous (short and wide), what a Plimsoll line is. *My* head hurts now—how can Ian absorb this?

But he does. My Ian is so smart, and Mr. Andrews is shaping Ian's intelligence and curiosity into something that will stand him good for the rest of his life. He's taken Ian under his wing and is teaching him to fly! And Ian is so grateful to him; he often wishes he could properly thank Mr. Andrews for all he's doing for him.

Alas, this means I don't see Ian as much as I used to, which is far less than I'd like to now. I want to spend all my waking moments with him as I spend at night in my dreams. But I must be patient, for this is the man I love and who loves me back. And we've years to be together. I know that I must be the dutiful wife (to-be, I add but only for now) to offer strength and support to my beloved and the future he envisions for us together. I've been as if in a daze for the past three months—ever since Ian proposed marriage and I accepted. We've been asked the date, but we've not thought that far ahead. It's too soon! Just knowing I'm betrothed is enough for my feeble female mind to accept. I can't speak for Ian, but I'm sure he has his mental state of confusion as his excuse as well.

And every time I try to think of life with Ian, I panic!

Married? Me? I'm but a child—I *can't* be getting married! My mother assures me that I'll be fine, and she agrees with both Ian and me that there's no rush. We've all the time in the world. We're both young, and we've a long way to go before we actually have to commit ourselves in matrimony. We're both still in school, and that leaves at least three years since my schooling won't be finished until then. Ian's two years older, so he'll be able to find employment in the meantime and pursue his career goals—perhaps becoming an apprentice at Harland and Wolff as he dreams of!

And this is a future that really shouldn't be because we're of a lower class! Only those born to privilege can gain a position and prestige such as Mr. Andrews is making available to Ian! Our people have no money for schooling of this nature! To be an engineer, responsible for the design of such majestic creations as these ships! Or of *any* of the marvels being envisioned by our enlightened society! Aeroplanes! Automobiles! Locomotives in the last century. Wireless communication as opposed to telegraph! Telephones! Poppa's been thinking of getting one since our village has now got a central switchboard and several of our neighbors are on the circuit. It would be so much easier to call somebody to talk or ask for something than it is to walk or ride over and find nobody's home. But he hasn't yet. And he refuses to get an automobile. I can't say I blame him. I *still* think they're infernal!

Ian came by tonight, but only for an hour. He's been looking so exhausted lately, with his schooling during the day and studying the engineering information (Manuals? Texts?) that Mr. Andrews sends him home with after his weekend visits— those weekends at Harland and Wolff whenever he can find transport to and from the yards. I beg of him to find time to rest, but his response is that the time with me is the most blissful rest he can have. I see that his countenance is brightened while we are together. I am so glad I can give that to him!

He's gone now, and it's time for my slumber. I must set you aside, my dear diary. Until tomorrow!

Diary Entry—June 1, 1911

I'm so sorry I've not written in you for the past two days, but what an *amazing* two days it's been! To walk the deck of the *Olympic* as an invited guest—to *sail* on her from Belfast to Liverpool, to *sleep* on her, and take the ferry back to Belfast today!

And it all came about from an invitation to watch as *Titanic* was launched, extended by Mr. Andrews to Ian and myself!

How do I sort out and recall all that went on in my life since Wednesday? Everything that happened is so foreign and so outside of the world that is mine that it's as if it happened to somebody else and I was privileged to witness—and to *feel*— the experiences of another. That *couldn't* have been me who lived it, could it?

And yet, it *was*! I still can't believe it.

I'll start at the beginning, and to do that, I'll briefly recall what I've earlier written in your pages leading up to the point where I so carelessly neglected to write over the past couple of days the events as I lived them, though you were in my handbag the whole time!

Ian came over late on Sunday, all out of breath and with his cheeks flushed with the exercise. I feared something had happened to someone in his family, that there was a sickness or—God forbid!—but he was smiling. Broadly. He motioned me to hold my questions until he could catch his breath; he'd run all the way from his home on the other side of the village.

He'd received a telegram from Mr. Andrews at Harland and Wolff. Would he care to join him and other dignitaries from the shipyard and White Star to witness the launch of *Titanic* and then have lunch with them afterward? Ian breathlessly accepted—and may he invite his betrothed to join them?

Mr. Andrews graciously said yes!

And now to begin.

Mr. Andrews arranged for an automobile to pick us up early on the thirty-first and convey us to Belfast. We arrived shortly after ten o'clock in the morning. We alighted at the office entrance to an enormous building, which Ian told me was the main drafting office, where the ships were initially conceived and designed and where the construction plans were created. We went inside and announced ourselves, and we were escorted to Mr. Andrews' office.

This was my first meeting with the man to whom Ian had been so full of gratitude and thankful for his patronage. And I found him to be the most marvelously *gentle* man I've ever encountered (aside from my Ian, of course). Yet he was a man who commanded the utmost respect from his subordinates, as I was soon to find out. His superiors appeared to rely heavily on him and deferred to him for answers—both simple and technical—to questions asked in regard to the two beautiful ships we were to see later today.

We spent some time in the drafting room, where Mr. Andrews proudly showed us the drawings for both *Titanic* and the new *Gigantic*, which was about to undergo construction next to her in the spot where *Olympic* was built.

Shortly after this, he transported us to the shipyard itself where we saw the crowds of people already assembled to watch the launch. We were guided down to the floor of the dry dock, and Mr. Andrews escorted us along the entire length of the ship—from bow to stern and back again. Nine hundred feet long! We were accompanied on this trek by Mr. Andrews' wife Helen. She is such a gracious and charming woman and a perfect companion for this pleasant-mannered man—a match that I hoped soon Ian and I would be as well.

In the distance ahead of us, we saw two gentlemen who were making the same journey as we. Mr. Andrews pointed them out as Lord Pirrie, owner of the Harland and Wolff shipyard, and Mr. J. Bruce Ismay, managing director of White Star Line and thus "owner" of *Titanic*. They were too far way to see with any great detail, though the gentleman identified as Mr. Ismay held a walking stick in one hand as he and Lord Pirrie discussed who knows what, but to me it appeared obvious. The majestic *Titanic* could be the only subject worth discussing at that time!

I found out later that day that Lord Pirrie and Mr. Andrews were related—uncle and nephew.

As the time approached for the launch, Ian and I begged off from accepting Mr. Andrews' invitation to join them on the grandstand to witness the launch from up close. Instead, we stood back and to one side—close to where *Gigantic* would be taking shape—and watched from that point. It was shortly after noon when the signals were given. Two rockets launched a few minutes apart, and the immense ship slowly began sliding backward and into the water awaiting her.

It was an impressive sight! And the noise of the crowd cheering, tens of thousands of voices raised in celebration as the newest and largest of the world's ocean liners took to the water for the first time. In spite of having nothing yet installed above the railings where the boat deck was, she was still sleek and inspiring, giving the appearance of immense strength and speed though she lay still and silent: no lifeboats, no smokestacks, no masts. These would be added soon enough.

And then a luncheon at Belfast's Grand Central Hotel; the public lounge had been reserved for the occasion! Such a huge, cavernous, open, and bright room! And so much food, so much to drink. I avoided most of it, I found myself too shy (me—shy?) to do more than nibble and sip as I sat with my beloved in the presence of such illustrious people! Heads of industry, lords, ladies, people of wealth and power and fame. And there I sat among them, a simple peasant farm girl! I was so self-conscious—was my hair done right? My dress is so plain and ordinary—and my sun-darkened complexion. These *ladies* with their glamour, their culture, and their perfection. Thank the good Lord that Mrs. Andrews was so much of a down-to-earth person; she made me feel *so* at ease.

We sat with Mr. and Mrs. Andrews, and they both ensured that we weren't left out and adrift among all this finery. Mr. Andrews and Ian discussed Ian's ambitions in engineering; Ian bashfully confessed that he wasn't certain what specific field he'd be settling for and finished by saying that he was looking at obtaining a broad education for the moment before deciding what to specialize in. Mr. Andrews listened solemnly and offered to advise him when he was ready—and he grinned when he said he'd be advising him in the direction of naval architecture for that's his own background!

Mrs. Andrews and I talked about the similarities and goals we shared and how little difference there was between us! Though she was born to society (her father had once served on the board of directors for the shipyard, and her brother was a member of the chamber of commerce in Belfast), she claimed to have no more ambition than to be a strong and supportive wife to Mr. Andrews and the raising of his children. They currently have but one—a daughter they called "Elba" for her initials (Elizabeth Law Barbour Andrews) who is so adorable!

My ambitions are much the same though *my* background, as you know, dear diary, is so much more simple.

But I hope to be much more though: always to be at Ian's side!

I wish I could go into more detail about the luncheon, but I can't! There was so much, and it was all so delightful! Maybe later I'll go back and add an addendum to this entry and describe the meal once the grandeur all wears off, for what followed still seems to me to be as if I'd dreamt it!

A trip from Belfast to Liverpool on board the brand-new RMS *Olympic!*

Ian and I were among a select group comprising the owners, builders' representatives, and guests who boarded a small passenger ferry after the luncheon and transported out to the *Olympic.* Ian and I merely thought we'd just have a quick tour of the ship before it set out for Liverpool later that afternoon. But just as we were preparing to leave the ship and return to shore, Mr. Andrews and Lord Pirrie invited us to remain aboard and share the journey with them. This came as Mr. Andrews introduced us to Lord Pirrie, explained to his lordship that he was "mentoring" Ian and was his guest at the launch, which was when we were asked to remain aboard.

I thought my heart would stop! *Olympic* was empty, her only passengers being the few dozen traveling back to England, and we'd have this vast floating palace practically to ourselves!

I know I went pale, and I prayed that Ian would cordially decline the offer—I saw him make the attempt—but then he solemnly bowed in acceptance to the offer and answered that it would be our honor to remain aboard and extended his humble thanks for the invitation.

I was speechless; all I could do was a shaky and clumsy curtsy. Mrs. Andrews gently slipped her hand around my arm to support me, and as soon as Lord Pirrie turned away, I leaned against her in a swoon!

Remaining aboard would mean that we'd be dining with these lords of industry and their ladies! In first class! And J. Pierpont Morgan, the American millionaire, would be there as well; I knew he was on board as he'd been pointed out to us earlier!

When I was small, maybe no more than six, I remember standing in the shallows of the swimming hole near our farm and watching my older brothers swimming out where it was deep. I hadn't yet learned to swim. Something floated near me, and I stepped toward it, intending to reach out and see what it was. I wasn't aware I'd stepped off the shallow shelf until I dropped into deeper water. I was in over my head!

That's exactly how I felt yesterday afternoon and toward evening as the time to join our hosts in the first-class dining room approached. We were underway and had been since shortly after four o'clock when the anchors were raised and *Olympic*'s engines were started and the small tugboats nudged the ship into the center of the North Channel, pointed her toward the Irish Sea, and we set off for Liverpool.

Ian saved me then. I hoped he could save me now. I was so afraid that I'd embarrass both myself and my beloved husband-to-be with my lack of breeding and culture. I tried to beg off as sick. I was certain I could be convincing as I'd never been out to sea and was sure I'd be ill, but Ian saw through my ploy. He strove to reassure me that if he'd had the merest glimmer that I'd debase myself, he'd never have agreed for us to remain aboard.

The faith and trust he had in me were reassuring, and he eventually managed to steady my nerves enough to go. A wee bit of brandy also helped. But only a bit, for I'm not used to spirits—and to indulge would render me unable to control my impulses (of which I have many for I'm normally such an impetuous spirit!) that I'd be sure to do the very thing I most feared and shame myself and my life's love!

Thank the Good Lord for Mrs. Andrews. She sat near me and constantly gave me gentle smiles of encouragement and support throughout the meal. I risked only one glass of sherry (oh, but the taste was exquisite!) through the meal, and this helped me maintain a calmness and gave me courage (false, I'm fully aware, but welcome!) to survive the evening.

The ship's orchestra serenaded us throughout the evening, and we were also joined by several of the ship's officers, those who were not on watch. Captain Smith (Edward, I believe his first name is) hosted the dinner, and I must admit it was eerie with the few of us (perhaps three dozen people) in such a vast room. It seemed as if there were more stewards than there were diners! I was so unaccustomed to be served, and I was unsure of the proper protocol during the meal.

And what a meal! Roast brisket of lamb. A fish of some kind—I think I was told halibut—with a sweet and sour honey and lemon glaze. Potatoes in their jackets and seasoned so deliciously! The soup was a vegetable base, and I couldn't tell what else was in it, but it was flavored generously with onion and seasoned with a hint of garlic. I felt it had just a bit too much salt; I could taste it lightly in the broth. Several vintages of wine and champagne. I skipped the wine other than the sole glass of sherry, which I'd sipped sparingly, though I did accept a glass of champagne when it came time to toast to the success of the RMS *Olympic* when the time came to set out on her maiden voyage in a fortnight.

I was beginning to relax throughout the course of the meal, and I was realizing that—in spite of their wealth and position in society—these people were just that. People. Well-educated and privileged people to be sure, but beneath that—people. That's not to say there wasn't an edge of snobbery and class distinction for there is in all of us, even in myself though I pray not *too* much! As the evening progressed, I felt so comfortable among these people who would otherwise not be a part of my world, nor I theirs, and I wondered what my fears were based upon!

And by the end of that evening, I was so tired! The stress and the anxiety had completely exhausted me. Not being wed, Ian and I were assigned separate (but adjoining) staterooms on A deck. Luxury suites! With a shared promenade deck! Cabin A-32 was mine; Ian had A-30. These were on the uppermost passenger deck, and while not as exclusive as the "millionaire suites" one deck below and behind us (and in use by Mr. Morgan, Mr. Ismay, and their guests on this night), we certainly felt it so! An oak four-poster bed with velvet drapes and goose-down pillows and a spring mattress! The washstand was also oaken with a marble top and steel basin. The paneling was a rich mahogany, and the trim around the ceiling and doors had carvings of mythological figures such as Zeus and Apollo. I suppose this was in keeping with the Greek basis of the ships name, but I'm only guessing.

Above us was the boat deck, with cabins for the officers, and below us was B deck, with more first-class staterooms, including those "millionaire suites" on both sides of the ship. Their private promenade decks were segregated from the rest of B deck's promenade, which ran the full length of the ship (as did the one on our deck). My cabin looked out onto the upper promenade deck, which itself was open to the sea, providing fresh ocean air to the passengers. One would think that it would be rather exposed in bad weather, but right now, it was warm and calm. We weren't actually "out to sea," though the channel separating Ireland from England is called the Irish Sea. We could clearly see the English coast from our cabins on the left side of the ship—and almost see Ireland in the far distance on the right.

It was late, and we knew we'd be docking in Liverpool shortly before dawn. But we couldn't sleep. Ian and I tried. We bid each other a good night and retired to our separate cabins but soon found ourselves up and out, watching the horizon as the ship glided serenely through the Irish Sea between England and the Isle of Man as we steamed in a straight path toward Liverpool. We soon found ourselves up on the boat deck where we had a more unobstructed view and remained there until early this morning when *Olympic* slowed and was guided to her dock by tugboats and her engines were stopped.

As we made our way to the gangplank, we kept our eyes out for Mr. and Mrs. Andrews. We fortunately spotted our hosts since we didn't want to leave without giving them our most sincere thanks for such a rare and unique treat. Mr. Andrews assured us that the pleasure was indeed all his, and he gave us a letter of introduction to the manager of White Star's Liverpool office where there were tickets awaiting us for a return ferry to Belfast (I hadn't thought how we'd get home!) and from there, conveyance would await us to bring us back to the village. He and his wife would be remaining with *Olympic* for another day when Mrs. Andrews would head back to Belfast. Mr. Andrews would stay aboard on the journey to Southampton tomorrow, to help outfit the ship and make it ready for receiving paying passengers, and from there eventually to New York. It was his duty, he told us, to sail on the maiden voyage to take note of how well the many components of the ship worked and to make note of improvements that might benefit *Titanic* and *Gigantic* to follow.

And so now we're home, and I've finished my long and long-delayed accounting of these glorious two days spent in a world I'd only ever dreamed of visiting. I know over the years I'll be reviewing these pages with my beloved and reliving once again this brief but remarkable time spent in a palace of the gods!

Olympic. Named after an ancient mythical race of Greek Gods. As is *Titanic*. I don't know where *Gigantic* fits in unless the three are meant to convey size and supremacy. That must be it. If I wasn't so tired, I'd give it more thought, but it's late (early—the sun should be up soon) and though I began this entry on June 1, it's now well into the wee morning hours of June 2. I'll not change the date however. June 2 will have its own history to be recorded. Most likely our families' reactions to our adventures as we tell them, for we had to put off their questions until we'd rested. At least I did. I can't speak for how Ian handled the curiosity at his home since the driver let me off first. I stood in the dooryard of my sweet little home and blew kisses to follow Ian as he was driven off to his own.

Good night (or good morning!), my beloved diary!

And sleep tight, my sweet prince!

Diary Entry—July 6, 1911

I hate him! I hate him! I hate him! Oh, how can he be so mean and viciously cruel!

Is this how all men are? Poppa sometimes will argue with Momma, but it's usually over something important like money or how much of the crop harvest to keep and how much to sell or something practical and necessary.

But Ian! He tells me he wants to marry me, then he talks with that hussy Frieda Jorgesson!

That Finnish fiend!

She, with her blonde hair and her blue eyes and pearly white teeth and large bosom and fair skin and wide hips and oh!

I'm only fifteen, and I've got the worries of generations of women on me now, and it's not fair! Since we were children, it's been a given that we would be wed and now he *dares*— *DARES!*—to talk with her!

The nerve!

Oh!

And he enjoyed the attention she paid to him!

Her family just moved to our village last week; her father was brought over by Lord Pirrie at Harland and Wolff to lend his expertise in ensuring that the *Titanic* outshines her older sister ship that was launched a few weeks ago. It seems that though the owners are quite happy with *Olympic,* which has been in service for several weeks, they want *Titanic* to be even better.

So Lord Pirrie enticed Mr. Jorgesson to his company from a shipyard in Germany. He'd been involved in the design of the *Kaiser Wilhelm II* in 1903, and he was still in negotiations to be involved either in the completion of *Titanic* or become involved in the third ship, *Britannic* (this is the actual name that was chosen, *Gigantic* being too presumptuous), which is under construction in the spot where *Olympic* was built.

Or both.

That's all fine.

But he brought *her*!

That Viking vixen!

And Ian's captivated by her, and it makes my blood boil.

And she *knows* he's been partial to me!

The gall!

Look at her, her dimples and her rosy cheeks and her flawless complexion.

Seventeen years old. The same age as Ian.

She must take me for a child, the way she saunters and curtsies to her elders, and her *please, thank you, yes, sir,* and *no, ma'am.*

With that lilting Bavarian accent she picked up from years living in Stettin, where her father worked and where she plied her sneaky wiles and her devious seductions among all the boys and young men she encountered.

The trollop! The tramp!

I can still see her now, smiling *ever so sweetly* in my direction and looking me in the eye all the while she spoke with my beloved Ian. And I the fool, the withering, cowardly daisy. Trembling as my petals droop and fall under the heat of her gaze. Trying to pretend that I didn't know what she was doing! Trying to pretend that all was innocence and harmless and unthreatening. So cool, so casual. Like the glaciers on the highest peaks of the mountains from where she was born. Does she take me for a fool? Does she think me naive? Am I so gullible as to think she isn't dangerous, that she isn't trying to steal my fiancée, my dreams, my *life*? Just what does she take me for? Does she consider me a peasant just because I'm not sophisticated, that I've not traveled, that I've not been cultured?

The idiocy!

And all because of those new liners White Star is having built in Belfast!

I hope they sink! I hope *she's* on board when they do!

And Ian! Why, oh *why* are you breaking my heart?

Can't you see what she's trying to do to us? She's been here only a week. She's seen what she wants, and she's going after it.

And *it* is you!

Are you so blind? Can't you see? I don't know why she hates me. We've never even met, yet she's out to destroy me!

And she'll destroy you to do it.

We'll both lose.

We'll both die!

Oh, why is she here? What does she want? Can't she find another? I have two older brothers; why doesn't she take one of them and leave me with the only love I've ever yearned for? Why does she have to take what's mine?

What did I ever do to her?

And what did I ever do to you, Ian, for you to turn your back to me and pay attention to her. I stand here, all alone and destroyed inside, while I see the back of your beautiful head of hair and your strong, broad, and muscular shoulders—and over them I see that disarmingly sweet, innocent expression. There she is, smiling at me as if she doesn't think I don't know what she's doing to us! To me!

I have to go.

I can't stay here.

I can't watch this.

It's more than I can bear—the pain! My heart doesn't want to beat anymore. It's so broken. It's pounding so hard, and I can't breathe! I can't catch my breath!

I need to cry.

I need to be alone. Oh, God! Why does love have to be like this? It hurts, I can't bear this hurt. Nothing should hurt this bad. Please take me away from here. Please stop the pain! I can't stand it. I can't! I just want to run away and not stop until I'm far, far from here. And I'll never come back. I'll never be happy here. I'll only know misery.

Oh!

I don't want to love anymore.

I don't!

Oh, what will I do? What will I do? Love is so hard! Please, Lord! Make it stop hurting!

Diary Entry—February 6, 1912

We've set the date! We are to be wed on April 9 of this year, and we'll immediately board a transatlantic ocean liner to emigrate to America!

It's so sudden, I know, and I'm all in a frenzy! I've only two months to decide who to invite, choose my maid of honor and bridesmaids, decide what I can take with me and what I'll need to leave behind, which of those my parents will have to send to me when we've settled in San Francisco (almost half a world away!) and which could either be given away or disposed of.

San Francisco! The "Golden Gate" on the Pacific! A grand old town in the Western Territories of the United States. California! Gold and Indians and more excitement than this young farm girl from Ireland can think she could ever handle!

And earthquakes!

It was only six years ago that the Great Earthquake and Fire of 1906 destroyed the town. I remember well the relief efforts that we'd contributed to which were sent to the destitute citizens of that devastated city and the newsprint that showed the incredible destruction. The unquenchable spirit and drive of the city's denizens astonished the world. Six years later, the city's been wholly rebuilt and thoroughly modernized. Ian and I will become the newest—though certainly not the last— arrivals in a city that welcomes hundreds of people from every nation through her portals each day.

Why are we rushing to marry? I can still hardly believe the news, yet Ian had assured me that the reasons were sound.

Ian has an offer for employment with a new firm specially chartered and structured to participate in the upcoming world's fair, which had been decided last year would be hosted in San Francisco in 1915. Specifically, the company he'll be working for (as an apprentice engineer) will be involved in the design, construction, and outfitting the displays for the Palace of Machinery; one of the "palaces" and buildings to be erected on the site of the exposition. He has been offered this opportunity by, of all people, Mr. Andrews, through a cousin of his who was living in America and had a high position in the firm involved. Mr. Andrews had been asked if he knew of any fresh new talent in engineering who would like a unique opportunity to be involved in such an enterprise and—if he proved his mettle—would be able to advance rapidly in this field. Any training or education lacking would be supplied as the candidate progressed, but he must have an aptitude for learning and hard work—and unbridled enthusiasm was definitely a requirement for the position!

Ian had received a telegram sent to his father's bank last week from Mr. Andrews, asking him to please come to Harland and Wolff as soon as possible to discuss "a potential position in America that could set him on his course for the rest of his life." Nothing else was said, and Ian arranged transport the very next day in a heightened state of curiosity.

He returned two days later stunned, thrilled, and humbled. His two days in the close company of Mr. Andrews rendered him speechless from mental fatigue and uncertainty. Another day would pass before he spoke of his visit to his father and asked his advice. Ian had already accepted the position but was graciously given some time for the offer to truly sink in before his acceptance would be binding.

Mr. McLean told him to take it. Though Ian didn't have any true experience to speak of, he must have had something in him for Mr. Andrews to recommend him. Of all the people he personally knew in the engineering realm, he chose Ian—a novice and an outsider!

A day after that, Ian came to me. Initially he wanted to break the news of the offer and tell me that he'd be going away for at least three years and that he'd write me daily.

I would have none of that—let me assure you! I told him that if he didn't take me with him, then he might as well forget me. I wasn't going to sit at home in Ireland, lonely and miserable and missing him while he went to America to make his success. Either we succeed or we fail as a couple—or there will be no couple. Or he doesn't go! My fate is to be with him, for better or for worse. Those are the vows. Now or later: it doesn't matter when success or failure strikes, and we'd be stronger together than we would be apart.

I made it clear I wouldn't stand for his leaving me behind for any reason, that he might as well accept that and make his travel plans to include me.

It wasn't much of a fight for him. He knew I wouldn't let up until I had my way. Ian McLean is my man, my future, and my life. He knows this. And I am his; he knows this too. What little dissension he presented in his defense was for the sake of convention. He knew he'd have to take me—he knew it all along.

And with that, we set the date. He was required to be in San Francisco in June. He could delay his departure no later than mid-April to allow for any travel impediments. After checking the schedules of the various shipping lines leaving from Ireland or England in April, we decided we'd sail on the *City of New York* and be married on April 9.

THE DIARY—ON
BOARD *TITANIC*

What follows are the intact and consecutive entries beginning with the wedding of Ian McLean and Glynnis Smith, which took place on April 9, 1912, in the small village where they'd been born. From there, they would take the train south to Queenstown (now Cobh) where they would board the tender and be ferried outside the harbor to finally board the *Titanic* at her last stop before heading east to America. This sequence ends with an incomplete entry begun in the late hours of April 14, when Ian returned from investigating a commotion in the hallway outside their suite.

In these pages are descriptions of the wedding, the travel to the port, and their first glimpse of the majestic liner anchored in the deep water outside the Queenstown harbor.

Once on board, Mrs. McLean gives her impressions of the ship's interior and accommodations—and in what has to be almost unique among any passenger's shipboard recollections—accompanying the captain and builder on a thorough inspection of the world's newest vessel while under way. This alone justifies the publication of the memoirs; nowhere in the official transcript or evidence is a description of the various working areas of the ship given by a neutral and unbiased observer.

All recollections previously published have come from those intimately involved in the areas described, but here we hear from a passenger who was suitably impressed to record her observations as best she could remember of an environment completely foreign to her at the end of what was obviously an exciting day.

She also relates her observations about some of her fellow passengers without any pretense or gossip. She knew that she was surrounded by the "cream of society," but she was so secure and stable in her own background and place that she failed to be impressed by anyone or anything she saw in others and could only be swayed by the opulence of her surroundings and personal experiences. By those who were so far removed from her world, she found no commonality, she was unimpressed, and she therefore dismissed them from more than a passing consideration.

Move this young girl into our current society, and she'd probably be the most balanced and self-assured person one could ever hope to meet—and one who most definitely could not be swayed by celebrity.

SB.

Diary Entry—April 10, 1912 (Dawn)

We are wed; we are now Mr. and Mrs. Ian McLean! I can't quite contain my tears of joy and happiness! It seems that all our lives, our youthful companionship and flirtations were destined to place us where we are today! It seems odd, for I've never looked at or thought of another boy as I have Ian for all my days. Some might say that it is because he's ensured that I'd never have the opportunity, but that's just not so! Ian has been not around far more than he has of late, and I've met a lot of other young potential suitors in my school and my church who might have made a proper mate for me, but I never once considered them in this fashion. I'd have made mention in you, dear diary, and you would thus contain the truth in your pages.

Proper is not acceptable—not to me! Ian is *perfect,* and that is what every bride should have: the *perfect* mate and life's partner.

Our betrothal has been just a bit more than a year. We would have been wed in another year or so, but Ian's opportunity in San Francisco meant that it would have to be now. Neither of us was willing to part and wait until he was established. *I* wouldn't have stood for it, and I was clear on that part. My place is by his side and whether he succeeds or fails in his endeavors, it is my duty to be his strength—his Rock of Gibraltar—and stand beside him through his trials and tribulations. If he fails, *we* fail. And if he succeeds, *we* succeed. Suppose he went alone and got established, then sent for me and we were wed? Then suppose his establishment should crumble as so many did in the earthquake six years ago almost today! We'd be exactly where we'd be earlier. Whether he fails now with me beside him or twenty years from now as we were advised to wait for his success to be on solid footing (I exaggerate, but my point will be taken), we'd be together—and only time would be the difference. We'd still be married, and my fate would be bound to his.

I won the argument. A bittersweet success, for it's not likeable to myself to be so emphatic in my desires.

Our wedding was midmorning yesterday. Oh, such a beautiful ceremony! I know my father went deeply in debt, but as I am his only daughter, he felt that the extravagance was his pleasure. I know he must still be lying awake and wondering how to repay his creditors! Dear, sweet Poppa! I love him so—and how I'll miss his strength and wisdom over the coming days and weeks and months and years!

And Momma! Oh, how she cried as Poppa escorted me to the altar. I, a lass of sixteen, was still so very much a child and now to become a woman, now and forever. Tears flowed from my eyes as I saw them in the church, looking still so young to me but probably feeling so very old at this time—as I'll feel someday when my own child (boy or girl) will be about to wed.

My beautiful maid of honor, Frieda Jorgesson, who less than a year ago was my sworn eternal enemy. Oh, how wrong I was about her! So dear and so sweet, she's been my best girl friend, as if we'd been created from the same mold and raised in the same home! I begged her forgiveness when I realized how I'd wronged her, and she was so dear and sweet and eager to assure me that I'd not hurt her. She understood, and she'd been wronged before by those who judged her by her looks and not by herself! Yet I couldn't accept that I'd not caused her the pain that I knew I had; if it were me, I'd have died under the weight of just *half* the sins I cast upon her.

I dearly love this sweet, unassuming, innocent, young woman—may God strike me dead if my heart isn't in these words I commit to you, my dear devoted diary! I wish I was one-tenth the person she is with her strength, calm, and inner peace. The least I could do was to ask her to support me on my day of wedded bliss, to be my maid of honor—a place of high honor—as partial atonement for the injustice I had her subjected to.

And I'll name my first child after her, for surely God will grant me a girl so that I may offer this infant up in glory and honor to her by giving her the name of *Frieda* to forever bond the atonement that I make to this beautiful, adoring girl for whom I'll forever keep a special place in my heart and my life.

And Ian! My darling man! So handsome in his very best suit, which he insisted he earn and purchase himself, he'd not allow his father to do even this thing for him. He stood so tall and brave, yet I could see how he shook and how his skin was gone gray. I felt as he looked, and I'm sure I was as white as my gown. If I wasn't so proud to join my life to Ian McLean, I'm sure I'd have turned and run from the church—from the future—as fast and as far as my strong young legs could carry me!

It took forever, it seemed, as neither my father nor myself really wanted our journey to end. It was such a short walk from the vestibule to the altar, but there was more than enough time for me to remember *all* the other walks I'd made with this strong handsome man beside me: his holding my tiny fingers as a baby as I learned to stand up, our walks through the fields as the young plants he'd sowed grew, my first days at school, all my days at church, and trips to town when the weather was just too fine to bother harnessing our horses to the wagon and choosing to walk to the village center instead. All with this gentle redheaded bear to guide me.

As he had through all my life, so he did now—for the final time, I fear—walking me, escorting me to meet my destiny, to give me to the man who would guide me through the rest of my days on this earth.

Then I was beside Ian. My father gave me a tearful kiss on my cheek, placed my hand within Ian's own, and slowly turned away to join my mother in the first pew. I fearfully looked up into Ian's green eyes and read the confidence that fought with the fear he felt for the tremendous responsibility we both were taking with our lives and our futures!

The rest of the ceremony is a blur. All I can remember is that I'd removed myself from the time and place of my wedding and began daydreaming of life with my Ian. I was so lost in my dreams that I almost didn't hear when the reverend turned to me and asked, "Do you take this man …"

I stammered! I couldn't find my voice! All of a sudden I felt the urge to run, to escape! What was I doing here? I can't be married. I can't be somebody's wife! I'm only sixteen. I'm only a child! What am I doing here?

I said, "I do."

Ian was pale and perspiring heavily in spite of the spring chill in the air as we turned to face each other for the final part of our vows. I'm sure I looked the same to him as he did to me. Our eyes were wide, and our smiles were fearful as the reverend said, "With this ring, I thee wed."

Ian placed the ring on my finger as he repeated those words—a ring that he also insisted to his father that he would earn and buy himself. He was so much the mature man; from the moment he asked me to marry him, he'd set all his goals and milestones along the way as best he could so that everything would be as perfect as he could make it.

Then the reverend said, "You may kiss the bride."

And he did.

He kissed me!

Our very first kiss! Oh! *Why* did I wait so long for this? Why did I refuse to let him kiss me before when he wanted to? It was heaven!

It was *perfect*!

It really was!

I don't remember the reception; it's all still such a blur. It's almost like I wasn't even there, like I was watching through somebody else's eyes—or on a motion picture screen. It couldn't have been *me* everybody was congratulating! I didn't deserve this happiness, this bliss!

I remember all the hugs and kisses from friends and family—both families—for now I had Ian's parents to cherish as my own as well! And I remember the musicians, playing all the gay and lively Gaelic tunes that we all loved so well—tunes of our Celtic ancestors—and even some of the new songs of today that we had never before heard being rural folks and quite some distance removed from the cities, which were far more advanced than we. They had us dancing and joyous nonetheless. They were so bright and catchy! And the toasts to our health and fertility (I blush even now writing that word!), and wishes for our long and fruitful future in America!

Ah, it was so grand!

By and by, people started going home; none failed to stop by and personally give their blessings to us. We were all so tired and rather dizzy from all the ale that flowed freely last evening. 'Twas not my first mind you, but I rarely have the opportunity—or the desire—to partake of spirits. We've rarely any in our home, and Poppa doesn't approve except in the most proper circumstances as an ingredient for a special celebration. I've no wonder now as I ponder this that I don't remember many details or events that I'm certain to find myself recalling in puzzlement over the coming days and weeks.

Ian and I have a small room at the inn here in the village. Our true honeymoon will take place on our voyage, but tonight we're here: our first night as husband and wife and our first night alone together. We've spent nights out as part of a group and always chaperoned—but now!

I saw several of the male guests at our reception giving Ian a wink and a little nudge in his side with their elbows as they passed out the door while leaving the reception, and I know what *that* meant. I tried to pretend to Ian that I hadn't seen it, but he's fully aware how observant I am and that I could hardly fail to have missed the implications! And he was turning red; he knew I'd not fail to notice or misunderstand the reasons.

I was turning red too. Then *and* now with the recollection.

Ian knew what was expected of him, and I knew it too. Ah, so fearful we were tonight. Quietly slipping into our room, hoping nobody would see us, but knowing that our stealth only advertised our intentions. A solitary candle on the bureau was all the illumination we had. The door was closed and bolted behind us once we entered, and we faced each other from either side of the bridal bed.

White with fear, we slowly began to undress: he his coat, vest, and shoes and I my dress, shoes, and veil. He unbuttoned the collar of his white ruffled shirt, and I removed my garter and stockings.

Thus we found ourselves sitting on opposite sides of the bed, afraid to go any further and afraid to look each other directly in the eye.

We began to talk. About anything and everything except for the action we were expected to make. We *did* hold hands and eventually slowly moved onto the bed until we were side by side, sitting with our backs resting against the headboard, still holding hands, and the soft down-filled pillows supporting our spines.

Still talking.

We stayed that way until just a short time ago, when Ian drifted off to sleep after we'd paused to rest our jaws.

Communication in place of consummation. Poor, timid Ian—how nervous and shy he was with me just now. And I with him! We could do naught but sit up and talk all the night! We'll sleep on the train, or *I* will because Ian still sleeps on. I find that I can't right now; slumber eludes me. For we are bound for Queenstown in the afternoon; we'll board *Titanic* tomorrow and begin our new lives together.

How can our lives begin so gloriously? We were ticketed to sail first class on the *City of New York*, but the coal strike, which had been running since February, had only just been agreed to be settled—though only after devastating the sailing schedules of so many vessels. Ours was among those canceled.

God bless Mr. Andrews! He immediately arranged for us to transfer our accommodations to the newly finished *Titanic*, and we'd be enjoying her on her maiden voyage! This made us so much more nervous because *Titanic* is the newest, grandest ship on the seas today! We had invited him to our nuptials, but he sadly declined. He would be on *Titanic*, preparing her for our honeymoon voyage!

Perhaps we'll be more at ease once we're out to sea. Perhaps, with *everything* being so different from all we've ever known, we'll come together as husband and wife as the newness of our union will be more familiar than the alien experience of journeying to the New World.

I pray that it is so.

I want to be Mrs. Ian McLean.

Fully.

In *every* way I can be.

Addendum—April 11, 1912

It seems to be a good place here to put an overheard conversation that Ian and my father had yesterday following our wedding ceremony as our guests were leaving for the night.

As Ian said good-bye to his mother and father, he glanced over at me with *my* family and noticed my mother lean and whisper in my ear. I replied to her in turn. He knew what this was about—my own father had done the same with him just seconds ago. Ian told me what he said later.

"Son," my father said to Ian, "I know you'll do everything in your power to make my daughter as happy as she deserves to be. I've liked you from the moment I met you, and I know your proper manner with her is genuine. I'm very proud to call you 'son,' Ian. I know you'll be good to her. And she'll be good to you. Take care of her and bring her back to us someday."

"I will, sir." Ian accepted my father's outstretched hand and shook it with a firmness that sealed a pact. "And thank you for your trust. We *will* be back. And with the grandchildren Glynnis tells me you wish to spoil soon."

I almost felt like I'd been bought and sold. Men!

My father chuckled at this, and I blushed as my mother and I moved to join them. "I want them soon as well," my father said. "A word of advice on being a father, Ian. Always be firm. *Never* let a child believe that he can control you. If you do, you've lost. It is a parent's responsibility to exercise discipline sparingly but with tact and be generous with fairness. Don't play favorites between children or between their mother and them. You are head of household; you must have final say over all disputes. You must also listen—and consider—anything your wife and children say, for they are affected by your decisions and have a right to give their opinions.

"And above all: lots of love and patience. It is not easy being all these things, but a child is all the better if a parent is as broad a person as possible. You are not raising soldiers—nor are you educating a classroom though it may seem so. You are shaping a future for the world. Do not forget that. Look within your child and find the talent the child possesses and nurture it. Do not make the child into an image of you. Do not hold the child to fulfilling your own dreams. Let that child follow his own destiny. This is what I have done with my children. And the results speak for themselves. You married one of them, therefore you must approve of my methods."

Ian nodded. "And a fine job you've done, sir. All your children have turned out marvelous. I shall cherish the one I've chosen and protect her with my life should I ever be called to do so. And I will take heed to your advice, sir. I can tell you now that you will be proud of the children we will bring back to you. My own father raised me the same way and I will carry that onward."

I sit here tonight, entering this recollection into you, dear diary, not to reflect on what promises were made in the past but to make it clear in the very beginning of our lives together. I have no doubt whatsoever that Ian will keep this promise he made to my father in that overheard conversation just last evening and the promise made to me when he recited his part of the vows to me—and in my reciting my part in turn to him.

I am Mrs. Ian McLean.

I am whole.

Diary Entry—April 11, 1912

Oh, what a majestic ship: *Titanic*! She is certainly much more elegant than any that has sailed before her. I've heard passengers say that she's possessed of far more than even her sister ship, *Olympic,* in her accommodations and style.

And she is! It was just a year ago when Ian and I boarded *Olympic* as guests of Mr. Andrews when she was handed over to White Star upon the conclusion of *Titanic*'s launch festivities and sailed (steamed) from Belfast to Liverpool. We disembarked before the ship continued to Southampton to be made ready for *her* maiden voyage. And the changes Mr.

Andrews hoped to make based on his observations on board *Olympic* at that time—though subtle—were evident to Ian and I when we viewed the same limited areas on board this newest of luxury liners.

We boarded just after eleven thirty this morning from a tender that took us from the dock in Queenstown to where *Titanic* was anchored in the mouth of the harbor. Once we'd gotten aboard, had our tickets verified, and received directions to our suite, we hurried out on deck to watch as the ship began sailing away from land and rounded the point from Queenstown, past the Old Head of Kinsale, and away off into the North Atlantic toward New York where we're expected to arrive early on Wednesday morning.

Today is Thursday.

Once we'd lost sight of land, Ian and I took a little bit of time to explore the immediate area of the ship near our cabin. We visited the dining salon, which was set aside for our class, the barbershop (Ian did need a bit of a trim, and I found some *lovely* trinkets to remind me of our voyage), the promenade deck set aside for second class, and the library. We returned to the dining salon for dinner, but we were too overwhelmed with the foreign surroundings and strange new experiences to have much of an appetite.

So following dinner, which we'd attempted early because we'd not eaten at all this day, we again embarked on a stroll along the second-class promenade and found our way eventually up to the boat deck. As we were on the left side, we could not see the setting sun, which was ahead and to the right of us, but we could see the approaching night from the rear. It was a bit chilly, but since I'd gone back down to our cabin for my wrap earlier, I was insulated somewhat from the cold.

Sometime during the late afternoon, prior to entering the dining salon, we were met by Mr. Andrews. He was on one of his unceasing inspections of the ship. *Titanic* being a new ship, he was aboard for the crossing—as he was for the *Olympic* last year and previously for the first voyages of every ship he oversaw the construction of—to ensure that all was as designed and to note any changes or improvements needed to that particular ship or future ships of that particular class. Indeed, and as I already mentioned, many of the alterations recommended by his voyage aboard *Olympic* were incorporated into *Titanic* during her construction and would later be done with *Britannic* in her time.

When Ian and I were aboard the *Olympic* last year, we had cabins A-30 (Ian's) and A-32 (mine). His was next to mine, and mine looked out on the promenade deck on the left side of the ship. That deck was open and exposed to the sea, and even though our short overnight sailing was at reduced speed, the spray kicked up by the ship's bow knifing through the water got us rather wet.

On *Titanic*, however, this area was enclosed; large windows protected the first-class passengers from the spray that came up from the forward motion of the ship—and made worse by the breeze the ship's passage made. He'd already received his thanks from passengers who'd sailed previously on the *Olympic* for this welcome improvement to their comfort.

Mr. Andrews also told us that the stern promenade on B deck seemed underutilized on the *Olympic*; in this ship, more first-class staterooms had been added on the port side. On the starboard side, and exclusive to the *Titanic*, was the Café Parisien, a small bistro staffed by French waiters that was added to *Titanic* only a month previous, rather than the staterooms like had been added on the port. Mr. Andrews told us that while *Titanic* was delayed due to repairs needing to be made to *Olympic*, it was decided by Mr. Ismay, Lord Pirrie, and himself to include a seagoing replica of a Parisian sidewalk café for the younger first-class passengers, which was something he would have enjoyed if he had the time. The café and the enclosed forward A deck promenade were very much last-minute changes; Mr. Andrews pointed out how they were the most obvious differences between the two sisters. However, if these changes were as positive as White Star expected them to be, they'd be incorporated into *Britannic* as well as added to *Olympic* the next time she was docked for service.

I so much enjoyed the few minutes spent conversing with Mr. Andrews. Such a kind and gentle man, so courteous and attentive. One would never know from his bearing that he was so intelligent and so powerful. One was made to feel that as one spoke, he listened and absorbed what one had to say. And I felt no sense of patronization; he *was* genuinely interested in my opinion when he asked what I thought of the ship thus far. I was certain that I'd like to have him as a guest in my home; his warm and comforting personality would always be welcome in my life. If all goes for Ian in San Francisco as we both fervently hope, perhaps we can meet socially upon our return to Ireland. I could become reacquainted with his charming wife Helen, whom he speaks so lovingly and longingly of. And his baby daughter Elizabeth, whom I still hadn't met. Just hearing her name alone causes me to yearn for my own child—and soon!

Ian has gone out for a short stroll, leaving me with this brief amount of time to write down my impressions of our first, though short, day on *Titanic*. I eagerly—and not a little bit nervously—wait for his return.

My *husband*. I tingle and shiver as I think of the word and what it means to me! *My* husband.

My heart swells with pride.

Diary Entry—April 12, 1912

What a fabulous and active day—and all done without the benefit of much sleep!

Ian and I were so nervous last night that once again we did not much more than talk, though we did undress and hold each other all night. We talked of us: our future, our expectations of life, and our marriage. I won't say that we defined our individual roles in our household, but we did agree to disagree where agreement is difficult to achieve. In other areas, our positions are well defined by tradition.

Yet we still were unable to "do our duty." It's as much my fault as his, probably more because—for the first time in my entire life—I kept getting the giggles. This only served to make my poor, beautiful man even more nervous—and self-conscious—and our clumsy fumbles and groping were made to stop.

But oh, how nice it was to kiss. And kiss. And kiss. And placing my hands on his manly chest and my body tight against his and with his hands and body the same with mine—I blush and burn with the *naughtiness* of it. I knew boys were different; living with three brothers, I can't help but know that but to see—and to *touch*—well!

Tonight. I know it will be tonight. And I can hardly wait!

This morning came, and with it, the bugle for breakfast. Ian and I, bleary-eyed from hardly a wink of sleep but still tight within each other's embrace, arose, dressed, and left our cabin for the dining salon. We reviewed the menu and marveled at the rich, delightful choices available to us, but ultimately we settled on fruit with cream for, as hungry as we were, our main meal has always been the noon dinner. Our constitutions would not have stood for anything heavy so early in the day.

Following this, we went outside and settled ourselves on two vacant deck lounges near the rear portion of the boat deck, on the left side of the ship. From our vantage point, we could see farther toward the stern where the open spaces were enjoyed by the steerage class. Children played, older ones danced to bagpipes, fiddles, and mouth organs. (Older? They're *my* age!) The adults on deck either watched the children (theirs and others) or enjoyed the fresh sea air as did others on the boat deck with us (first and second class alike).

We relaxed on our lounges in this fashion until we felt it was time that we once again toured the ship; hoping to find other delights to amuse and amaze us, and this time we had Mr. Andrews as a personal escort! What a treat! I'm certain few others in second class would have enjoyed the privilege of viewing the first-class dining salon and other magnificent sights found in that part of the ship—and the pleasure of dining with Captain Smith! He was hosting a gathering at his own table with several distinguished-looking gentlemen and ladies but rose and came to greet Mr. Andrews as we entered. We had the honor of officially meeting the charming and debonair master of *Titanic*, an opportunity that hadn't quite materialized when he was in charge of *Olympic* the year before. At that time, we were seated at a separate table and could only observe him from afar.

Looking back on the events of this day, I find that to be the highlight. In my mind, I'd always imagined ship's masters to be authoritative and stern, no-nonsense types. And this, he was. But he was also humorous and inviting. He spoke at length with Ian about his goals in San Francisco and asked his opinion of *Titanic*. Ian apologetically replied that he'd not yet formed one but volunteered that he'd stood on the unfinished deck of *Olympic* while on a visit to Belfast and looked across the way at the frame of *Titanic* and thus was impressed with the design and construction. He had a rather "unique" opportunity to view so much of what went into the manufacture of a ship that most others of his background would never see for themselves.

The captain and Mr. Andrews chuckled at this, and at that point, we were both invited to join the two of them as they inspected the ship after the luncheon. Would we honor the company with our presence for lunch? To this, Ian and I were both quick in accepting, and we were escorted to the first-class dining salon, where we sat down to our meal. This time, we ate less sparingly; the light meal we'd partaken in our own dining class had long since settled.

I find it odd yet thrilling in a perverse sense that in being exposed to the environment of the "elite," I find that I am adopting their vocabulary, patterns of speech, and other mannerisms. I've *never* talked like this before! Or *thought* this way! Or *acted* this way! I'm becoming one of *them*! How strange.

Haaaiii! (That's the literary way to write a sigh. I think. Long, drawn-out exhale).

And now I giggle.

But to commence (shame on me!).

After an hour in conversation with Mr. Andrews, during which I'd enjoyed a lamb with mint sauce and Ian ordered the roast beef, both Ian and I starting with pea soup and adding baked potatoes in their jackets and finishing with tapioca pudding and seemingly gallons of coffee—black, to offset the effects of the wine we'd had with the meal—we set off with Captain Smith and Mr. Andrews on their rounds.

A curious beverage, coffee. I'd never had this before, and I rather enjoyed it—in spite of the bitter tang. How alert and awake it made me feel!

As we were in first class, Mr. Andrews took the opportunity to allow us to linger in these opulent areas and absorb the beauty and scale of the grandest ship on the seas. We were awestruck at the beauty and grace of the grand staircase, with its carved oak railings and newel posts. One would never know that there was steel and iron underneath the wood, so tight and well matched was the grain.

And at the top of the stairway was the most glorious clock I'd ever seen. Mr. Andrews told us it was called "Honor and Glory Crowning Time." I was sure there had to be a symbolism there somewhere, but the meaning escaped me—and I didn't see fit to ask what it could be.

We left the main entrance to first class and found ourselves on the boat deck, on the left side of the ship, but farther forward of where we'd relaxed that morning. We went to the bridge, where the officers who run the ship are stationed.

I've never seen so many brass fittings in my life! The whole area simply gleamed! And there, in the center, was the large oaken ship's wheel, with eight spokes and so highly polished and evocative of strength and control! The ship's telegraphs, which connected with the engine rooms below and behind us, telling the engineers what the officers wanted the ship to do—slow ahead, full speed ahead, all stop, slow astern, full astern—and separate for each of the two main engines. I'm told the third engine was a turbine, good only for forward motion and unable to be utilized for reverse commands. There were a series of communication devices—telephones—primarily for the lookouts and watch stations in various areas of the ship to allow them to communicate with the bridge as needed. Also on the wall was a lighted board showing the status of the watertight doors down below. At this time, all fifteen lights were off, indicating the doors were open, and there was free passage from one end of the ship to the other in the boiler rooms, engine rooms, and whatever else was down there. Mr. Andrews told Ian and me we'd be going down there shortly as part of the inspection rounds. We also saw a bulletin board where various messages concerning the operation of the ship were posted for the notice of the officers on watch.

Very impressive to see the command center of this virtual "city on the sea." And looking straight ahead out the windows of the wheelhouse (which is where the ship's wheel is, naturally!), we could see through the bridge windows and straight ahead past the mast and beyond the bow of the ship on to the horizon. Straight ahead was our destination: New York!

Our tour carried us into areas on the ship not normally accessible to passengers. There was a passageway that ran the entire length of the ship, from "stem to stern," called "Scotland Road" by the crew. From here, the crew could get to any part of the ship without having to negotiate the passenger hallways. It seemed to me to not only be very efficient for accessibility but also, since many of the crew members were from the engine rooms or were stokers for the furnaces, they were understandably dirty, greasy, and grimy—not fit to be seen in such a manner by the "refined" upper crust of British and American society.

I, on the other hand, found all this quite thrilling and exciting. I'd always suspected this type of activity behind what was normally exhibited to me as normal life, but to see it at last? This would be valuable knowledge to me as the wife of a future engineer myself. I looked forward to seeing Ian come home some days looking just as these hardworking seamen did now, though I didn't relish the fact that I'd have to learn to properly launder his clothing to remove as best I could the signs of his activities.

We went to the furnace rooms first. It was hot and dusty, and the men shoveling coal into the furnaces (boilers, I must remember the correct names for things!) were sweaty and dirty, shirtless in the heat. Yet this was my impression of specific items my eye lit upon. On the whole, the boiler rooms were exceptionally clean, as one would expect in a brand-new ship.

Mr. Andrews pointed out to me what I was seeing. Basically, the room (or rooms, there were several) was divided into back-to-back boilers, with coal bunkers opposite the boiler faces. Coal was shoveled by the stokers from the bunkers and into the furnaces (*boilers!*). Stray coal was kept picked up as quick as could be so as to prevent the turn of an ankle by accidentally stepping on a piece. "Trimmers" were men whose task was to keep the coal level in the bunkers to be easily scooped by the shovels of the stokers.

The rooms were broken between rows of boilers and bunkers by the watertight bulkheads that stretched across the width of the ship and as high as I could see in the dimness above the immediate lighting. The bulkheads had doors that were raised and kept in the open position for access between compartments.

Mr. Andrews noticed my interest in these and explained what I was seeing. "Those are the watertight doors for the bulkheads. You'll recall the panel of lights up on the bridge above a map showing the ship's watertight compartments, all the lights off? That indicates the doors are open in a nonemergency situation. In an emergency, or if water should enter the ship through a faulty seam in the plates, the door would automatically close and seal the compartment, making it watertight. The light on the bridge would come on once the door is sealed."

I nodded and asked what I thought to be a dumb question. "So when those doors are closed, *Titanic* is unsinkable?"

There were polite chuckles from Captain Smith and Ian.

Mr. Andrews merely smiled slightly. "No ship is unsinkable. *Titanic* most definitely *can* sink. The intent is to reduce that likelihood. To enable the ship to stay afloat long enough for rescue to happen. Perhaps even long enough to be towed to a proper spot for grounding and repairs if close enough to land. But definitely not to make her unsinkable. We've not come quite that far in shipbuilding."

Ian and I both nodded in understanding.

"So how long would the ship stay afloat if water were to come in?" I asked.

Mr. Andrews gestured about him. "We've got sixteen watertight compartments. Depending on the breach, how fast the water was coming in, how many compartments were compromised, the ability of the pumps to control the flooding—we could either stay afloat indefinitely—that means we could continue to port provided we still have engine power—or in worst case, we'd sink in minutes."

He smiled as I gasped. And he hurried to reassure me. "Worst case is not likely to happen. We could stay afloat if two, three, and perhaps even if four consecutive compartments were breached. It would depend on which ones—how badly and if the pumps could keep up. We don't anticipate more than two at any one time to be breached, and that would be from a collision—somebody hitting us. The opposite scenario, where we hit something—we'd lose one or two in the bow. In either event, we'd remain afloat long enough for rescue. Most likely long enough to affect emergency repairs and proceed to port, either under steam or under tow.

"Note a comparison between us and the new Cunard ships: *Lusitania* and *Mauretania*."

There were jeers and good-natured shouts of "blasphemy" at the mention of the names of *Titanic's* bitter rivals.

Mr. Andrews smiled in response. "We have 'transverse' bulkheads, which means they cross the width of the ship. Any flooding would extend, naturally, across the width, and we'd remain more or less on an even keel, though down noticeably either by the bow, stern, or total depending on the breach. The Cunard ships have 'longitudinal' bulkheads as well as 'transverse,' which means the compartments are honeycombed. Without cross-flooding, the ship will list to one side or the other. This would pose a problem when trying to lower the boats. You want a level deck for that. More than a 15-degree list to one side or the other and the boats on the 'high' side can't be lowered properly—if at all—because they'd scrape the side of the ship and perhaps become 'holed' by the rivets. Consequently, those on the 'low' side will swing away from the ship and become dangerous to load. The Cunard vessels would have to be cross-flooded to restore the balance in that event. We *hope*, of course, that we'll never have a breach. Nobody wants to be on a sinking ship."

Ian and I nodded as Mr. Andrews stepped back and gestured toward the rear of the ship. "Shall we continue our tour?"

We proceeded through the remaining boiler rooms and into the generator room, stopping long enough for Mr. Andrews to explain that steam diverted from the boilers turned the generators and the resulting electricity powered nearly everything on the ship from the lights, to the elevators, refrigerators, wireless room, telephone switchboard, and galleys (kitchens). From there, we entered the huge engine room.

One would expect the engine rooms of a ship to be hot, dirty, smelly, and noisy. Not so *Titanic*. Being a new ship, the spacious areas were as clean and crisp as the bridge above. Everything shone brightly, and several men were kept busy polishing the exposed surfaces of the engines and the pipes and supports. Others were busy checking and recording readings from the gauges (Ian said that's what the dials with the indicator pointers were called) and oiling the moving parts to keep them free and quiet.

The chief engineer, whom I learned was named Mr. Bell, came to us and spoke with the captain and Mr. Andrews, answering their questions and smiling broadly as he did so. His report was simple: everything was running flawlessly. He passed along to Mr. Andrews the compliments of his crew for building such a fine ship and for giving them such well-built machinery to maintain. He stated the same from the stokers in the boiler rooms who had little to do but to keep the fires burning evenly and maintain steam pressure and temperature. All in all, there were no complaints or requests for improvements. A full and complete report would be drafted and submitted by the time we reached New York.

Ian and I were briefly introduced to Mr. Bell, who shook Ian's offered hand and gallantly tipped his cap to me. He invited Ian to come down at his leisure and said he'd be honored to give him a more detailed inspection of the machinery at anytime he pleased. Ian thanked him and accepted, stating he'd be honored at such a privilege. We then left the engine room crew to their work and proceeded back toward the upper decks.

We visited many areas of the ship from there, including passing through the Café Parisien where they were just setting up for dinner. It was sunny and comfortable, very much giving the atmosphere of a sidewalk café with its narrow yet lengthy size, wicker furniture, and greenery. With the view out the windows over the ocean, one *could* imagine it as a "street." I would have loved to stay and dine, but it was exclusive to first class and we were second. We dreamily followed Captain Smith and Mr. Andrews through the café and made our way back in the direction of the bridge.

At the end of the tour, we thanked Mr. Andrews and the captain for their graciousness and hospitality. We made one final stop at the wireless "shack" (actually, it was a room on the port side of the boat deck a short distance behind the bridge). We were introduced to the two operators; Mr. Philips was the chief officer, and Mr. Bride was the junior. Mr. Bride had just gone off duty and was about to prepare for bed when we arrived, so we were fortunate to meet them both.

Ian was fascinated by the idea that coded information could be sent over the air, hence "wireless," and received and understood at the other end by another operator. The technology fascinated him and, for him, the tour of the ship ended here. It would be hours before I would see him again. He was enthralled by the education he was getting from Mr. Philips and Mr. Bride. I found myself completely dismissed from Ian's immediate attention, and I turned with false moroseness to face the amused expressions of Mr. Andrews and the captain.

"Alas, my love has cast me aside for a new mistress! Ah, fate!" I said in false drama, causing the two older gentlemen to laugh happily. Captain Smith even applauded!

Mr. Andrews offered me his arm. "Come, Mrs. McLean," he said. "I'll escort you to your room where you may pine your heart away and devise evil retribution to the harlot who has stolen your love away."

More laughter, including from me, and I cast a quick glance over my shoulder at Ian as we left the small confined room.

He didn't even hear, so immersed was he. He later told me that he took the opportunity to send a Marconi-gram to our family back in Ireland.

Family. Singular. Mine was his, and his was mine.

And would be forever!

I was instead, at my request, escorted to the second-class library, which was located under the dining salon for our class. I browsed the selection of books, finally choosing one that seemed as if it would be interesting, signed it out with the clerk, and made my way back to my cabin.

I began reading, but the activities of the day, while not physically demanding, were nevertheless tiring for a lass who hadn't much sleep in two nights. I quickly dozed off before getting very far.

It's now 3:00 a.m. ship's time. I've slept all this time. I must have been exhausted! I awoke still fully clothed, excepting my shoes, to find Ian sleeping deeply beside me and wearing his nightshirt. He must've entered, seen me slumbering, and chosen to let me sleep rather than wake me. I've no idea how long he was gone—or even if he'd had dinner.

But my man was here with me and so beautiful in his repose. I hadn't the heart to wake him. I couldn't drop back to sleep, and I didn't want to touch him for fear he'd awaken (he needed his sleep as much as I did). I turned a light on low, shielded it from the bed so as not to awaken him, and jotted what I could remember into you, my diary, which clearly is a lot!

Such a marvelous trip we're having—an experience we'll not have again for some time to come. I know I'll always remember the joy and happiness I'm experiencing every time I open your pages in the future. I hope I am getting the right words to describe these events, but I pray that the flavor of these happenings is being captured as well.

I've nothing more to say. I believe I've written all I can. I shall read a bit until fatigue should reach out to me and then lie back down beside my adoring husband until we can awaken together.

Diary Entry—April 13, 1912

Today is Saturday. Ian and I slept through the breakfast bugle and awoke shortly after ten o'clock.

Refreshed, we dressed rather lightly and spent the bulk of the day where we spent yesterday morning: on the aft (that means rear!) boat deck, port side, basking in the sun, and people watching. It was great fun for us, observing our fellow passengers as they strolled, conversed, and generally enjoyed the voyage in their own ways as we were doing in ours.

There were several others like us, lounging on the many deck chairs arranged on the open areas where we chose to relax. Some were in conversation, others were reading (as I was), and even one or two were napping. Occasionally, I would look up from my book if I chanced to observe something from the corner of my eye and watch as children played in pairs or groups under the watchful eyes of parents or servants. I think this held my attention more than watching people stroll the deck in couples or trios, conversing softly with each other. I was not far removed from being a child myself, and I could still relate to the children.

Such fun they were having: playing tag, spinning tops, hopscotch, and other pursuits to expend energy that youth had in abundance. Laughing! Life was fun for them, and I smiled as I watched.

Like yesterday, I could see toward the stern of the ship where the third-class passengers assembled. They weren't doing all that much different from us in second (and first, with whom we shared the boat deck), but their activities were less restrained—and louder—but no less fun for them as ours was for us. I enjoyed watching.

I wasn't alone in this either. There were some people, most of them solitary, who leaned on the railing and looked down at the third-class passengers, observing—as I did—their means for recreation. The same small group of musicians—they had to be from Ireland as I was, their music was so familiar and welcome to me in being so—entertained boisterously, and a number of their fellows were dancing and clapping in time to the tunes. I couldn't resist tapping my foot in appreciation to the sound, and I saw several others on the boat deck doing the same.

This was how Ian and I spent most of our day. As inviting as the public rooms in this ship are, the fresh ocean air and the blending of so many different types of people were by far more enjoyable to us. I'm glad we weren't alone in this feeling.

Mr. Andrews passed by several times on his inspection of the ship, usually with one or more of his assistants in tow. Three or four times, when he was not preoccupied, he would smile warmly and nod to us. One time, when he was passing alone, he stopped to join us, bringing over a vacant deck chair to rest. It was not yet time for supper, and the air was cooling—and the shadows on the deck were lengthening. I had my shawl over my shoulders and a steamer blanket to keep my legs warm; Ian had retrieved them from our cabin a short time earlier. I was ensconced in my book and unaffected by the chill in the air, which had increased enough to cause many of the passengers to seek warmth inside. I'd become so absorbed in the story that I hadn't noticed Mr. Andrews arriving until he spoke.

I shall describe this excellent book when it is complete; for now, I'm not yet halfway through it. Perhaps by late Monday.

Mr. Andrews asked us again if we were enjoying our journey and how we liked the ship. Was there anything we could suggest for improvements? No matter how small or insignificant the suggestion, he was seriously considering all—not just for *Titanic* but for upgrading *Olympic* the next time she'd be put into dock for servicing and for *Britannic*, which was still under construction.

Neither of us could think of anything—not I as a mere passenger nor Ian as a student of engineering. As it was, the ship was such a marvel so far beyond anything we'd ever experienced that there couldn't possibly be anything we could suggest. Much of what we'd seen was so far beyond our ken that we'd have never thought the like could be possible; there was no imagining for such as we that these marvels not only could be dreamt but could be built!

Mr. Andrews beamed when we told him this. One could tell how proud he was of this pinnacle of technology, yet he was humble enough to know that there was no perfection; things could always be made better.

Ian, recalling what we'd discussed yesterday while in the engine spaces, asked why the *Titanic* was being billed as "unsinkable," which many of the newspapers and journals (and passengers on board whose conversations we sometimes couldn't help but overhear) were claiming.

Mr. Andrews replied, "She's as near to that as human minds and backbone can make her. But there's no such thing as 'unsinkable.' Even wood, most of which has natural buoyancy, can sink. *Titanic* is made of iron. She can sink. But we've minimized that possibility. You recall the watertight doors below?"

We nodded.

"You'll also recall *Titanic*'s divided into sixteen compartments, separated by fifteen watertight bulkheads. At the flip of a switch, or a sign of water in the compartments, the doors can be closed, sealing those compartments from one another. This ship is designed to stay afloat with any two of her compartments breached and opened to the sea. She can float with any three—even with her first four under extreme circumstances. Eventually she may sink despite this, but she's designed by this virtue to almost be her own lifeboat. It's expected that she'd remain afloat long enough to allow help to arrive and remove all her passengers and crew to safety. Our wireless office is manned at all hours—not just to accommodate the passenger's idea of the novelty of sending messages to friends and family from a ship at sea but also to send and receive reports pertaining to the conditions *at* sea. To warn of hazards, to pass along warnings from one vessel to another, and to come to the aid of a ship in distress. You may or may not know of *Republic,* which sank off the Massachusetts coast three years ago because of a collision. Wireless was new then, and her operator called for help immediately upon extricating himself from his berth. It took the ship thirty-six hours to sink; all but three persons were saved, and those three died in the collision itself. *Republic* was a White Star Line ship built by Harland and Wolff, just like *Titanic.* We learn from our experiences.

"So, no, my young friends. *Titanic* is *not* unsinkable. But she is as close as we can make her following a collision. She's designed to stay afloat under the most extreme conditions we can imagine and act as her own lifeboat, along with the twenty we carry aboard, until summoned help should arrive."

He smiled at us and patted my hand reassuringly.

"But don't you worry. *Titanic* may be a new ship on her maiden voyage, but she's under the command of a veteran crew. Captain Smith, Chief Officer Wilde, and First Officer Murdoch are all veterans of *Olympic,* as are many of the crewmen below and the deck crew above. They know how to sail a ship this size; they know what she can do. Fear not. You'll see New York safely."

He stood up, apologized that he had work to finish, and bowed once again before continuing on his way.

Neither Ian nor I were ever concerned that the *Titanic* was unsinkable, and we needn't worry about our safety. But rumor had also gone around that "God himself could not sink this ship!" That rumor was attributed—multihanded, obviously—to a member of the ship's crew or agents. One could never learn which. I wanted to know who had the *audacity* to offer an affront to God. God could do anything; wasn't he omnipotent and all-powerful? This was a boastful challenge—and one that would tempt fate someday if ego and arrogance weren't reined in by humility.

We relaxed for a while longer until the bugle for supper was sounded. Ian and I ate lightly, strolled along the promenade deck until it was too cold to remain outdoors, and then went inside one of the public rooms to get warm. It was too early for bed since it was not quite nine o'clock, and I could hear the faint strains of a string quartet coming from somewhere in the first-class area of the ship. The music was gay and soothing, and I closed my eyes to listen with pleasure.

It was maybe ten thirty when Ian suggested retiring for the night. Hand in hand, we strolled leisurely down to our cabin. He is already in our bed and is waiting for me to finish my entry so I may join him.

Ah, but I am so enjoying this trip. It is so relaxing and so invigorating. I feel so blessed to share it with my new husband—the joys of new experiences with one whom I love so.

Thank you, God. Thank you for bringing us together and filling our lives with so much happiness.

Diary Entry—April 14, 1912

It is Sunday, and it has happened. I don't know why it took so long or why we were so nervous; it was the most natural and uncomplicated thing in the world!

We are united now. We came together as husband and wife for the first time, and it was so easy and so beautiful. For whatever reason, the fear we'd felt over the past several days was not present. As we came together and joined, we both knew an ecstasy that could never be described even if one were to have the words and the courage to attempt, which I don't, so I won't.

My darling sweet and loving young man! How he filled me so with his love and his strength. If a mere mortal could be transported to heaven to cavort and converse with the angels, he brought me there. And I've not come down yet.

We were two flushed and quiet children at the Sunday service, which was conducted by Captain Smith in the first-class dining salon today, and we were sure everybody could tell what we'd been up to last night. I'm certain it was written all over our faces! We felt as if we didn't belong there, that what we'd done was evil and we'd be spotted and cast out by God's mighty servants, but of course that didn't happen. It wouldn't—and it couldn't! What we did was as natural as breathing; it's how children are conceived! And we're married, united in a ceremony that took place before God in his home, which is the church! So we hadn't sinned.

But it felt like we had—we'd enjoyed it so much!

I'm aflame with embarrassment as I write this, but I'm alone in the room at the moment. We heard a commotion outside in the hallway, and Ian's gone out to investigate. Thus I have the chance to record today's events before he returns.

And then? I daren't say!

After the service, which was held at eleven, we proceeded to the second-class dining salon for our dinner. We sat across from each other as we ate, speaking only with our eyes and sly, mischievous smiles. Each knew what the other was thinking! And perhaps we might have a time getting through the rest of the day until we would

Note: The entry ends in this abrupt manner due to Ian's return to the cabin and his insistence that his bride get dressed and go on deck with him.

The commotion in the hallway was attributed as the result of *Titanic* colliding with the iceberg, stopping her engines, and blowing off built-up steam in the boilers.

Mrs. McLean would not complete this entry. Her next entry—reproduced later in this publication—would be written aboard *Carpathia* after the rescue.

SB.

BACKGROUND ON THE "LOST" DEPOSITION— WHEN AND HOW

The deposition given to Senator William Alden Smith, Republican from the state of Michigan, by Mrs. Glynnis McLean, born Glynnis Smith and currently known as Mrs. Glynnis Branigan, is now placed intact at this point to help provide historical continuity. To do so, a bit of the background behind the deposition must first be presented.

By this time, Senator Smith had conducted seventeen nonconsecutive days of hearings, first in New York City, commencing on the morning of April 19, 1912, and continuing within days in Washington, DC. His last scheduled day would be on May 25, when he would tour the RMS *Olympic* and interview her captain, her wireless officer, and *Titanic*'s lead fireman, who was now working aboard this older sister ship. After this day's efforts, he would proceed to finalize his report and submit it to Congress on May 28—along with the testimony of one final passenger who was still in New York, living off the remaining money she had brought with her from Ireland (her home, as we've learned earlier in the story). She had recently received by wire the necessary funds to return to her homeland;

she was to set sail as a steerage passenger aboard *Olympic* later that day.

Senator Smith didn't know what information he'd be getting from Mrs. McLean that he hadn't already received redundantly from the many witnesses he and his committee had seated before them over the course of the previous month. But as he had the day free, he decided to visit her and let her tell her story. The scenario is as thus:

It was just past seven on a cold Friday morning. The mist was still rising from Central Park, but it was far from quiet. This was New York City, the financial and cultural center of the United States, and so the city had been awake for quite some time; in many respects, it hadn't gone to sleep at all. It had long been the entry point for new arrivals who came to begin new lives and pursue the American dream. Just midway through the twelfth year of the twentieth century, New York had long ago supplanted Washington as the focal point for the country, although the political power still remained in the Capitol, nearly 250 miles to the southwest.

A shiny black Premier motorcar came to a halt at the Fifth Avenue address of the Plaza Hotel. Sitting in the rear passenger compartment of the automobile was the chairman of the Senate committee investigating the *Titanic* sinking; he would conduct one final passenger interview.

William Alden Smith was a self-made man. Supporting his family as a twelve-year-old by selling popcorn and working as a newsboy, he also put himself through school; eventually, he earned a degree in law and was admitted to the bar. He'd become an expert in railroad law and finance as the general counsel for two railroad entities in his home state before becoming elected to the House of Representatives from Michigan's Fifth District. In 1907, he was elected senator and had held the post for five years. He had recently announced his intention to run for a second six-year term in an election to be held later that year, which he would win. He was a vibrant fifty-three-year-old who, though gray haired, still resembled the down-home rural boy who'd ingeniously supported his family after his father's illness. Forty years later, he was in charge of the Senate inquiry looking into the events leading up to the sinking of *Titanic*. Its purpose was to determine the cause, fix responsibility, and to enact legislation that could prevent another tragedy.

He'd heard some amazing and startling revelations from the testimonies he'd collected in the five weeks since the start of the inquiry—from the hazards of travel in the North Atlantic, the insufficient capacity of the lifeboats most ships carried, and the behavior of the passengers and crew, both noble and shameful. Tomorrow he'd be touring *Olympic*, the older sister ship of *Titanic*, as part of his investigation and would be speaking with her captain and a couple of others among her crew who were participants in the saga. He was just about finished with the report; his aides were compiling the testimonies, evidence, and documented facts to present them to the full Senate within the coming week.

He was at the Plaza Hotel that morning to keep an appointment with a passenger who would be the last new survivor he intended to interview. Though her willingness to testify before the committee had been known to the senator and his staff for several weeks, her presence hadn't been deemed necessary. However, he changed his mind the day before when word reached him from New York that she was still available and amenable to meet with him should he wish to speak with her. He wasn't certain what she could add to the information he'd already collected, but in the interest of being thorough— and as he'd be in the city on related business—he boarded a midafternoon train from Washington to New York on the twenty-third and preceded his visit with a telegraph informing her that he would like to hear what she might have to say.

Their conference would be timely. She was due to depart on *Olympic* back to her home in Ireland without the body of her young husband (they'd only been married six days at the time of the tragedy and were en route to America to begin their new lives together), and it was known that the British Wreck Commissioner's Inquiry, conducted at the request of the British Board of Trade, was more concerned with questioning the crew of *Titanic* as well as her builders, owners, and the officials of the British Board of Trade than they were about questioning passengers (at the conclusion of which only three passengers—J. Bruce Ismay, Sir Cosmo Duff Gordon, and his wife Lady Duff-Gordon, better known as the well-respected fashion designer *Lucille*—were interviewed). Senator Smith knew that valuable information was best obtained from all potential sources, regardless of standing or technical knowledge, and he made every effort to be as well-rounded in his questioning and the subjects of his interest as he was about the technical specifications of the ship's construction, the route taken through the North Atlantic in April, and the involvement of the relatively new field of wireless telegraphy.

His goal was multifaceted. *Titanic* was a British-built ship owned by an American conglomerate, sailing on her maiden voyage as part of a trio of ships serving the Southampton to New York route and carrying American passengers. The results of the inquiry would be designed to force changes in the construction, operation, and upkeep of any ship that was destined for or sailing from American ports and carrying American citizens.

Higher watertight bulkheads.

Adequate lifeboats for all persons.

Mandatory twenty-four-hour watch on the wireless and better control over its use.

Double-hulled construction rising farther up the waterline.

And other improvements. It was already happening. *Olympic* (the first of the three giant liners constructed at Harland and Wolff Shipyards in Belfast, Ireland, for the White Star Line) was already carrying more than enough lifeboats for her passenger rating and was due to be dry-docked for retrofitting on much of the rest later in the year. The unfinished *Britannic*, still under construction and yet to be launched, was already being worked on. Other ships would follow.

Senator Smith had a full day to talk with this final witness.

Glynnis McLean seated herself gracefully upon leading the senator and his stenographer from the foyer of her suite into the sitting room. Mrs. Altford, Senator Smith's stenographer, noted the setting as Edwardian, tastefully arranged, and open. Just through the half-closed door, one could make out the bedroom; the bed was made tightly, and no sign of linens were evident. In the sitting room, the drapes were open; sheer curtains were in place over the windows. The room was subtly lit by the sunlight that filtered through, and dust motes hung suspended in the soft illumination of the seating arrangement. Mrs. McLean invited them to be seated. The carpet was colorful, tastefully accentuating by its design the furnishings in the room. On the table was a carafe of iced tea and several glasses; a container of ice was in a stand nearby. Mrs. McLean poured for her two guests and seated herself before them.

She faced Senator Smith with a calm gaze and prepared herself to answer questions that she knew would hurt her to have asked.

The senator stared back at her. He'd interviewed most of the crew who survived, the remaining senior officers, and a number of passengers—including J. Bruce Ismay, managing director of the White Star Line—and this was the first time he felt he'd met his equal. The woman seated before him had lost her husband of only six days, yet she appeared rather collected and composed. The senator knew that she was about to speak for Ian McLean instead of about him.

What follows is her deposition word for word, and emphasis on words within the dialog is specific in the original documentation, not later editorial assumptions. Included as well, in italics between Senator Smith's questions and Mrs. McLean's answers, are observational notations made by Mrs. Mary Altford that would not have appeared in a version submitted to the board but is common on original notations even today. On the original, these notes are bracketed.

SB.

THE "LOST" DEPOSITION

Senator Smith straightened his notes, cleared his throat, and began.

Senator Smith: Where were you and your husband, Mrs. McLean, at the moment of the collision with the iceberg?

Mrs. McLean takes a cautious breath before answering.

Mrs. McLean: Since we struck the iceberg at 11:40 from what've heard, my husband and I were in our stateroom. We did not feel the collision, so I can't be more specific than that.

Senator Smith: When and how were you informed of the collision?

Mrs. McLean: I believe it was near midnight—maybe a few minutes after. My husband and I heard noises in the corridor outside our cabin, and he went out to find out what it was. He was gone just a few minutes, and when he returned, he told me what he'd learned.

Senator Smith: Which was?

Mrs. McLean: That the ship had struck an iceberg and the captain had ordered the ship stopped to inspect for damage and wait for a clear path through the ice.

Senator Smith: Whom did he learn this from?

Mrs. McLean: Ian had caught up with a steward he'd spotted a few cabins down from ours. It would have been from him.

Senator pauses questioning and accepts cup of iced tea from Mrs. McLean.

Senator Smith: Thank you. Let us continue. Tell me what happened next.

Mrs. McLean pauses in thought.

Mrs. McLean: Ian had asked me if I'd like to go up with him, but since I didn't feel like going to all the trouble of dressing, I told him no, that I'd just as soon wait for him to return and he could tell me what he found, so he left our compartment again. When he came back that second time, he said he'd gone up to the promenade deck and was about to make his way to the wireless room when he noticed Lieutenant Lightoller and a crew of seamen preparing to uncover the lifeboats. Ian said he went to the lieutenant and asked what was going on. Mr. Lightoller told him that the captain had ordered the boats swung out and to be ready to fill them with women and children and stand by for orders to lower them. Ian asked if the situation was dangerous, and he told me that Mr. Lightoller looked around him and then answered quietly that it was. That's when my husband returned to our cabin to tell me what he'd found out, and then he told me to get dressed. He got our life belts out of the wardrobe as I did and helped me tie mine on over my clothes.

Senator Smith makes notes, looks up puzzled.

Senator Smith: You say that Mr. Lightoller told this to your husband *quietly*? Your husband specifically used that word?

Mrs. McLean: Yes, that word specifically.

Senator Smith: Odd that you should remember that. For what reasons do you suppose he did this?

Mrs. McLean: I've no idea, sir. I'm only telling you what my husband told me, and I didn't think to ask what he meant. At the time, I hadn't even caught the tone of the word under those circumstances. And weeks later, I'm sorry that I can't answer that to yours or my satisfaction.

Senator Smith nods.

Senator Smith: We could guess that it was a message intended to avoid panic, but guesses aren't facts. To continue; you said that your husband was intending to go to the wireless room. Why do you suppose he wanted to go there?

Mrs. McLean: Ian had made a fairly good friendship with Mr. Bride. I can only suppose that if there were any real danger to the ship, the captain would have requested the wireless operators to send out a call for assistance. This naturally made Mr. Bride the most likely person to speak to.

Senator Smith: Did you, at any time, believe there was any danger?

Mrs. McLean: Not at first. Seeing the lifeboats being swung out and made ready for loading and launch of course had us concerned. But we were on a brand-new ship with a seasoned crew. And the ship *was* equipped with the most modern safety features. So we initially thought that it was all just a precaution and that there really was nothing for us to be concerned about.

Senator Smith consults notes from folder with previous testimony.

Senator Smith: Was there, at any time, a call to report to the boat stations?

Mrs. McLean: Not that I'm aware of. Of course we were already on the boat deck, so a call at that place would not have done any good. Maybe there was below decks, but we weren't there when it would have been issued.

Senator Smith: Did either you or your husband return to your cabin after you first went on deck?

Mrs. McLean: No. We'd considered it, but by that time, we *knew* the ship was sinking. The tilt toward the bow was becoming obvious, and we were afraid that if we went back to our cabin, we might well go down with it.

Senator Smith refers again to notes.

Senator Smith: Where were you at the time the rockets were being fired?

Mrs. McLean closes her eyes and thinks; the pause lasts several seconds.

Mrs. McLean: I'd guess we were still on the boat deck, about even with the third funnel. It's not that difficult to remember, though I'm not able to be perfectly certain either, because just before we noticed the rockets, we'd stepped inside the French café and had been there for at least ten minutes, getting something to wet our throats. I imagine we forgot the situation we were in. It was the second time we'd gone in there; the first time we'd just quickly passed through, and other times, we'd looked through the windows from the outside as we were so struck by the decor. So beautiful! It was after we'd left that I noticed rockets being fired. The café was on the right side of the ship—the same side from where we saw the rockets being launched and even with the third funnel. So that's where we must have been.

Senator Smith: No call to lifeboat stations?

Mrs. McLean: Again, none that I know of.

Senator Smith: Tell me about the crew loading the boats. How were they?

Mrs. McLean: Those I remember seeing were very good. They were calm, and they followed their officers' orders quietly and efficiently.

Senator Smith: Do you know who the officers were?

Mrs. McLean pauses to think, and then she shakes her head.

Mrs. McLean: I definitely remember Mr. Lightoller as being one of them. Mr. Lowe as well, and Mr. Boxhall might have been there from the testimony I've read in the papers, but I can't recall personally. I didn't get to know some of their names until I met them on *Carpathia*. Until then, most of them were nameless to me.

Senator Smith: I see. How was Mr. Lightoller's conduct?

Mrs. McLean: I think the way he was handling the situation—very much in charge and very firm, but calm—helped ease my fears tremendously. My only complaint is that the boats weren't nearly full enough. But that's hindsight. Nobody thought the ship would actually sink before help arrived, and most of the passengers on deck at that time didn't want to go in. I was of the opinion that Mr. Lightoller lowered the boats halfway full for the simple reason that he couldn't find enough people at the time in question to put into them.

Senator Smith frowns at her.

Senator Smith: Considering that over 1,500 souls were lost, including your husband, one would think there were *plenty* of people to fill the boats.

Mrs. McLean: Indeed there were. In hindsight. But you'll also notice that the boats Mr. Lightoller was in charge of contained mostly women and children. He was adamant about that. No men, except to crew the boats, until all the women and children were off. As you can see by the hostility toward those men who were saved, if Mr. Lightoller *had* filled the boats with men, then there would be an even bigger outcry than there has been to this point. I'd say that the lieutenant is caught in a "damned if you do, damned if you don't" quandary.

Senator Smith raised his eyebrows at her oath and smiled slightly.

Senator Smith: I stand rebuked. So you feel the lieutenant was justified in the way he handled the situation? Including the half-empty boats?

Mrs. McLean: Yes and no. The fact that he refused to allow any men on board was correct. But in hindsight, he should have found and forced the women in whether they wanted to go or not. Much as my Ian finally did with me. Mr. Lightoller was in conference with the captain. And with Mr. Andrews. I saw this myself, and I knew Mr. Andrews. We'd met at *Titanic*'s launch a year before, and he'd been quite fond of Ian and me. He was all over the ship and was constantly dropping below to check on the progress of the water as it filled the ship. He knew approximately what time *Carpathia* was due to arrive, and he knew that *Titanic* couldn't last that long. In my opinion, Mr. Lightoller should have forcibly thrown what women he could find into the lifeboats and lowered them full. He may have wound up in trouble with his superiors after arriving in New York, but a lot more lives still would have been saved. But again, that's in hindsight. At the time, we really didn't understand our true situation. He did the best he could with the resources at hand.

Mrs. McLean is very forceful in her defense of Mr. Lightoller. Senator Smith smiles again.

Senator Smith: You may well be right about the trouble, though if he had, you can be sure he'd have been favorably cited by this court of inquiry for his conduct. And that would have tempered his punishment—if any—from his superiors.

Senator Smith pauses as he turns to next page of questions.

Senator Smith: And on to his superiors—did you notice Mr. Ismay at any time that night?

Mrs. McLean: I did. He was on the boat deck. Starboard, the right side of the ship. I don't remember his ever leaving it until shortly before Ian put me in my boat.

Senator Smith: What time was that?

Mrs. McLean: I've no idea. Before two o'clock, I think.

Senator Smith: What was Mr. Ismay doing?

Mrs. McLean: Besides making a general nuisance of himself?

Senator Smith looks up sharply.

Senator Smith: A nuisance, you say?

Mrs. McLean: He was trying very hard to be helpful, to give him the credit he is due. Many lives were saved due to his involvement in getting passengers to board the boats. He knew the ship was sinking—I've no doubt of it—and he did not shirk his duty in his actions. But he seemed to be quite frantic and kept getting in the way of the officers who were trying to keep calm and order while loading the boats. He could have caused a panic had it not been for the countering attitude of those officers.

Senator Smith: Did he scare *you*?

Mrs. McLean pauses to think.

Mrs. McLean: A little. But I knew he was very much out of his element. He was a businessman, not a sailor. I doubt very highly he'd ever been in a situation of this nature—or of *any* nature, for that matter. He was clearly panicked at the inevitability of the disaster's conclusion, and I know he meant well in his efforts to get as many people off the ship as possible and save as many lives as possible, but in his haste, he might have caused a riot. Thank God that didn't happen.

Senator Smith: Do you think that Mr. Lowe might have been justified in his oath to Mr. Ismay? I pray that I don't have to repeat it, though I understand you were near the scene at that time and heard it for yourself.

Mrs. McLean: You need not repeat the oath to refresh my memory, Senator. I did hear it when originally spoken. Ian and I had wandered over to the starboard side to see what was happening there, and we were just minutes before and thus in time to witness the exchange and the cause of it. I must say that Mr. Lowe *was* justified, but one cannot blame either him or Mr. Ismay for the exchange. The situation was very stressful. There was no boat drill, as you know, and this situation was something nobody was prepared for—though they should have been. My complaint about Mr. Ismay—and Ian had voiced it to me as well—was that Mr. Ismay would have been more helpful if he was inside the ship and insisting that people put on their life belts and report to the boat deck instead of standing out *on* deck and yelling "Lower away. Lower away!" Let the crew do their jobs—that's what they've been trained for is what Ian said.

But Mr. Ismay *did* make me nervous. The president of the company and thus technically the owner of the ship behaving in that manner? Not something likely to instill calm in a situation that needed as much as it could get.

Senator Smith: Were there any other instances where hysteria was displayed by either passengers or crew?

Mrs. McLean thinks for a moment.

Mrs. McLean: I can't really say there were until near the end. Women who refused to board the lifeboats without their men. A final rush for the one or two remaining collapsible boats as the bridge was going under. Up until then? For the most part, people stayed inside, it was so cold. Also, the ship's orchestra was on the boat deck, playing some fairly lively music. How can one panic when one's feet are tapping time? As the tilt toward the front became more pronounced, I noticed some anxiety and a sense of urgency become more apparent from passengers and crew alike, but for the most part, there was utter calmness.

Senator Smith: Did you notice any of the crew behaving badly? I would say, more precisely, in an *ungentlemanly* manner?

Mrs. McLean: No, none that I saw. The crew was behaving in a very professional manner, and they had the presence of the officers to instill discipline and order should any be required. They set a fine example, and this kept the situation relatively stable. I saw the captain on deck several times. He was in and out of the wireless room, he was ensuring his orders regarding the boats were followed, and he was available to answer questions briefly. And he assisted any who needed assistance—be it a life belt or clarification of the situation. There were times I *didn't* see him—not that I kept his whereabouts at the front of my mind because of all *I* was trying to understand—but I would imagine on a ship that size that he had many places to be. He had to see for himself what the current situation was, and I'd assume he was also in various areas of the ship to see how high the water was rising and trying to determine how much time was remaining before *Titanic* sank. He looked stunned throughout, but that was understandable. How does one deal with a situation like that? However, he was definitely in charge.

I saw several of his officers. Mr. Lightoller was the most visible, and I also saw Mr. Lowe. Others whose names I only came to know later on. Mr. Ismay, of course. And Mr. Andrews. No bad behavior from any of the officers or crew. Not in my presence.

Senator Smith: Tell me about Mr. Andrews. I've heard a lot about him regarding that night, but I'd like to hear from you if I may.

Mrs. McLean smiles. Her smile appears radiant, and it is obvious she feels fondness for her subject.

Mrs. McLean: What can I say about Mr. Andrews? So strong and so quiet. If he was in any way distressed, he certainly never displayed it in my presence. Mr. Andrews was all over *Titanic* in those final hours. Much of his time was spent assisting women and children into the lifeboats. He also upbraided Mr. Lightoller—and one of the other officers—for not filling the boats with enough people. I seem to recall, but please don't take this as certain since I didn't hear it myself, that Mr. Lightoller had replied to Mr. Andrews that he was concerned that the boats would not be safe to lower with their full complement, and that he'd sent a group of sailors below decks with instructions to open the doors in the side and the boats would be filled from there. Mr. Andrews firmly informed Mr. Lightoller that the boats were tested in Belfast, each and every one of them, with a weight load in excess of the capacity and that there was no danger of overload and to please fill the boats henceforth. Mr. Lightoller then began doing so. I believe the other boats were lowered with more passengers from then on, but by that time, there weren't many boats left.

Senator Smith: Did Mr. Andrews speak with either of you at any time?

Mrs. McLean: No, sir, he did not. He did nod to us in recognition a couple of times in passing, but it is my belief that he didn't truly realize it was us. He was under an incredible amount of stress, you realize. The last I saw of him was when he entered the first-class dining room.

Senator Smith: What boat were you on?

Mrs. McLean: It was a canvas-sided one on the left side. Collapsible D. I understand there was another on the right. And I know of another on the roof of the officers' quarters above it, near the funnel.

Senator Smith: Yes, there were a total two to a side as you describe, but only one on each was actually lowered. The other two were planned to be launched, but they floated off as *Titanic* sank. Do you remember any of the passengers and crew with you?

Mrs. McLean: I'll have to think a moment.

Senator Smith: Take your time.

Mrs. McLean begins to speak hesitantly.

Mrs. McLean: There were two little boys, not much more than babies, really. I recall their father leaning past Ian to hand them to the officer who was in charge of lowering us. He passed them onto the women in the boat. I remember a little boy about six or seven. Michael, I think his name was. Several women, a few men. Two men jumped into the boat as it was lowering, and one missed. We picked him up when we were on the water. There was one married couple in their thirties; she was put into the boat before it was lowered, and her husband jumped from *Titanic* into the water just after, and we picked him up. Those poor men spent the night freezing wet. I pray they're okay.

Mrs. Futrelle, her husband was a writer of mysteries. Ian was an admirer of his work. Mr. Futrelle didn't join her, and I learned that he didn't survive.

Most of the passengers were from first class, and a number of third. I think I was the only second-class passenger. Most of us *were* passengers. Three or four male crewmen were controlling the boat plus those who jumped and we picked up. All told, there were about two-dozen people.

Senator Smith: Were there any bodies on your boat? I've heard in earlier testimonies that several people died while waiting for *Carpathia* to arrive.

Mrs. McLean: Not on our boat, no. I've heard the same, including that there were three on my boat just recently found by *Oceanic*. But that wasn't true. My boat was recovered from the water and brought back to New York on board *Carpathia*. There were no deaths on my boat.

Senator Smith: Do you recall the number of your boat?

Mrs. McLean: I'm sorry. I thought I'd said. Collapsible D.

Senator Smith looked at me, and I flipped back through my notes, nodding at him that she did give us this information. The senator continued.

Senator Smith: If I recall Mr. Lowe's testimony correctly—and I should as he was quite colorful—it was Collapsible A, one of the boats that floated off from the starboard side, which was found. He'd testified that he'd left three bodies aboard when he drew alongside and transferred the living passengers from it into his own.

Senator Smith accepted a refill on his glass of iced tea from Mrs. McLean, which she poured as he spoke.

Senator Smith: Thank you. Now, tell me about the lifeboats. Aside from Mr. Ismay and Mr. Lowe having words, was there anything you can recollect occurring at the boats that may have stuck with you? Anything outside of what would normally be expected in a situation such as this?

Mrs. McLean: No, Senator. What I did see was gallantry, a lot of tears and pleading from women who had to board while their men stayed behind. And from their children. I recall when Ian and I were on A deck, where a boat had been waiting empty since early on because the windows weren't open to allow people through, that a very distinguished gentleman escorted a young woman whom I first mistook as his daughter, but later learned was his wife, into the boat and asked Mr. Lightoller if he may board. I learned very soon after that this was Mr. Astor. He didn't seem too pleased as his wife was "in a delicate condition," I heard him say, and he'd wished to accompany her to ensure her safety—he didn't want to leave her alone. He asked Mr. Lightoller what number boat this was. He was told it was Boat 4. He nodded and quietly went back into the ship. Shortly afterward, I saw him again. He was helping load my boat. Ian and Mr. Astor each took an arm and lifted me from the deck and placed me into the boat as gentle as you please! Ian shook his hand and thanked him for his graciousness. Mr. Astor smiled and went inside the ship. That's the last I saw of him. I also witnessed Mr. Lightoller begin to refuse entry to a young boy because he appeared to be too old. The boy's father challenged this, saying that he was only thirteen and he could go with his mother. Mr. Lightoller allowed this reluctantly but vowed he would be the last.

We saw the rockets being fired from the bridge earlier on—at least six of them—but the scene was too hectic to be sure. Oh, they were beautiful—but we knew that it was *Titanic*'s desperate plea for help from anybody who could see her. It was a beauty of deadly irony set against the drama on the ship. I've read of the ship that was so tantalizingly close to us, but I never saw her. If there was indeed a ship nearby and watching, may God sink her and damn her crew!

Mrs. McLean seethes with anger for the first time since being questioned. Senator waits until she settles.

Senator Smith: You don't recall any signs of panic?

Mrs. McLean: None to speak of.

Senator Smith: What of class distinction? Was there any indication of people being refused entry into the lifeboats due to class or status?

Mrs. McLean: None whatsoever. I know what you're leading up to. I've read the claims in the papers. I can't obviously say definitely that there was no class distinction displayed by either officers or crew, but there was none that *I* witnessed. I *did* hear a fair number of those whom I believe were first-class passengers stating that they hoped the boats they were boarding were "first-class" boats. Others said that the forward boats were for first class and ship's officers; the ones in the rear were for second class, third class, and crew. But nothing like that from officers or crew. Anybody who approached a boat was granted admittance. In my personal presence, this was limited to women—crew as well as passengers. There was no refusal to the stewardesses or ship's nurses or children. *Regardless* of station.

As for the men, only if there was room, and that was not done in my presence at all by Mr. Lightoller. His rule was "women and children only" except for crewmen to handle the boat. Otherwise, Ian would be here with me now, and Mr. Astor would be with his young bride.

Mrs. McLean stops a moment to calm her voice, which was beginning to break, and then continues.

Mrs. McLean: Of course, I can only say what I witnessed. I wasn't everywhere, and I saw only a small fraction of the boats loaded and lowered. And as I was on the most forward of the boats on the left side of the ship, one would think there would have been no third-class passengers on it at all, unless they were pulled from the water if the claims of "class distinction" were true. As your records should show, half the people on that collapsible were third class.

Senator Smith nods in acceptance of her statement.

Senator Smith: What do you recall of events once your boat was lowered and in the water?

Mrs. McLean: We rowed. We didn't get far since our boat was leaking. The sides weren't secured very well, and water splashed in. We hadn't nearly the full complement of passengers, but I don't know how much more we could have held with the sides the way they were. We did pick up a few and spent the night bailing out water that kept sloshing in.

Once our seamen felt we were far enough away to be safe from suction, we stopped rowing and simply watched. I could not understand why there were still so many people on board by that time. It was after two o'clock, and I could see Mr. Lightoller and other men—I will go to my grave certain that Ian was among them—trying to free another boat from the roof of the officers' quarters behind the bridge next to the funnel. A tremendous amount of people were coming up from below decks and from within the public rooms. I don't know where they all were all this time or why they hadn't come up sooner!

And even though I saw several boats in the water before I finally boarded mine with plenty of room for more, it seemed as if there were more people on board *Titanic* than her boats could have possibly held. It seemed like hundreds!

Mrs. McLean's voice is a whisper, and she can hardly be heard. Senator Smith and I lean closer to hear better. She remains quiet for a moment before continuing.

Mrs. McLean: *Titanic* was beginning to stand on her head. Her bow was underwater, and the water was climbing up the face of the bridge and washing through the visible decks. You could see it through the window openings of A deck where Boat 4 had waited before it could be loaded. The stern was rising. We could just see the propeller from where we sat. We were far enough away from the ship that her massive side could not block our sight of it. The lights were still on, and the orchestra was still playing on the boat deck—not far from where Ian and I were when we last parted.

Mrs. McLean's breathing is rapid and her face is blanched.

Mrs. McLean: There was a sudden wave, and the ship moved downward. The stern rose higher. I saw the men washed off the roof where they were freeing the boat. It seemed they had just freed it and pushed it to the deck below when the wave took it—and them—and washed them away. I saw the first funnel break free and fall forward; it crushed a number of swimmers when it struck the water.

I saw the stern rise even higher—not quite straight up, but it was rapidly gaining that position.

Then the lights went out. They were on, burning brightly—and then they were out.

It took a bit for my eyes to get used to the darkness. We were close enough to the ship for the light to affect us, and when they were out, the darkness was near total. And while we waited to get accustomed to the dark, we heard screaming! Screams of fear, screams for deliverance.

And overpowering this—rumbling and crashing—the sounds of the ship breaking up.

It was the sound of the world coming to an end.

Mrs. McLean paused again.

Senator Smith: What did you do?

Mrs. McLean: There was nothing *to* do—nothing to *say.* As we got used to the dark and began to make out objects again, we were still looking toward *Titanic.* It appeared as if she'd righted herself, that all the heavy objects within her had crashed through her bows and balanced her. She seemed to have settled back down evenly and had even swung away from us. But she couldn't have, could she? We didn't take that long to get our night vision—not so long that she could have turned so much that she'd be able to present her narrow view to us so fast. It occurred to me then that she'd broken. I mean, she *must* have—her funnels were gone, all four, and the front end—full of water—was broken free and headed for the bottom. With all those brave men—my Ian among them—going with her. And her stern, empty of all but people, settling back down and remaining afloat. I thought it must have twisted when it was tipped up because I could clearly see most of the rudder and not so much of her profile.

And just as I had that thought, the stern tipped back over, partially on her side, and then raised her propellers once again out of the water and began to sink. The screaming never stopped, and I could hear it get louder. I could see people clinging to the rails, the silhouettes of people moving as ants would on a carcass. For that's what *Titanic* was now: a broken and dead carcass.

Then she was gone. It took less than five minutes from the last sound of the ship breaking in half until the flag at her very stern disappeared beneath the sea.

Gone.

Except for hundreds of swimmers calling for help in the freezing water.

And then they too were gone—silenced in death—very soon afterward.

A short time later, Mr. Lowe in Boat 14? Yes, I seem to recall that number. He approached us with a couple of other boats tied to his, and we joined up with him. He transferred most of his people to the other boats, untied from us, and went back to look for people to save.

He didn't find many.

Mrs. McLean wipes her eyes of the tears that have formed and stops talking. Senator Smith also wipes his eyes. Mrs. McLean is the first person to speak at length about her ordeal, and the senator is deeply moved. Mrs. McLean looks up.

Mrs. McLean: I believe I've said enough for now. I should like to have lunch brought up. Maybe we can eat. Afterward, if you're interested, we can talk more.

Senator Smith: Yes, I think that would be appropriate at this time. Thank you.

AFTER LUNCH: A DIALOG

What follows comes from Mrs. Mary Altford's own unpublished journals both professional and personal: her recollections of life as a functionary for the Senate Court of Inquiry, a position she'd held for the twenty-four years Senator Smith served in Congress (first as a member of the House of Representatives from 1895 to 1907 and then as a senator from 1907 to 1919). It is obvious that the senator recognized and appreciated this stenographer's abilities to accurately capture and record vital testimony without error or coloration; this can be ascertained by comparison with other records of earlier committees that the senator chaired in both houses of Congress. It is also obvious the stenographer's memory and understanding of the wide-ranging subjects she'd been required to record was phenomenal; comparing her original notes with those of other persons present displays a rare and intuitive grasp for detail and clarity within its simplicity. In no case where extant notes can be compared against each other and contrasted to the final reports can one find either error or embellishment.

The following dialog is written as if it were captured by a recording device and later written out in longhand, which it most surely was not. The importance in what follows is twofold: it is written descriptively and contains what must be accepted as direct quotes, though written from memory later that evening. It is also the only known instance in twenty-four years where Senator Smith relaxed in the company of his witness and held a conversation with—instead of collecting testimony from—his subject. It is important to the historian as well as the layman to recognize this change in attitude. The senator found himself comfortable for the first time since the hearings began, and he obviously liked this tragic young woman—or young girl. She was not yet seventeen, she was recently widowed, and she was alone in a foreign land among strangers she depended on for kindness and charity until she could return to her home and her loved ones. She'd witnessed and survived a tragedy few of us today can fathom (though with the ever-present specter of nuclear annihilation in the Cold War between the United States and the Soviet Union, we can surely relate), a tragedy that could not—and should not—have happened but for the overconfidence placed in the advancement of modern technology. She was still stunned by the events, and it was clear she still didn't fully grasp what had happened.

Yet, it is clear that she *did* understand. Though she was an innocent and naive young farm girl from the countryside beyond Belfast, she was not unintelligent. She was a well-schooled, well-read, and clever young girl. Reading her diary excerpts (beyond those examples first published here) serves to reinforce the conclusion that she was nobody's fool. She could and did understand all that was within her limited world, and she had an intuitive yearning to reach out and discover more that was outside.

Much like Senator Smith himself. The senator was self-educated, and he instantly recognized her as a kindred spirit. Of all the people he'd dealt with in his life, there were few like this child-woman who captivated the humble boy that the senator had once been.

For the remainder of the senator's visit with Mrs. McLean, they talked. He talked about the construction of *Titanic* and her sisters—one finished and to be visited the next day, the other waiting to be launched and completed—and what he'd learned about their construction, their operation, and the misguided perception that they were unsinkable. She detailed her activities on board the liner, concentrating in narrative what the interrogation could not hope to reveal: her observations, the actions of her fellow passengers, and her feelings and realizations that the voyage that held so much promise for so many people was about to turn to unimaginable horror.

The following is taken directly from the personal journals of the court stenographer who set down within hours the candid conversation between Senator Smith and Mrs. Ian McLean. There has been no attempt to dramatize the narrative beyond that which is part of the journals themselves. The stenographer took little part in the discussion; as her training had required, she was there merely to observe and record all that went on around her.

This job she did extraordinarily well, and her journals are unique in their historical context. Few others are known to survive. It can only be hoped her descendants someday see fit to publish these journals as unique windows back to a time in our nation's history where the inner workings of our government existed only as dry legalese, with nothing of humanity remaining in the dusty recesses of our National Archives.

SB.

MRS. McLEAN'S REMEMBRANCES

"We boarded the ship in Queenstown, which was her last stop before continuing on to New York," began Mrs. McLean. "Originally we were booked on a smaller ship, the *City of New York,* out of Southampton by way of Liverpool, which is across the Irish Sea from Dublin. Dublin is rather south of Belfast, where the ship was built, and Belfast is in Ulster Province, which is where Ian and I are from. We were going to take the ferry from Belfast to Liverpool."

The senator nodded in understanding and motioned for her to continue.

"Due to the coal strikes, however, many crossings were canceled. We were booked first class on a steamer from Liverpool to New York. But with the coal strike, we found our passage rebooked onto *Titanic.* Ian and I discovered a number of other passengers were on board for the same reasons."

"Did anybody have concerns about sailing on *Titanic* as opposed to any other ship?" asked the senator.

"None that I recall," came her reply. "We all who were reassigned considered ourselves fortunate to be able to sail on *Titanic* for the same price we'd paid to be on our originally ticketed, then canceled, ships. Many of us would never have dreamt we'd ever afford to sail in such luxury under any other circumstances. No, Senator Smith, the coal strike was thought to be a blessing in disguise for us. We'd otherwise be on a much older, slower, and smaller ship.

"Most of us had never seen such a ship up close, though Ian and I had both seen *Titanic* before. We were guests at her launch, and we'd sailed on *Olympic* from Belfast to Liverpool prior to *her* maiden voyage. We'd also caught a quick glimpse of *Titanic* two weeks before our voyage after she had finished her sea trials and left Belfast for Southampton, where she would depart for New York on April 10. We boarded the next day. We were told that our second-class cabins on *Titanic* would be far more luxurious than the first-class cabins on almost any other ship. The pictures we'd seen before agreeing to transfer—and our recollections of our time on *Olympic* the previous year— made it appear to be very much so. We told each other that if this truly were the case, we'd probably not want to ever leave the ship in New York for our new home. We were still on the tender when we said this. The ship was docked in the harbor, as she was too big to enter and be boarded at the pier."

The senator nodded. "So you crossed from Liverpool to Queenstown—how?"

Mrs. McLean smiled. "Actually, we didn't. We'd received word early on that our original booking had been canceled, and we'd been given the opportunity to sail second class on *Titanic* instead. Naturally we were thrilled, and Ian quickly made inquiries to find out where and when we could board her. Queenstown was our best option and would give us an extra day before it would arrive. We hurriedly arranged transport to Queenstown from Belfast by train and arrived the afternoon before *Titanic* sailed into sight and dropped anchor just outside the harbor. We had been informed that there would be two tenders standing by to transport passengers and luggage from the dock to the ship. Once we were alongside, we'd board through doors in the side of the ship, have our passes checked, and receive directions to our cabins. Our luggage would be brought up to us shortly afterward.

"The members of our family had come to see us off. God only knew when we would all see each other again and the good-byes were tearful and heartrending.

"We had a final toast presented to us—blessings for our marriage, the voyage, and our future here in America—and then we all turned in for the night. It was late, and we didn't want to risk missing the ship when she arrived to pick up the passengers the next day."

Mrs. McLean paused while she reached for a glass of water, tea having been fully consumed an hour earlier. The senator and I remained silent while waiting for her to continue.

"The next day came, and we were on the dock, ready. *Titanic* swept majestically into sight and dropped anchor right on time. It was eleven thirty in the morning, and we were already on the tender, watching this huge luxury liner that would take us to our new home in America!"

The senator nodded. "What were yours and your husband's impressions?"

A twinkle came into Mrs. McLean's eyes. "Grand! Marvelously so! As I said, we'd sailed down the Irish Sea on the *Olympic* a year previous, and we'd also seen *Titanic* leave on her trials two weeks earlier, but this was different. We were to actually *board* her and spend nearly a week living on her! And once we did, we were astonished! She was *Olympic* renewed! She was a new ship by looks and by smell. Fresh paint, everything clean and tidy. Beds made just so, and the mirrors and glass fixtures were without a smudge or a speck of dust anywhere. The carpets in our suite were thick and soft and *better* than *Olympic*—just as Mr. Andrews had said she'd be! We were sure we were in the wrong part of the ship."

Mrs. McLean was deeply within her remembrances. The senator remained motionless and silent as he waited for her to continue.

"Ian asked me if I was nervous, and I said I was. I told him I'd miss my old home and my friends and family, and he told me that he would as well. But he strongly and happily said, 'We'll make our fortunes in America, we'll return home in one of *Titanic*'s first-class suites, and we'll be the envy of them all!'"

Mrs. McLean smiled.

"When Ian said it, I knew it was true. He was always optimistic and worked hard to make things happen for us. This is how it had been all our lives—since we were children—and I knew it would be true going forward."

Senator Smith nodded.

"So what did you and Mr. McLean do next?"

Mrs. McLean poured herself a fresh glass of water.

"We'd inspected the suite and marveled at the appointments; the room was done in white, and the furniture was a muted brown. A bunk bed on a wooden frame with a washbasin on a wooden stand at the head, a small sofa, polished wood dressing table, a small desk at one end of the cabin, and a wardrobe near the foot of the bed. There were lavatories with bathing facilities shared by the adjoining suites and separated by genders—trivial for White Star as I've learned but equal to standard first-class accommodations on most other steamers. We quickly unpacked our belongings and went out to explore the ship.

"*Titanic* was a virtual floating city. From where we stood— at the second-class promenade deck just past the fourth funnel and outside the second-class passenger's entrance—we looked left and right down a seemingly endless corridor with doorways and passages leading off at right angles. The view ahead of us was the sparkling sea. Our cabin was on E deck, below the second-class dining room, and only three flights of stairs down from the deck we stood on. We jockeyed for position among the hundreds of other passengers lining the starboard side railing all along the promenade deck and waved good-bye along with all the other passengers to our loved ones on the departing tender and on the shore—as if they could see us at that distance!"

Mrs. McLean was flushed, lost in the memory of her departure day's excitement. She went on breathlessly.

"Soon all the whistles blew, and the ship started her engines. The sea at the stern of the massive ship began to churn—the engines were now powering the ocean liner—and *Titanic* headed away from the mouth of the harbor under her own power. The small harbor tugboats stayed alongside to help nudge and direct the ship until it was well past the entrance to the harbor and was then finally pointed out to sea and on her own until our arrival in New York, which was to be early on Wednesday morning. It was only Thursday.

"Once out at sea, Ian said to me, 'I'm game to explore the ship and see what she has to offer. We'll be living on board her for the next six days, and we'll have plenty to do. Would you care to join me?' I replied that I'd lie down a bit, but for him to go on ahead. I'd join him for dinner later. He offered to pop down into the cabin shortly, and if I felt up to it, we could take a stroll on the upper decks. He'd point out to me what he'd seen already, and we could dine at our leisure afterward, would I mind? I told him not at all, but I'd love for him to escort me to the cabin. I believed I'd have gotten lost if I tried to find it alone."

Mrs. McLean smiled as she recalled this and unconsciously gallantly offered her arm to his memory.

"'It would be my pleasure, your ladyship,' he chided me. 'If you will come right this way.'"

Mrs. McLean took a sip of water and then continued.

"The two of us entered the ship at the second-class entrance just forward of the smoke room. From there, we made our way down to E deck and parted with a kiss. He promised to be back within a couple of hours and left to explore the sections of the ship accessible to him.

"This was the beginning of our trip—we spent the next few days exploring *Titanic*, wondering at the sights and meeting all types of people whom we'd never in our normal lives interact with. Ian sent a wireless message home on Friday, keeping it as short as possible to conserve our money but anxious to let our families know of the beauty and the splendor that was the *Titanic* and how the memory of the voyage would stay with us for the rest of our lives!"

Mrs. McLean sighed and opened her eyes. She looked directly into those of Senator Smith.

"In ways we'd never fathomed—that has surely become the case now, hasn't it, Senator?"

Senator Smith nodded solemnly.

"Tell me about that last day on *Titanic*, if you would please?"

Mrs. McLean took a deep breath as if to prepare herself for a dreaded ordeal and let it out in a long sigh before she spoke.

"Ian and I attended the Sunday service as guests of Mr. Andrews in the first-class dining room late that last morning. Captain Smith officiated. The sermon was beautiful and conducted in accordance with the Protestant faith, which is the Church of England, but it was also styled to include tenets

SCOTT STEVENS

of other Christian Faiths. Basically nondenominational, but Christian throughout.

"We had a luncheon in our own second-class dining room following this and spent much of the rest of the day relaxing on the second-class promenade deck. I read, and both of us watched random activities around us. Mr. Andrews stopped by for a brief chat while making his survey of the ship and once again received our compliments on the well-built, sturdy ship he had designed.

"It was getting cold by this time, and we went in to prepare for dinner. We'd been hearing rumors of ice warnings all that day, and by the sudden drop in temperature, we were certain that ice was near. We couldn't see any when we looked over the railing. It wasn't yet dark, though the sun was low on the horizon ahead of us, and I'm sure we'd have seen ice if there had been any.

"That final dinner on *Titanic* was the best I'd ever eaten in my life; the meals served in the dining room here at the Plaza pale by comparison! I couldn't eat it all—it was so generous—but I sampled nearly everything on my plate. And I helped myself to some of Ian's too!"

The senator smiled at her.

"Do you remember what was served in your cabin? Your dining room?"

Mrs. McLean smiled back.

"You're probably familiar with meals like this, I'm sure, and for my part, I'll never forget it. I had baked haddock covered in a tangy sauce. Ian had curried chicken on a bed of rice. Both of us had this with green peas and roast potatoes. We had our choice of plum pudding, coconut sandwich, or American ice cream. We chose that last one for the novelty since it was new to us. Creamy and delicious. We were served fruit, cheese, and nuts. Our digestion was soothed by coffee served throughout the meal. There were other items on the menu from which to choose, but this is what we ate that night.

"Afterward, we walked off our dinner by taking a casual stroll along the boat deck. We stopped by the wireless room to say hello to Mr. Philips, who was on duty at the time. This would have been close to seven thirty or eight o'clock. It was dark by now, except for the lights from various locations on the ship. We could see inside the boat deck entrance to the grand staircase for first class, though we knew we couldn't go in without an invitation and escort since it was not our area of the ship.

"So rich and luxurious! And the dress of the passengers! This would be the last festive night out, as we learned we would arrive in New York either late Tuesday night or early Wednesday morning. Monday would be set aside to begin packing and preparing for docking—plus remember this was Sunday, and everybody seemed dressed in their best evening wear that night. I seem to recall one woman in particular being singled out for praise in designing the evening wear many of the ladies were draped in. Lucille, I believe I heard was her name.

"None of the other nights aboard were as showy and extravagant as this.

"I'm aware that the elite of American and British society were on board *Titanic*, though I wouldn't have recognized any of them by sight. My world was so isolated from theirs. I saw a lot of money and style in that area, and from where I stood—on the outside looking in—I must say I was a bit wistful, wondering what it would be like to be such as they.

"But only in passing. I am quite content with my life for it is all I have *ever* known, and I am happy with it. Besides, as regal as the first-class men I observed and as elegant as the ladies were, I had my Ian—and he had me. We wanted for nothing else.

"At about ten thirty, Ian suggested we return to our cabin. The cold was now chilling our bones. We had been outside the entrance to first class for some while now, leaning against the support for a lifeboat and listening to the ship's orchestra. The music reached us faintly and clearly from within the ship and soothed us with its strains.

"We proceeded back to our cabin, but we were not in any hurry. Tomorrow was Monday, and we would sleep in.

THE COLLISION

"We arrived back at our cabin shortly after eleven o'clock. It had been a peaceful day, but the night had turned bitterly cold. We'd enjoyed ourselves tremendously and were tired and wanted to turn in. Tomorrow would be the last full day aboard the ship before we'd have to prepare for Wednesday's arrival in New York, and we hoped to make it another full one. I was hoping to send a Marconi-gram of my own if I got the chance."

Mrs. McLean's voice grew pensive.

"As we removed our coats and gloves, we smiled shyly at each other. We were becoming used to being married and sleeping together. Snuggling tightly was now very comfortable. We'd succeeded in breaking down the barrier keeping us from consummating our marriage the night before, and we were eager on this night to give each other the physical pleasure our marital union allowed."

Mrs. McLean blushed as she confessed this to the senator.

"But we weren't in *that* much of a hurry. We undressed far enough for comfort but retained decorum. I had on my petticoat; Ian wore his trousers and undershirt but was in his stocking feet. I suppose we were still nervous and shy, and we'd approach each other with care. We were certain we'd have plenty of time.

"We talked as we sat in the room: I at the desk, and he on the edge of the bed. This was something we'd hoped would become a lifelong habit, talking to unwind at the close of the day and meeting for slumber and more if we weren't too tired afterward.

"'I don't want this trip to end,' I said to Ian, and he looked back at me and smiled. 'This is bliss. It's heaven. It's how I always dreamed my life would be.'

"Ian chuckled. 'That's why we're here, my sweet. So that, regardless of any hardships we might face in the future, we'll face them together. And we'll always have *this* to look back upon.'"

The senator was rapt with attention as Mrs. McLean recalled that night. Mrs. McLean's eyes were closed as she pictured the scene in her mind.

"We sat silently, looking across the room at each other and probably saying sweet little phrases to each other. I suppose it was to 'get us in the mood' and relax us all at once. I've no experience in this, so I can't define it. I simply recall that I felt at peace with my new husband and he with me. We were both eager to approach each other but both shy and hesitant as well."

Mrs. McLean was blushing furiously as she opened her eyes and focused on the senator.

"I feel so vile, speaking of this to you who might be old enough to be my grandfather—and a perfect stranger at that. Your assistant, however, would understand my emotions, her being a woman. However embarrassing this is for me, I must make you aware of my condition at the instant my world changed. What I had. And what I have lost."

Mrs. McLean sighed and shifted her position to make herself more comfortable. As she did so, she gently placed her hand flat to her breast to feel her heartbeat.

"I hoped that feeling would never end. I wanted it to go on that way forever. In my heart, it still does. My heart has broken into thousands of pieces, yet it races as if it were made whole again when I recall that moment. Our last in peace and in joy.

"Shortly before midnight, a commotion could be heard outside the corridor. We tried to ignore the noise, but the mood was soon broken.

"Ian looked toward the door and moaned. 'I've never been fond of drunken revelry at others' expense,' he said. 'It sounds as if there's some sort of a problem. Maybe I should go see what's the matter.'

"I stood and went to him to put my arms around him, and I hugged him close.

"'We've still the rest of the night,' I told him. 'They'll soon quiet down. I'm sure that other passengers will complain to the stewards if it keeps up, and they'll take care of it.'

"Ian nodded as he stroked my chin, and he kissed me. 'I certainly hope so,' he said. He looked at me and smiled tenderly. 'Nevertheless, my love. I enjoy being with you like this just as much.'

"I smiled back at him and said, 'As do I. Ian, I need you. Make me happy. Make me yours.'"

Mrs. McLean was blushing again, but her gaze was direct into the eyes of Senator Smith.

"I wanted his child. We'd joined only once before, on the previous night. I wanted to give him a child, one he wanted as dearly as I, and until I 'kindled,' we were going to continue our union, come what may. Please don't think what I am relating to you is indicative of any other motive. I couldn't bear to be thought of as brazen."

The senator quickly moved to reassure her. "You needn't go on with this subject, Mrs. McLean. It's not pertinent to the investigation."

Mrs. McLean shook her head. "I'm afraid you're wrong there, Senator. It is. You see, we didn't get together that night. If I'm carrying his child, and I feel I am—for a woman knows these things—then our single mating was a success. Ian will live on with me through our child. I will know for certain shortly."

Mrs. McLean sat quietly in thought for a moment, and I could tell the senator was uncomfortable—nearly as much as Mrs. McLean, but for a different reason. I pitied him, but I still rather enjoyed it. It's not often I see Senator Smith in such a state.

Mrs. McLean finally returned her attention to us and continued. "We were stopped again as the noises from the corridor grew still louder. 'I swear, Glynnis, it seems as if we're going to war what with that racket out there.' Ian turned back toward the door.

"'It doesn't sound like they've been drinking, I know that sound as do you. *This* seems more urgent. Like there's something bad happening to cause concern.'

"Ian listened a moment, nodded, and began donning the clothing he'd removed earlier. 'I ought to go out and see what's the matter then. Perhaps it's nothing, but I'd like to know the reason for all the commotion.'

"He looked over at me with a twinkle in his eyes as he buttoned up his coat.

"'You stay right where you are. I want to see you looking just like that when I come back. And we'll finish where we left off just as soon as I return.'

"His gaze lingered on me in just my petticoat, and I felt as if were naked before him. He came over and kissed me as I ran my hands through his hair, and I recall sighing. Then he released me and stepped back, but I could tell he didn't want to leave me. 'I'll be back in just a few minutes, dear,' he said.

"His finger traced a line down my cheek as he strode out into the corridor. I stared at the door a moment, went back to the desk, and sat down to enter the day's events in my diary."

The senator's expression became more interested.

"You kept a diary of the voyage?"

Mrs. McLean smiled and nodded. "Yes, I did indeed. I've been keeping one almost daily since I was eight. I had it with me on *Titanic*, and it's all I saved when I boarded the lifeboat. I made note of everything we did on the ship: the things that struck me with wonder, which I was sure I'd never experience again in my life for our children to read of when they're older—should we have any."

Mrs. McLean sat quietly for a moment.

"I've not opened it since then. I'm not sure I'd want to. I can recall quite clearly what transpired on board *Titanic*, especially on *that* night. I'm sure I'll never forget it."

The senator nodded.

"Ian was gone for about fifteen minutes, enough for me to enter a couple of pages before he returned. He told me to get dressed, and as I did, he told me what he'd learned. The passageway was not filled, but there *were* a number of people in it—all talking rather excitedly and not very quietly. Ian told me he spoke to a cabin steward.

"'We've struck an iceberg, sir. There's no cause for alarm, but we've stopped so the captain could determine if the ship has been damaged. I expect we'll be on our way again in the morning as soon as he can see the way through the ice.'

"Ian was mildly concerned, and he pressed for more information. 'Is there a lot of it about?' he asked.

"The steward shrugged. 'I've not been up on top, sir. But I suppose there is. It would only make sense for our stopping at this hour of the night.'

"Ian came down briefly to tell me this, and he asked if I'd like to go up on deck with him to learn more. I told him I'd prefer to stay in our warm cabin and would wait until he came back and told me what he learned. He kissed me and left to go up on deck. He was back in less than ten minutes.

"Ian told me that he then made his way back to the elevators that took the passengers up as far as the second-class smoke room. From there, he stepped out onto the boat deck and stood off to the side quietly and watched. He could see the portside lifeboats near him being uncovered and swung out in preparation for lowering. He went back through the smoke room and emerged on the starboard side.

"The same thing was happening there. From the quiet orders being given by the officer in charge, Ian determined that the situation was far more serious than the steward had indicated. He glanced toward the bridge and through the windows he could just see Mr. Andrews, Mr. Ismay, and Captain Smith in close conference. He could see Captain Smith's face and said he looked quite grim. Ian stayed where he was a few moments longer to make certain of what he believed he saw, and then he hurried back down to our cabin. When he told me the boats were being swung out, I was stunned.

"'Is it really that serious?' I asked.

"He nodded as he went to the wardrobe and brought out some warm clothes for the two of us to wear on deck.

"'It rather appears that way. I'm not taking any chances, however. If this ship is to sink, I want us in a lifeboat. If not—we'll lose only a little sleep and have something exciting to write our friends back home when we get to New York.'

"He brought out our life belts. 'Regardless, I want us on deck and ready for whatever may happen.'

"I remember nodding slowly, and then I rose from my chair to do as my husband suggested. As I dressed, Ian removed our few valuables and put them on the bed. I asked him why and he said, 'Should *Titanic* sink or be damaged enough to where we're transferred to a rescue ship, I want us to have something to support us until we reach San Francisco. And I'm entrusting it to *you* since the rule is women and children first. Just a precaution. I'll take enough cash to see me through until we're reunited.'

"He finished what he was doing and helped me into my coat. Or rather, *his* coat. He held open his large, warm greatcoat for me to slip into. 'I don't want to take any unnecessary chances, darling. I doubt we'll even have to leave the ship. This is most likely just a precaution. We'll more than likely be back on board before sunrise. But just in case.' He left this statement dangling as he wrapped his arms around me and held me tightly.

"I nodded and smiled confidently up at my husband. 'If you feel it is necessary, then it is so. I have complete trust in you— or else I would not have married you.' I turned around in his arms to face him, clasped him to me, and kissed him. 'That's a promise that we'll stay together and see this through. Promise me we'll both be okay?'

"Ian nodded and answered, 'I can only promise that things will be as best as fate allows. And that I'll do *my* part to make it true.'

"I held him close again, and then I released him. 'That's all I ask, my beloved,' I said with a smile of what I hoped was assurance. 'I guess we'd better go up and wait to be told what to do.'

"We looked around our cabin quickly to make certain we hadn't forgotten anything, and we put the valuables he'd set aside into the deep pockets of the coat he placed over me. Besides the money we'd brought, there was our marriage certificate and my diaries—and one last thing I pressed into Ian's hands was a small doll, the likeness of me as a small child, which Ian had given me for Christmas years earlier.

"I said, 'Take this with you. Should we become separated, then know I am still with you. It would give me peace if you'd carry it until this is over.'

"Ian smiled, and then he kissed the doll, then me, then the doll again. He placed the doll in his left-hand vest pocket and secured it. 'It will remain here, next to my heart where your love lives, until we return. Now let's go. I've a bad feeling about this.'

"We stepped out into the corridor, locking the door behind us as we did so. We then went up on deck. We never went back. This would have been almost an hour, more or less, after the ship had struck the iceberg. I recall Ian checking his watch and stating that it was nearly twelve thirty. I'm not certain, however, if Ian's watch was set to the ship's time or not. I know he set it just prior to the Sunday sermon, but I don't know if he'd corrected it since."

ON THE BOAT DECK

"We emerged on the boat deck and stayed off to the side to watch. We could see dozens of people outside, but most of the passengers were staying indoors where it was warm. Many members of the crew were still preparing the boats for lowering, but none had gone as yet—not that *we* could see at any rate. There were several officers nearby who were calling for women and children to board the boats, but few were willing to do so. The men were told they'd have to wait until women and children were loaded, but some crewmen were allowed in to handle the boats—at least the boats we were near."

"Which boats were these?" asked the senator.

"The ones near the stern. This was where the second-class boat deck was located. The boats in the rear—so I was told—were for our use, the lower classes. I remember the one nearest to where we came out on deck was Boat 14."

The senator's attention was focused. "Who told you this?" he asked sternly.

Mrs. McLean brushed off his concern. "One of the first-class passengers. *Not* one of the crew. And this was our first day out, not that night. On *that* night, at *that* time, not much was said by anyone. Shock and then acceptance were still setting in regarding our situation.

"Not very long after we came up on deck, we saw that the boats closer to the bow were swung out and lowered. I recall seeing one of them lowered only one deck, and then left to hang on the ropes—empty—while others were prepared and dropped all the way to the sea. At this time, the ship was obviously lower in the water in the front, and the lifeboats closer to the bow were being used first.

"We stayed where we were, silent. After a few minutes, Ian suggested we go across the ship to see what was happening on the other side. As we made our way there, we could see that one boat from the right side was already in the water and drifting behind *Titanic*. At first, I thought we were moving and that we'd leave the boat behind, but I soon saw it was being rowed. *Titanic*'s engines were stopped, and she'd earlier released all her steam pressure. We'd heard the noise even down in our cabin, but it had stopped before we came on deck.

"Ian started leading me toward the nearest boat. 'Perhaps you'd better get in now, Glynnis, before things get worse.'

"I shook my head. 'I can't see the urgency. We've stopped, and boats are being lowered, but I don't see any indication that we're in danger. Besides, it's much too cold out. How much colder will we be in the water away from the warmth of the ship?'

"Ian faced me. 'If we wait and the ship truly is in danger, there may not be time to reconsider. You really need to get into the boat now.'

"I shook my head. 'You will come with me, won't you? Because if not, then I won't go.'

"Ian knew how stubborn I could be, and he looked rather exasperated with me at that moment. 'The rule is women and children first.' He smiled at me. 'I'll get a later boat, and we can all keep warm by rowing around *Titanic* and chasing each other until morning. Or until it's deemed safe enough to bring us back aboard.' He laughed. 'Men versus women rowing contest! Won't that be fun?'"

Mrs. McLean's eyes were slightly raised as she recollected this attempt at humor by her husband. Then she looked back at the senator and me.

"Ian grew serious. He knew I wouldn't get on that boat without him—not at that time anyway—so he shrugged, and we turned away from the boat. 'Let's see what else is going on,' he said. 'Maybe we can get some better idea of the condition of the ship from one of the officers forward.'"

She paused, looking down at her fidgeting hands in her lap. Senator Smith and I waited for her to continue at her own pace and in her own time.

"Soon after, a white rocket was launched from the bridge. I guess it was getting on toward one o'clock by now. The rocket was white, with exploding stars that rained down on the surface of the water."

"No colors?" asked the senator with interest.

Mrs. McLean shook her head. "No, sir. None. Plain white. The rocket went up quite high in the sky and then exploded into white stars with a loud bang. There were several of them before the sinking—maybe ten minutes apart. Time has a way of getting away from one in a circumstance such as that, but I'd guess they were sent up at ten-minute intervals."

"How many?" the senator asked.

Mrs. McLean had been asked this same question during the deposition and couldn't answer it definitively then either.

"More than six. Less than a dozen. I can't say more accurately than that. I really didn't pay much attention after the first two or three that had caught my notice."

The senator nodded. "Please go on," he said.

Mrs. McLean nodded and took a deep breath. "It was now past 1:15. If my timing is correct, the fourth rocket had just been fired from the roof of the officers' quarters. We were back on the portside boat deck and just a bit nearer the bow than when we first came out, and the sight and sound were both blinding and deafening. Ian turned and held me at arm's length. 'Glynnis, you now see the danger we're in. The captain's desperate for any ship to see the rockets. Not *all* ships have been equipped with wireless, you know.'

"I told him that it can't be all that bad. I pointed out to him that there are lots of ladies—and even *children*—still aboard, and few seemed too concerned. I argued with him that it was just a drill. And I complained again about the cold.

"Ian couldn't argue the last point. It was *deathly* cold on the open boat deck. And if he hadn't seen Mr. Andrews' expression as he apprised Captain Smith of the situation, he wouldn't have believed that the huge liner could be in danger. But in danger it was. It was now more than an hour and a half since the *Titanic* had brushed the iceberg, and he knew there wasn't much time left. Already we could see the ocean—when Ian pointed it out to me over the rail, it appeared so calm and deceptively serene—as it drew closer to the forward deck near the bow, that lower part where the hatches and mast were. It wouldn't be long before that deck was flooded. And the ship would only have moments left to live at that point."

Mrs. McLean shook her head.

"I still couldn't understand fully what had happened. Ian couldn't seem to convince me of the seriousness of the situation. 'Glynnis I beg of you. Get into the lifeboat.'

"I looked once again from Ian to the boat nearest us—Boat 12, I believe—then back to Ian. 'Must I, Ian?' I asked.

"'Yes, dear. You must,' he replied.

"We approached the lifeboat, but we stopped a few feet away from where it was being loaded. We observed that passengers were being assisted across a three-foot gap and into the waiting arms of the men in charge of the boat."

Mrs. McLean rubbed her temples and poured herself a glass of water; the ice in the carafe was melted into bare slivers by this time. After drinking down half the glass, she continued.

"'Dear, *please* get into the boat,' Ian said.

"'Not just yet. Let me spend just a few more minutes with you. Just in case.'

"Ian looked at me and slowly nodded. We then proceeded forward on the boat deck, past the empty davits, which just moments ago held Boat 10.

"We were halfway down the boat deck, moving toward the bow, and we passed the first-class lounge in the direction of the entrance to the first-class foyer with its magnificent grand staircase and glass dome. This brought us to the davits for Boat 8, which had been lowered perhaps fifteen minutes earlier, and we were alongside the second funnel. We stopped to watch the confusion that surrounded the loading of Boat 4 ahead of us. Nobody seemed to know where to go for boarding it. It hung at the level of the A deck promenade, waiting for the windows of the closed deck to be opened—or smashed out—to allow the loading of the women and children who were waiting with increasing impatience. We moved forward and stopped again to watch Boat 2, the furthest forward, as it was loaded.

"'There seems to be no panic, Ian,' I said as I observed the apparent calm of the passengers—many of whom preferred *not* to take to the open sea. 'Maybe we can get on in a moment or two.'

"Ian shook his head. 'They're simply waiting for someone to tell them what to do,' he countered. 'There is no officer in charge here, and the crew members on deck don't seem to sense the urgency. Look.' He pointed toward the bow of the liner.

"By this time, the ship's name was disappearing under the surface, and the point of the bow would soon be under. Already, seawater was just a few feet short of lapping onto the well deck—between the bow and the superstructure—and the ship was starting to list to starboard.

"'There's not much time, my dear. You *must* get into a boat.'

"From behind us, several gunshots rang out. Ian and I, along with a number of other passengers, turned at the sound. An officer was standing near the rudder of a lifeboat and aiming a gun along the side of *Titanic* in an apparent attempt to prevent passengers from leaping from the liner's deck into the crowded boat. The attempt appeared to work; the boat was lowered safely with no further problems and was rowed a safe distance away. It was Boat 14. We also saw that, while Ian and I had strolled forward, Boat 12 had been lowered. There now remained only three more regular lifeboats on the portside—one in the rear and two up front. One of those was lowered to A deck and was still empty. The collapsible next to the davits for Boat 2 had yet to be launched.

"We decided to cross over to the right side of the ship. We were just in time to witness an altercation between one of the officers and a man who appeared to be a passenger. He was dressed as if he'd rushed out of bed and had thrown a coat over his sleepwear. I didn't recognize him, but Ian did. It was Mr. Ismay. He was shouting and urging passengers to get into the boat nearest him. 'Lower away. Lower away!' He seemed panicky and near hysteria, and this caused the officer to turn on him and shout an oath, which I clearly heard, before ordering him to step back and shut up. It sounded like he said, 'Would you see me drown the whole lot of 'em?' I was too far away to hear clearly, but I got the general tone of the situation. *Titanic* was not going to remain afloat for much longer. 'Ian, I'm frightened.' I turned to him and drew him close to me.

"Ian nodded. I could tell that he was scared too. But he wouldn't let me see this. 'There's nothing to be frightened of. Come. I'll prove it.' He took me by the hand and led me back across the ship to the port side once again.

"Earlier in the voyage, we had toured the ship in the company of Captain Smith and Mr. Andrews. In the process, we'd spent a considerable amount of time admiring the furnishings and decor of the luxuriously appointed public rooms. While on our tour, we'd stopped off at the Marconi room, and Ian spent quite a bit of time talking with Mr. Philips and Mr. Bride. He even sent a wireless message back home. Ian had struck up a friendship with Mr. Bride, and the two of them—only two years apart in age—had gotten along famously. It was to this room that Ian now took me.

"We'd just missed colliding with Captain Smith. The captain seemed not to recognize us as he rushed past en route to the bridge. He was too concerned with the fate of his ship. Ian merely glanced at him as he led me inside.

"Mr. Phillips was bent over the telegraph key, sending a steady stream of distress signals to any ship near enough to receive them and copying down signals sent by those ships that responded. Mr. Bride was assisting him as best he could, taking messages and running them to the bridge if the news was something the captain, or his immediate subordinates, needed immediately.

"Mr. Bride sat back for a moment to catch his breath and rubbed his aching thighs vigorously. The muscles had cramped from his nonstop dashing to and from the bridge. It was all he could do to keep the cramps from causing his collapse to the deck. He looked up and noticed us in the doorway. 'Mr. McLean? What are you doing here? You should be putting your wife into a boat, quickly. We've not much time is what the captain told us.'

"Ian nodded. 'That's why we've come, Mr. Bride. You're the best men to ask—you and Mr. Phillips. What is the situation?'

"Mr. Philips had taken one ear from the headset upon our arrival and thought how best to answer the question. Ian read the hesitation correctly and said, 'I'm a steady man in a situation, Mr. Philips. It is my wife who needs to hear the news. I'll take responsibility for her reaction.'

"Mr. Philips looked toward Mr. Bride and gave a nod.

"Mr. Bride turned back to address us. 'The *Carpathia* is the closest, but she won't be here until near on four o'clock. She's putting on all steam and coming to us—her speed is rated 14 knots, but Captain Rostron is pushing for more if he can get it.'

"'The captain just told me that the boiler rooms are flooding. Water is about to wash the well deck. Cargo holds and forepeak bunker flooded—the forward steerage berths and crew berths as well are gone. He said Mr. Andrews doesn't give her another hour.' He turned and addressed me directly. 'You'd best find a seat in a boat while they're still here, ma'am. I'm told there's none left starboard—and the port boats are almost all put out as well. And hurry. You've no time to lose.'

"I had gone pale at the news. Ian thanked Mr. Bride for the information and led me to just outside of the room. 'Those are the men who know the situation, dear. They're the ones the captain keeps informed so other ships in the area know our urgency. *Again*, I beg you. Get into a lifeboat.'

"The accuracy of the information Harold Bride had given was verified by Captain Smith, who'd returned to the Marconi room with more information. The captain said, 'All starboard boats have gone—as has Collapsible C. Mr. Murdock has informed me that they are trying to remove Collapsible A from the roof of the officer's quarters and fit it to the davits for Boat 1. Please inform *Carpathia* that all boats will have been launched within the next fifteen minutes. And to please hurry!' The captain turned to go without waiting for an acknowledgment from either of his wireless operators. He caught sight of Ian and me standing a few feet from the door to the room and stopped for a moment. 'If you heard my order to Phillips and Bride, then you know the urgency of the situation. There are still a couple of boats left on this side of the ship. I suggest you board either Boat 2 here or Boat 4 down on A deck, though Mr. Lightoller seems to be having a bit of a time with Boat 4. You've little time left. If you'll please excuse me.'

"The captain dashed off to the bridge and was met by Mr. Andrews, and the two men went off to the first-class foyer.

"Ian and I looked at each other as the stern-most boat was lowered. It was nearly quarter to two by the clock in the Marconi room. As we looked toward the stern, the crewmen manning the falls began lowering Boat 16 to the water more than ninety feet below. The increased height was due to the worsening tilt as the bow slipped lower beneath the sea; the stern was rising as if on a pivot.

"Ian turned to me and took my arm. 'Sweetheart, we've not much time. You heard the man. You *must* get into one of these boats.'

"'What about you? I won't go without you!'

"Ian was beginning to lead me to Boat 2. The crew was trying to assist passengers across the widening gap between it and the ship's railing, but Ian stopped and faced me straight on. 'Don't make me have to worry about you while I try to save myself. I'll have a hard enough time as it is. It will be easier for me to do whatever I have to do if I know that you were safely off the ship. Now, darling, *please* get into a boat. I'll see you when this is all over.'

"As he said this, one of the officers, I don't know his name, shouted, 'Lower away.'

"Boat 2 was quickly dropped to the ocean. I looked over the rail and saw how nearly empty it was. 'There's only about two-dozen people in there. *Surely* they could fill the boat with more! Put some of the men in there!'

"Ian shook his head. 'Women and children only, they're saying. But I know they *should* put men in to fill the boats if there aren't any more women.' He looked around at the people still remaining on the forward boat deck. 'The mere fact that I don't see any women about doesn't mean there aren't any still on board. Why, there were hundreds of women and children in third class; we saw them ourselves just yesterday!'

"'Then where are they?' I demanded.

"Ian just shook his head. 'I don't know. Perhaps they've boarded the starboard boats. Perhaps they're still down below, waiting for instructions. We *still* haven't heard a call to report to lifeboat stations, and we've not had a drill so far on the voyage. I doubt anybody even *knows* their stations. But I do know one thing. Those half-filled boats mean that people can still get into them if they swim for them. And that's what I'm going to try to do. So please. Get into this next one. I'll get off the ship as soon as I can and swim to a boat. I'll see you on board *Carpathia* when she gets here.' He was cupping my chin in his hand and tilting my head up so he could look into my eyes.

"I was trying my best to hold back my tears and was fairly successful up to this point, though one coursed its way down my cheek. Ian saw this and gently kissed it away.

"'Promise me, Ian? Promise me that you'll be saved!'

"He pulled me to him and kissed my forehead. 'I can't promise that. I can only promise that I'll try. I can do no more.'

"I smiled up at him. I knew he would if he could. 'Then I'll accept that promise. I know you'll fight to do your best.'

"We heard the muffled splash as Boat 2 reached the water. The ropes were cast aside, allowing the lifeboat to be rowed a safe distance from the sinking liner. We made our way down to A deck, where Mr. Lightoller and two seamen had resumed working on Boat 4. We stood back out of the way to watch.

"I was to learn later from Mr. Lightoller that Boat 4 had been a problem the entire night. Over an hour earlier, it had been lowered—empty—from the boat deck to the A deck promenade where a number of passengers were told to assemble for boarding. The promenade deck had windows—a feature not found on *Olympic*—and the windows had to be opened with a special tool or be broken out. The passengers were told to go up to the boat deck, and the boat would be raised for them. 'First you tell us to go up—and then you tell us to go down. I wish you'd make up your mind.'

"Finally the windows were broken open, and passengers were ordered down to A deck to begin boarding. They followed Mr. Lightoller, who began helping passengers through the window, across the gap between the boat and *Titanic*'s side, and finally into Boat 4.

"We were among those who went down to the A deck promenade once we learned the windows were removed. We listened to Mr. Lightoller as he expertly instructed the women to watch their step, move to the rear of the boat, and try to keep the weight load even. We saw another couple—holding each other as close as Ian and I were—approach Mr. Lightoller. 'Might I board with my wife, sir? You see—she's in a rather delicate condition.'

"Mr. Lightoller looked the elegant gentleman and his pretty young wife in the eyes as he gave his answer. 'I'm sorry, sir. Women and children only.'

"'I must protest—'

"'Sir, my orders are to see that the women and children *only* are put into the lifeboats and taken away from the ship—and that is precisely what I am doing. There will be no men put aboard any boat until after the women and children are off *Titanic*'s decks. I'm sorry.'

"The gentleman seemed taken aback by Mr. Lightoller's strict attitude. He smiled grimly and nodded. 'Very well, Lieutenant.' He helped his wife across the gap to the boat, and then he stepped back, ignoring her pleas that she remain with him. He stood silent for a moment and then attracted the officer's attention. 'What is the number of this boat, if you please?'

"'Boat 4, sir.' Mr. Lightoller turned to those passengers nearby. 'Any more women? You, ma'am. Come on. Get into the boat. We've not much time.'

"He was speaking to me, but I was watching the end of the scene just playing out before me. The gentleman nodded at Mr. Lightoller's answer and began to walk toward the first-class entrance to the grand staircase from that deck. I was later to learn the gentleman was Colonel Astor.

"My attention was returned to the events at hand when Ian nudged me in the ribs with his elbow. 'Glynnis, darling, he's calling for you to enter the boat.'

"Mr. Lightoller was gesturing impatiently to me. I shook my head and looked to Ian.

"'I can't. I won't leave you.'

"Ian took me by the upper arm, and I feared him for the first and only time in my life at that moment. I was certain he was going to pick me up and throw me into the boat. Instead, he pulled me close and put his mouth beside my ear. 'My precious, we've been through this before. I'll find a way off the ship. So help me, I'll do it. But I want you safely off the ship. Now get *in*. I'll see you when we're rescued.'

"He couldn't overpower my protests, and I broke from him and ran back up to the boat deck, through the first-class entrance leading from A deck, up the grand staircase, and back out to the boat deck. I passed Mr. Astor as I did so. I reached one of the collapsible boats that was being fastened to the lowering devices where Boat 2 had been and stopped, barely controlling the panic that was threatening to engulf me.

"Ian raced up after me, caught hold of me, and turned me around. He didn't speak to me, and I wouldn't look at him. I was watching other passengers as they began to board. We saw mystery writer Jacques Futrelle—one of the few passengers Ian and I *did* recognize on *Titanic*—as he escorted his wife over the side, and then he stood back to wait for the boat to be lowered."

"How did you recognize Mr. Futrelle?" asked the senator.

Mrs. McLean smiled. "Ian was a great fan of mysteries, especially those from American writers. He says that the mysteries written by the English are too dry. The Americans have a wit and a drive about them—a wildness and lack of inhibition—that makes their work more intriguing. Apparently, Ian wasn't alone in this belief. Mr. Futrelle's works were widely published in Great Britain. Ian especially liked Edgar Allan Poe and Mr. Futrelle. It was really Ian's only escape from the seriousness of his career goals. As for me, I didn't like Mr. Futrelle's stories. They gave me the shivers." Mrs. McLean actually *did* shiver as she concluded this statement. "We'd stepped up alongside of Mr. Futrelle—or rather he back to us—as his wife was seated.

"'She's listing badly now,' Ian said. 'There shouldn't be this much of a gap between the lifeboats and the ship's side.'

"Mr. Futrelle turned to him and nodded. He saw me and smiled gallantly to me. 'That she is. But they say *Carpathia*'s steaming at full speed to us and should be here any minute. Nevertheless, I'm not taking chances with my dear wife. I'll try to get into another boat, perhaps that one there'—he gestured to the collapsible above us, fastened to the roof of the officers' quarters—'and escape the ship. But at least I know *she'll* be safe.' Mr. Futrelle looked at Ian with a firm eye and said, 'I suggest you put your wife into this boat and then join me, sir. We've a little time, but I wouldn't delay if I were you. Unless you can swim in ice water—especially in all your ladies wear. It will take you straight down.' The writer tipped his head, walked off through the first-class foyer, and disappeared from view.

"Ian faced me. 'Glynnis, you *must* get on this boat! It's the last one left. You *must* go!'

"Mr. Lightoller had arrived by this time and was checking to see the ropes were properly secured before he ordered his crewmen to swing the boat over the rail and prepare it for loading. He turned to me just then and came close. Mr. Astor had joined us.

"Mr. Lightoller said, 'Ma'am, you must understand. For your husband to have any chance at all, you must get on this boat. I, for one, intend to survive this, but I won't leave until my duty is done. This ship will have to sink out from under me. When she does, I plan to swim for the nearest lifeboat and save myself. Your husband can certainly join me. It truly will be every man for himself at that point.'

"Mr. Astor said, 'Give your husband a chance at life. With you to distract him, he'll surely die. Get into the boat so that he might save himself by knowing you are out of danger.'

"Mr. Lightoller nodded grimly and said, 'Please, ma'am! There is no time left!'

"I turned to look toward the front, and I could see the position we were in. The forward deck was completely submerged, and water was rising swiftly and visibly up the structure supporting the bridge. I turned to Ian and Mr. Lightoller. They must have felt I would continue to protest, though I was actually prepared to give in to them.

"Before I could speak, Ian had already broken my embrace, and with Mr. Astor on my other side, I was delivered into the waiting hands of Mr. Lightoller. I allowed myself to be placed into that last boat. After a quick kiss from Ian, he stepped back—and I was alone.

"'No more?' Mr. Lightoller shouted. 'All right then! Lower away, now! Gently! Keep her level! Steady now! Steady!'

"Ian moved forward against the rail and looked down at me and me up at him, wondering if we'd ever be together again. I noticed Mr. Astor had disappeared; he must have gone back inside the ship. Ian smiled to me and gave me a jaunty little wave—a gesture that was the hardest I'd ever have to see. I blew him a kiss in response, and he jerked back as if he'd received it directly, smiling down at me in shining gratitude. He reached into his right-hand vest pocket and withdrew a cigarette, which he smoked as he watched while the boat I was in reached the water, was released from the ropes, and quickly rowed away.

"It didn't dawn on me until later that Ian didn't smoke! Where he got the cigarette and what incredible stress he was trying to hide from me were questions for which there would never be any answers. I wasn't sure I'd ever want to *know* the answers. I just wanted to awaken from this nightmare, safe and warm in my bed in the safety of our cabin and the security of Ian's arms.

"This had to be a nightmare, one that was caused by the stress of all the newness my life was taking, so quickly and in ways I'd never have imagined for myself—just a young colleen from Ireland. It *had* to be a nightmare. It couldn't be real. It just couldn't.

"But it was. It was all *too* real. And the awareness made it through my disbelief in the form of the cold, salty air and the sight of *Titanic.* I could see the whole length of the ship, clearly sinking and with almost no time left."

ADRIFT ON THE LIFEBOAT

"We were rowed away from *Titanic* as quickly as the men in the boat could pull. We retrieved three or four people who'd jumped from the deck after we reached the water and swam out to us. One of them was the husband of one of the women we had with us, and I remember them shivering miserably until we were picked up after sunrise.

"I never let my eyes leave Ian's form as he grew smaller in the distance. He stood at the railing, finishing his cigarette and ignoring the activity around him: getting the remaining collapsible freed from the roof of the officers' quarters and onto the boat deck where it would be attached, filled, and lowered with what remaining souls were available to be saved.

"I watched as Ian finished smoking and believed I could follow the ember of his cigarette as he flipped it over the side. He positioned himself to assist in bringing the collapsible down to the deck. We weren't so far off that we could not see the slats being positioned to slide the boat down, and I saw as those slats broke under the weight. The boat landed upside down on the deck!

"I thought I recognized Mr. Bride as one of the men working to free that final boat, but I can't be certain. I certainly recognized Mr. Lightoller, and Ian was unmistakable.

"*Titanic* was sinking faster now. The water was entering and filling A deck, below where my beloved was working to free the lifeboat, and it quickly climbed and began flooding the boat deck. The stern of the ship rose higher, and the screams of fright and fear from those passengers still on board will haunt my dreams for as long as I live!

"I watched as Ian disappeared in the rush of the water, and I prayed he would swim to safety. I saw as the first funnel, its base now underwater, broke its supports and crashed into the sea atop dozens of swimmers, crushing them. I saw the collapsible pushed aside by the wave caused by the funnel's collapse and several swimmers frantically approaching the boat and trying to climb onto it. We were too far to go to their aid—but not too far away to see that the boat was still upside down. I prayed Ian was one of those swimmers."

Mrs. McLean was gasping in quick short breaths, and she paused to drink the rest of her water.

Senator Smith, concerned, leaned forward and told her she needn't go on, but she shook her head at him.

"I must. I need to tell it. I need to get it out from inside me—or I'll be crushed by the weight of it." She remained quiet for a few moments then spoke in a quiet, mournful voice. "Ian was under that funnel. Mr. Lightoller saw his fate and was unwilling to tell me of it at first. But I made him. I had to know. I didn't want any false hope."

Mrs. McLean was quiet again, and a tear fell large and slow down her pale cheek—a tear she allowed to remain until it had dried of its own accord.

Through my own tears, which were flowing freely, I saw the most beautiful, brave, and gallant woman who'd ever entered my life. I knew the thought was morbid but true nonetheless. Her grief and the single tear gave her a beauty that, in my opinion, the world had never before—and never would again—see as long as human life existed.

"We watched silently as the ship's stern continued to rise higher above the sea. We were facing the ship as we rowed; those of us able to had grasped an oar, and we stopped when we felt we were far enough away to escape the suction the seamen told us would be caused by the ship when she went down.

"I'm told we stopped perhaps five or six hundred meters away. Distances are deceiving when you have no references—this I learned from Ian over the past few days of the voyage—but we were far enough away to witness what came next. In spite of the tragedy, it was awesome and beautiful in its display of brute power.

"*Titanic* was sinking by the bow, and the stern was rising out of the water. You could clearly see the portside propeller from where we had stopped. The base of the second funnel was now in the water, and the grand staircase and beautiful glass dome at the top were submerged. The ship began sliding forward into the water, and soon the second funnel appeared to break free—almost falling *backward* from the force of the water rushing against it. And the stern rose higher still.

"There came from within the ship a thunderous noise at about the time the third funnel broke off, and the fourth quickly reached the water. It was loud enough to drown out the screams of the people still on board crowding the stern. The lights flashed and went out, and all that was left was starlight—millions upon millions of pinpoints in the sky—and the ship was like a finger pointing straight up, blotting out many of them. The noise became a roar, and we could feel the vibrations pounding through the water through the bottom of the boat to our feet and seats.

"It's hard to tell what happened next. It appeared to me as if *Titanic* had righted herself, but it looked strange. It was like it had turned—and was still turning—to present her narrow end to us. As bright as the stars were, there still wasn't enough light to see clearly. But then, the ship rose back up on end and quickly slid into the water.

"Oh, the screams of the swimmers were terrible! Cries for help and mercy were in front of us where the ship had disappeared, and we could do nothing to help save those poor souls from freezing and drowning. Our boat was nearly full from those who jumped and swam to us as we were lowered, and we were somewhat afraid to go back. We were afraid we'd overfill and add our lives to those who had already perished.

"We did make an effort. We managed to turn the boat around and started to go back. We could still hold a few more people if we were careful and didn't mind the crowding. Then we noticed our boat was leaking. We were in a collapsible, and the canvas sides hadn't been properly raised. The water was able to get in if there was enough activity to cause our boat to rock. It broke our hearts to have to sit still, unable to come to the aid of any more desperate and dying people and to listen to them die. The sounds of their cries grew quieter as the night wore on.

"We couldn't even row out to where the other lifeboats were floating. We had no means of calling them to our aid. Only a couple of the men aboard had had the stamina to row, and the ladies never considered doing so. We had no idea what to do or where to go.

"After what seemed to me to be about an hour, we were sighted by one of the primary lifeboats. Mr. Lowe was the officer in charge. He'd gathered up a few other boats that had been drifting, tied them together, and towed them behind him.

He found us and took us in tow as well, after helping secure our sides a bit better. He'd been insisting that at least one of the boats go back and try to save people from the water. Many of those in this grouping argued against it, but he would have none of that. He transferred most of the people from his boat into those that still had room, freed his boat from the rest of us, and went searching.

"Unfortunately, it was much too late. He managed to rescue several people from the water, and he found the overturned collapsible Ian had been helping to free just before the wave washed it and everybody working on it overboard. There were nearly thirty survivors on that boat, trying to maintain their balance as best they could until they could be saved. I'd heard an officer's whistle a few minutes after Mr. Lowe left us; I learned it was from Mr. Lightoller. He was one of those standing on that boat—and so was Mr. Bride.

"Dawn was about to break. The sky in what I took to be the east seemed to be brightening just a bit. I saw a green flare being lit and waved from one of the other boats. There were cries of grief and discomfort over the otherwise silent sea. As the sky grew lighter, we began to notice that we were surrounded by ice—ice of various sizes and shapes, growing white as the rising sun reflected from them.

"And wreckage. Bits of wood, some baggage. Strewn as far as the eye could see.

"And bodies. Hundreds of them, frozen and floating, their faces as gray as the life preservers they wore, in all manners of dress and from all walks of life: first class mingled with steerage mingled with crew. No class distinction among the dead. And in the distance, steaming quickly toward us from the south, a ship, her one funnel billowing with thick black smoke and her horns and whistles blowing shrilly.

"It was *Carpathia*. I understand it was close to four o'clock in the morning, perhaps a bit later. It would be quite some time before she would reach us. She stopped to pick up the first lifeboat she encountered. It was the one with the green flare: Boat 2, I've been told. As the others rowed toward her, Mr. Lowe returned to take our group in tow once again. He raised a sail—the only lifeboat I recall seeing with one—and took advantage of the breeze that came with the dawn to quickly get us to the *Carpathia* and rescue."

Diary Entry—April 16, 1912

If I don't sort out my thoughts, I'll go mad! I've not been able to think clearly enough to write after the tragedy!
Ian is gone!
My love!
My life!
I don't know what to do. How will I live?
How will I go on?
I'll never forget the last time I saw him as the boat I was in was lowered into the sea. Though he was surrounded by several others who were trying to detach and lower the remaining collapsible from the roof of the officers' quarters, I only had eyes for him. Those others were shapes in the mist. He was leaning against the rail, so calm and so brave, a cigarette in his hand, which he would bring to his lips and draw upon. And he doesn't smoke!
I never once saw a sign of panic in him. He was confused in the beginning about where we should go and what we should do, but one thing was always paramount in his mind: we had to get off the ship. *Titanic* was sinking!

We could see dozens of our fellow passengers in various states of dress, milling about the boat deck, as the officers and seamen were readying the boats to be filled and lowered. We were on the port side most of the time, but we would occasionally move to the other side and observe the activity there.

Initially we didn't think it would sink. We both kept calling to mind the assurance we'd received from Mr. Andrews—just a day sooner—that *Titanic* was meant to be her own lifeboat in a situation such as this. That was the design and construction of her watertight bulkheads.

They're not so watertight now. She lies at the bottom of the Atlantic with all her compartments, cabins, public spaces, the first-class dining room, cargo holds, boiler rooms, engine room, and her bridge full of the water the bulkheads were meant to restrain.

I feel so brokenhearted for Mr. Andrews, whom I learned yesterday was lost. He was so certain he'd built the safest ship afloat, and yet he was the first to realize that it was all for naught.

So many people died before first light. I've no idea how many of us were saved, but *Carpathia* is such a small ship. She's able to hold us all plus her own, and I fear the loss of life was immense. My Ian was one of them.

My heart is broken; I don't know how I will go on without him. All my life, Ian has been a part of me. From childhood, when Peter first brought him home from school as a six-year-old pup until yesterday morning, my life has always had Ian as a part.

And now he's gone.

He was so manly in those last few moments before we were parted. By my understanding, I was on the very last boat off. I had chances to leave sooner, but I couldn't go without Ian.

And he wouldn't as long as there were women and children still aboard. We were on both sides of the ship, at first standing in disbelief that we were in any danger. We thought it was just a precaution, and we'd be back aboard by morning.

The tilt of the deck grew steeper toward the bow. When we got close to the bridge, the front of the ship was so low that it appeared ready to slip under at any moment. The distress rockets that had been fired from the bridge had stopped a short time before.

And Mr. Andrews—how many he helped save is incalculable! His increasing sense of urgency was the signal to us that we were in dire straits—and we'd best look for a way off the ship.

There'd be no going back in the morning. The ship wouldn't be there.

I recall when Ian first learned of the iceberg, when we were still down in our stateroom. He'd gone up on deck to investigate what he'd heard, then came back to alert me. He insisted we dress and go back up; the ship was in distress. What I saw and heard was terrifying, and I knew—we both knew—that *Titanic* was in trouble. I had already pocketed my valuables at Ian's insistence, which consisted of you, dear diary, deep in the pockets of the coat Ian held open for me. I gave him back the doll he'd given me for Christmas so many years ago!

I bid him to carry that doll with him until we were reunited—not yet knowing that I'd be reluctantly agreeing to board a lifeboat *without* him (my heart broke at that point!). He nodded somberly as he put the doll in his vest pocket, right next to his heart.

He reached into his right-hand vest pocket, withdrew his billfold, and pressed it into my hand. I knew it carried most of our cash, and my heart sank.

"You take it, Glynnis. Just in case. It will see you wherever you feel you need to go when you're rescued."

"When *we're* rescued!" I quickly responded.

He smiled grimly and nodded, his eyes never once leaving mine. "Yes. When *we're* rescued."

That was when he picked up his greatcoat and held it open for me. I believe now that he knew he'd never need it for himself again.

"You wear this." He nodded at my diaries, which were four in number. "The pockets are large enough to hold those safely."

I agreed, and he shrugged me into the coat, helped me put the diaries into the immense pockets, and put on two coats himself—one of them mine! We hurried out the door and back up to the boat deck.

Many of the boats were gone by then. One boat all the way forward that had been partially lowered early on was only now starting to be filled from the deck below us. There was a final boat just being attached to the equipment for lowering, and that's the one Ian raced me to. Mine would be the one life he saved that night.

We got to the boat, and the officer in charge, whom I learned after we were rescued was the second officer, Mr. Lightoller, was urgently loading the boat with all the women he could find in the vicinity. Many men were about, but aside from assisting getting the women in, they were generally standing back and watching quietly.

Ian and I slowed down as we approached the boat. The officer saw me and held out his hand impatiently. I turned to Ian and pulled him close. "Please get on with me. I can't leave without you!"

Ian whispered, "It's going to be all right, my love. You get into the boat, and I'll swim out to meet you." He turned his head and looked up behind him. "Or better still, I'll help get that one down and launched, and we'll row out to you. Don't worry. You just get in so I don't have to concern myself with your safety. If I know *you're* all right, it will be easier for *me*."

If only I could have realized what he'd meant. The water was washing against the base of the bridge, and I feared that Ian wouldn't so much as row off as he would be washed off.

I clung to him a moment longer before I let him release me to the officer who helped me in. I think I was the last to board, but I may be wrong. The activity around me is all a blur. All I can clearly know is that I never lost eye contact with my darling Ian.

"Be strong, my love. And have faith." Those were the last words I heard him say.

I tried to be brave, and I tried to smile my love to him as the boat began to drop to the sea. His image blurred from the tears in my eyes, but I was afraid to blink them away. I was afraid he'd disappear in that quick flash of darkness while my eyes were closed.

The water was just a few feet below us, and it took no time at all for the boat to reach it and for the ropes to be cut away. The crewmen in the boat quickly grabbed the oars, and the lifeboat was hurriedly turned and rowed as far from *Titanic* as it could go. We were but a few feet off when several men jumped over the ship's rail and tried to land in the boat—one of them struck half on and half off and was pulled in. Another, the husband of one of the women with us, landed in the water and swam to us.

"Ian, jump!" I called out to him in hopes he'd emulate their actions and thus be saved as they were.

I doubt he heard me. The last I saw of him, he was atop the roof of the officers' quarters, helping to free the remaining collapsible from its fastenings and trying to get it down to the boat deck so it could be filled and launched.

As painful as it was for me to hear, I forced Mr. Lightoller to tell me what he remembered about the fate of my husband. This is what I learned.

They got the boat free but had no time to lower it over the side. There was no true way of even doing so because it had landed upside down. The bridge slipped under the water at that moment and an immense wave, probably caused by the forward motion of *Titanic* as she slipped under, washed the boat—and all the men working on it—back toward the stern. At that moment, the first funnel snapped its mooring lines. The funnel toppled into the sea, crushing many of the hapless swimmers directly in its path.

The funnel nearly hit Mr. Lightoller; Mr. Bride escaped injury by the slimmest of margins and was washed away from the ship. Mr. Lightoller, however, was sucked under briefly before a blast of air from deep inside blew him to the surface.

He hesitantly told me that he feared that the funnel crushed Ian. I could see his sorrowful expression crack as he said these words, and tears were very near the surface.

I thanked him and turned away to be alone.

This was yesterday. I found a vacant deck chair on the fantail at the very stern of *Carpathia* and stayed there the rest of the day and all the night. I didn't sleep. I *couldn't* sleep. I stayed awake—all awareness of my surroundings unable to intrude on my remembrances of my life with Ian.

And thus I came to terms with the realization and acceptance of his loss.

How will I go on?

As best I can, I suppose. What choice do I have? I'm Irish. We persevere; that is our lot in life. We can be persecuted, but we can never be conquered. Not by people. Not by nations.

And not by life.

We will be in New York in a couple of days. Many of us who have survived have already begun to accept our losses.

And it's amazing. Those of us who have accepted it and steeled ourselves to carry on are of the lower stations of life—the steerage passengers or those much like myself. The ones who are "downtrodden" and born to suffer the fate of servitude and degradation. The ones who toil for their supper and reap the rewards produced by the sweat of their brows. We are the ones who are raised to survive indignities and disasters. We're conditioned to it; it's in our blood.

Those in the upper classes—not so much the second class as the first—can't seem to come to terms with what has happened. They are indignant that their husbands weren't rescued. They're concerned with the loss of their valuables. And they appear to be resentful of the "inconvenience" of *Titanic* sinking. Who was going to pay for their loss? Who was going to replace what was taken from their lives?

Their inability to be human made me *glad* I'm the girl that I am. It makes me even more proud that I'm of the earth, that hardship is part of me. It enables me to embrace my loss; while I might want to see blame fixed, I won't stop living to wait.

Titanic's surviving officers and crew are not much different from my people perhaps. Their lot in life is similar to mine: born and bred to a certain station, not able to rise above that, and so resigned and ready to meet all challenges as they come and to survive and continue on. No sense of injustice really. They were too used to things being the way they have always been. I'd heard talk as I grew up that a change was in the air—that the situation for the lower classes was going to be improved either by voluntary means from the aristocracy or through work stoppage and (God forbid) violence.

But that would probably be in a distant future that I might not live long enough to see. It doesn't change the *now*.

I heard that Mr. Ismay, the owner of *Titanic,* was under heavy opiates in the doctor's cabin. By what I witnessed and what Ian told me at the time, Mr. Ismay was the panicked passenger who was frantically urging the men in charge of the boats on the right side of the ship to hurry and lower the boats, that there was no time. I remember being there, and hearing the officer in charge lash at him most descriptively. He'd backed away at the rebuke, and I didn't see him again.

J. Bruce Ismay. On board to celebrate the maiden voyage of *Titanic.*

The *only* voyage of *Titanic.*

I've heard some people say he was grieving the loss of his ship—that it would cost him and his company millions in settlements and break him.

I've heard others, more charitable than the first, say the immense loss of life is what is breaking his spirit.

I want to believe the latter, but I've always been a forgiving person. God made me thus; I cannot (nor will I) change that in myself. Even though one of those lives was dear to mine.

I must put you down, now my dear diary. I have nothing more to say. I need to turn inward to try to find the inner strength I know I have in me to carry on alone.

It will be so hard.

THE CARPATHIA

"It was close to seven o'clock when we reached *Carpathia* and were brought aboard. Under different circumstances, I would think it such a beautiful sight to see: the bright sun, the clear sky, and the blue-green ocean studded with ice floes.

"But not this morning; for among those flows were the bodies and wreckage of *Titanic*. The sea was a grave now, and none of us wanted to imagine the beauty and splendor the scene *could* have been. The reality was much too unavoidably obvious and hard enough to bear.

"Once aboard, we were asked what our berths were on *Titanic* and then escorted into the various public rooms set aside by class and station. We were given hot broth, tea or coffee, blankets to warm us, and clothing; many of those who'd left *Titanic* were underdressed and suffering from exposure to the cold ocean air. There were several who were taken to the infirmary with varying degrees of frostbite and other injuries. Our boat had taken on enough water to where our feet were fairly well frozen, and I was grateful to be able to remove my sodden shoes and stockings and warm my feet by a steam radiator. I dried my shoes, and when I felt better, I put them back on and went outside where I stayed—voluntarily— until we docked in New York. I didn't want to be warm and comfortable while my Ian was cold and wet at the bottom of the ocean. It didn't seem right to me, and I felt I owed a penance for surviving while he died.

"I spent a frantic time in my exhaustion that first day on board looking for Ian, then trying to find anybody who might know what became of him. I soon encountered Mr. Lightoller, who reluctantly told me what had happened—what he had witnessed and what he believed happened on that basis. I felt life was no longer worth living, and I quietly went outside to the ship's fantail and stayed there the rest of the way in. I slept fitfully and ate hardly at all. Several people, including some fellow survivors, tried to bring me around, but I would have none of it. I tried to write in my diary and make sense of my experience, my survival, and my loss, and it was hard getting the words out. So I just stayed where I was, alone and in misery, until we docked in New York.

"Once here, I noticed with curiosity at first, and then revulsion, the hoopla—is that the word?—about the boats in the harbor and the people lining the dock. These were people looking at misery—voyeurs, if you will—who had come to look upon the face of tragedy like we were a circus sideshow. They were no different from a crowd that gathers around the scene of any type of accident, be it a train or a man stomped to death by a wild animal. It was a show, an event. Something they could say that they were a part of though all they were *really* were observers. Ghouls. Feeding on the misfortune of others.

"That isn't to say that there weren't people who were sincerely concerned and who wished to help. I'm certain there were many from charitable organizations or just plain good-hearted and giving people who were there solely to help care for those who had no place to go and no one to comfort them.

Those people were and are angels, but I initially couldn't tell the difference from where I stood.

"And the press. Out for their stories, their exclusives. Out to sell the most 'amazing' tales they could get—and if they couldn't get them, they'd invent them. Once I managed to get *here* to this hotel, I obtained the daily papers when I was ready to read them. And the stories they printed! Senator, I was *there*! I can't say I saw everything that happened, but many things printed I *did* witness. And I can't recall much of *anything* happening the way it was told in your American newspapers!"

Mrs. McLean was indignant as she spoke these last lines, and who could blame her? It was precisely the reason Senator Smith refused to read the news during the inquiry—and would not allow any information brought to him that did not directly concern the interview of a witness summoned before him. Gossip was not allowed, regardless of the source, unless it was under sworn testimony. And then, it could only be *assumed* to be the truth.

"Mrs. McLean, how did you avoid the press at the pier? How did you get off *Carpathia* without being recognized and accosted?"

Mrs. McLean smiled. "The ship's own passengers were allowed to disembark first, followed by the survivors. The ship's captain did this in fairness to his charges, as their trip was interrupted, and they'd been so accommodating to us from *Titanic*. As I was reasonably presentable in that my clothing was rumpled, but appeared clean and organized, I simply mingled with them and was lost in the crowd.

"By the way, you and I passed just before I left the ship. You were in a hurry; from what I later read, you were looking to speak with Mr. Ismay before he could leave the ship. You probably don't remember since you brushed past without seeming to see.

"Once off the ship, I came here. I should say the clerk must have thought I was a sight; this is a very high-class hotel. But as I had the funds required for this modest room—and I informed him my belongings would arrive shortly with my husband and valet—he could see no reason to deny me this suite. He had no way of knowing who I was, and within the hour, I was forgotten. He was far too busy trying to sort out the requests for lodgings by others who had come soon after to worry about one lone woman who had the means to pay.

"Except for purchasing additional clothing and going for a walk to sort my thoughts out—a trip to Halifax in hopes that my Ian had been found—a change of scene and to do something different, perhaps to dine somewhere other than my room or the restaurant downstairs, I've been here ever since.

"In another day, I'll be aboard *Olympic*, returning to Ireland. It will be difficult. So many things on board that ship will remind me of *Titanic*. And of Ian."

Mrs. McLean paused in thought. She was finished, one could tell. The afternoon was getting on, and it would soon be time for us to leave her. But it appeared that she wasn't *quite* finished with us yet.

"Tell me, Senator Smith. What have you learned in your inquiry? I want to know why *Titanic* sank. Was it in her construction? Was it in the way she was handled? Why did so many people die out there that night—not just my Ian, but all of them? And what is to be done about it? I deserve to know, and I won't be here in your country when your findings are released. I've told you my story. Now you tell me yours."

THE SENATOR'S SOLILOQUY

At this time, we don't have the full background on the construction of *Olympic* or *Titanic*. Over time, that information will become available; Mr. Franklin of White Star's New York office and Mr. Ismay have assured me of that. Suffice it to say, it has significant bearing on the subject and will be admitted to the records of the inquiry as it is obtained.

But there *is* much that we do know.

To begin.

A decision was made in 1907 to construct what would become the three biggest, most luxurious ocean liners ever built to sail the North Atlantic between Great Britain and America. They were commissioned by the White Star Line, whose chairman was J. Bruce Ismay. He'd succeeded his father and had been groomed to take his place upon his father's death or retirement. It was his death that provided the promotion. This was in 1899.

Olympic was begun first, in late 1908, with *Titanic* following in early 1909. They were built side by side at the Harland and Wolff Shipyards in Belfast, and were to be the pride both of the shipyard and of White Star. The intent was to beat out their rival company, Cunard Lines, which owned *Mauritania* and *Lusitania*. Those two ships had won awards for speed—crossing the Atlantic in record time and capturing the famed Blue Riband Award from the Germans. The Cunard ships had been built with the assistance of the British admiralty, which gave Cunard access to the latest turbine engine technology.

There was a price for that arrangement, but it doesn't necessarily concern us here.

Both White Star and Harland and Wolff knew they'd never compete with Cunard in the quest for the fastest crossing. It was thus their desire to build ships of size and luxury appointments that would never be equaled or surpassed. There is to be a third ship, the *Britannic* or *Gigantic* (there's some argument over the final name; White Star claims the former so I'll refer to her as that) to follow soon thereafter. Her keel was laid this past September, as I've learned through the testimonies. The three ships together would form the new Atlantic flagship fleet for the White Star Line for years to come.

These new ships were a marvel of engineering, as your husband knew personally, for you related him telling you that he stood on the deck of *Olympic* and looked across to *Titanic* while both were under construction. The Irish are proud of their shipbuilding skills; nobody builds them better. That is why an Irish ship is a reliable ship. And regardless of what company, what nationality, *owned* the ship, if it was built in Ireland, it was Irish.

The main of the work concentrated on *Olympic*. The intent was to get her into the water as soon as possible and ready to sail—the lessons learned from her would be applied to *Titanic* and *Britannic*.

Olympic was launched in October 1910, less than two years after primary hull construction was begun, and she was completed and ready for two days of sea trials in May 1911. She passed and was due to leave Belfast the afternoon of *Titanic*'s launch. She sailed to Liverpool, which at that time was the home port for White Star, and began service two weeks later.

There was nothing overly special about either *Olympic* or *Titanic* except their appointments. Twenty-nine boilers to power the engines, allowing a top speed of nearly 25 knots. Longer than the Cunard ships, but sleeker. More luxurious. More opulent. They weren't built any differently than any other liner before them except to account for the size; they'd have to be of thicker steel and have more solid bracing. That's a design feature based on engineering determination. Your husband would have understood this.

Titanic was launched on the last day of May 1911. She was towed to a graving dock, where she was completed and made ready for service. Lessons learned during several voyages of *Olympic* resulted in upgrades and improvements done during *Titanic*'s construction: more staterooms on B deck, the planned elimination of the ladies' writing room, and enclosing the A deck promenade to reduce the wind blast and spray generated by the ship's forward motion. Because of the new fad for sidewalk dining, which appears to be the rage in Paris, a French bistro, the Café Parisian, was added to *Titanic* that was not available on *Olympic*.

There were some other changes as well.

Because of this, *Titanic* was claimed to be both bigger and better than *Olympic*. This was only partially true; both ships were the same length, width, and height, but *Titanic* was several thousand tons heavier.

Both were considered *virtually* unsinkable. I'm stressing that word because nowhere has any representative of White Star Line claimed *Titanic* unsinkable prior to the sinking. All said "virtually," or "practically." All used qualifiers to stress her supposed invincibility to sinking and how her design would keep her afloat long enough for rescue ships called in aid to arrive.

The claim was never made until White Star's American agent, Mr. Franklin, was asked why he delayed the full announcement of the tragedy and the loss of life. He said, "We thought her to be unsinkable." After all, he had the wireless message from *Olympic,* which he received on the morning of April 15. He could simply have said he was awaiting confirmation before releasing any news. Perhaps that is what he meant, that her destruction was incomprehensible. Also, many wireless stations in New York and Canada were intercepting and mixing overheard wireless signals. This only served to compound the confusion.

Titanic sailed from Southampton shortly after noon on April 10. During the inquiry, it was learned from several people aboard that there was almost a collision between her and the *City of New York*—the very ship you and your husband *were* to sail on—as she was steaming down the river toward the open ocean. One of many ships left idle due to the coal strike changing so many people's travel plans.

This collision was averted by some quick thinking on the part of a tugboat captain and your own Captain Smith. But it was a near one. One wonders what would have occurred had *Titanic* not been delayed by this near miss—or if the two ships *had* collided. Would *Titanic* have been in the position to meet the iceberg? Would she have passed by earlier? Later? Not at all?

One wonders.

Incidentally, I once met Captain Smith myself, crossing the Atlantic on *Baltic.* That was about six years ago, and at that time, my son and I dined at the captain's table and toured the ship. Much like I'll be doing on the *Olympic* tomorrow.

Of course, I'll be looking with a more critical eye on this tour than I did when Captain Smith guided me through *Baltic* and explained his ship's appointments and safety features.

Everything I've ever heard about Mr. Andrews had been nothing short of honorable, including *your* description of him. He was a genius of a man—but a humble genius as well. He was loved—not just liked, but *loved*—by all who encountered him. He built a sound ship, the crew from below decks testified strongly to that. And I'll see that for myself when I tour *Olympic* tomorrow. I intend to go where most people never go. I want to inspect what I can of her plates, her rivets, and her framing. Her double bottom and her watertight compartments. If I could order her placed in dry dock so I can walk beneath her and inspect her keel, be certain that I would. I want to know what—in *Titanic*'s construction—caused her to sink that night. Calculations that engineers have made for me state that the size of the opening in the hull could not have much exceeded twelve square feet—that's rather small, Mrs. McLean. It's six feet by two feet. Or four feet by three feet. Or twelve feet by one foot. Any multiplier you can imagine: 144 feet by one inch is not very big. To give an example, twelve square feet is smaller than the door to your suite. A bit larger than the surface of your bathtub. Smaller than your bed. And described as a gash approximately three hundred feet long, based on the breached compartments. A pretty narrow gash to have admitted that much water if that's a continuous length. Some experts tell me it was most likely a series of holes, or sporadically opened seams and sprung rivets. But we'll never know. The ship is two miles down; there's no way to reach her.

Below-deck survivors talk about a gash. Mr. Ismay claims to have heard Mr. Andrews describe just that to the captain shortly after the berg was struck. But had anybody actually *seen* that gash? I think not, because anyone who had sight of it most likely drowned moments later, and only one witness from Boiler Room 6 lived to tell about it. This would have been the end of the tear, which extended about two feet behind the fourth bulkhead.

In my layman's opinion—shared by members of the board and is pure conjecture on our parts and not based on conclusive fact—is that *Titanic* settled slowly at first, then filled more rapidly as open portholes reached the level of the sea. The more open portholes, the more openings. Several passengers testified that their portholes were open to admit fresh, bracing air. One passenger even stated that ice broke off the berg and fell into his cabin from the porthole!

Which leads one to this conjecture. If the portholes were closed, the ship *may* have floated longer. But how much longer? One cannot say. Eventually, the water filling the very bow of the ship in the five compromised compartments would have spilled over into the next compartment back. Which is also exactly what happened, but sooner due to the open portholes. One theory was advanced privately: if the watertight bulkheads were opened after the collision to allow the water to flow evenly from bow to stern, would the *Titanic* have stayed afloat longer?

Several experts I've spoken to have said it would. The boilers would have to be dampened and the fires put out, or there would be an explosion when the water reached the hot metal. And that would mean no power to keep the lights lit. The wireless had backup batteries, but all else would be dark, complicating the evacuation. But the ship *would* have stayed afloat longer—at least long enough for help to arrive. The reason behind this theory is that if the ship settled evenly, then only twelve feet of opening would have been exposed to the sea the whole time, and the portholes would have taken longer to have reached the sea to allow additional water in. And then, only if they were to remain open. One would think that Mr. Andrews, in *this* scenario, would have had the presence of mind to order several teams of stokers, stewards, and the like to go through the ship and close them. Surely, they'd have missed some, but they'd have closed enough to buy more time for the passengers.

Perhaps nobody thought of that. Or perhaps they did—and reasoned that keeping the lights lit as long as possible would help keep calm on the ship. There's no way of knowing. You see, it's easy to solve a problem with the benefit of hindsight—when it's too late to apply that solution.

Therefore, you have the mechanics of the sinking.

Now to human error.

How much blame can be assigned to this?

Considerable, I'm afraid. Let me give you some examples.

There were at least six wireless messages, either meant for *Titanic* herself, passed on by her for other ships, or intercepted *by* though not directed *to* her.

Six.

It's not known if more than three ever reached the bridge; there was no standard protocol for delivering those messages. To me, it seemed that passenger traffic took precedence over navigational warnings though the officers and crew of several ships I've spoken to deny this. Not just those on *Titanic*. They all claim the safety of the ship takes precedence over passenger convenience.

Then why did Captain Smith give a wireless warning from *Baltic* to Mr. Ismay on that Sunday afternoon and allow him to put it in his pocket and keep it until nearly suppertime? A warning from *Mesaba* never reached the bridge at all, according to Mr. Bride's testimony.

And the *Californian*—which we'll return to. A communication from her stating that she was stopped in ice near where *Titanic* would herself arrive less than an hour later was cut off by Mr. Philips before it could be fully sent, and that one was specifically addressed to *Titanic*. That was *less than an hour* before *Titanic* struck the berg.

That's three detailed messages right there, all within a twelve-hour span before the collision with the berg and all warning of ice in the area *Titanic* was approaching. How many others that we'll never know about?

So what *did* the officers on the bridge know? Did they have all the information they needed to navigate in what we all now know were ice-strewn waters? Ice that drifted farther south than was considered normal, making what should have been a safe and clear crossing hazardous? The sea-lane is always switched south this time of year to *avoid* that ice, yet there it was. You saw that ice the morning after the sinking while still in your lifeboat.

How fast was the ship going? Too fast for conditions, obviously. But did they know the conditions, based on sightings of ice from other ships in the area? Mr. Lightoller passed on instructions to his relief when he went off duty at ten o'clock that night that the lookouts had been instructed to watch for ice. So they knew ice was near, yet the ship never slowed.

The lookouts were told to keep a sharp eye for ice, yet they had no binoculars. It's questionable whether that made a difference. I'm told the naked eye is better for seeing things at a distance. In a broad field, the glasses would help them identify an object in detail once it was spotted, but glasses would not help in the initial spotting. And Mr. Lightoller believed they'd be sighting ice by nine thirty—fully two hours *before* the collision!

And yet the ship never slowed.

Once the berg was sighted—was "hard a-starboard" the correct command? Some say the ship should have struck the berg directly, it would have crumpled the bow and killed dozens of crew and passengers in the very tip, but the ship would have remained afloat. And the engines were "full astern." Others say that if the engines were allowed to remain "full ahead," the ship would have better steerage and would have responded to the helm faster.

However, a witness from the engine room stated that the collision had already occurred by the time the engine room telegraph gave the alert of the command from the bridge; in that event, the ship was still "full speed ahead," making that option a moot point.

The number of lifeboats. Granted, *Titanic* was intended to be her own lifeboat; the design of the watertight bulkheads was meant to help keep the ship afloat long enough to allow rescue ships to arrive and transfer her passengers—and perhaps some cargo and luggage if there was time for that.

The bulkheads didn't go high enough to keep the water out as the bow sank lower, and the water spilled over into dry compartments, causing the ship to sink deeper and deeper as time went on—and not much time at that—so the compartments they were intended to protect weren't watertight after all, were they? Ultimately, the ship was nothing more than a large lifeboat with an open plughole in her bottom—and there was no plug to stop it from filling. The open portholes expedited matters.

Back to the lifeboats. You realize that there were more than 2,200 people on *Titanic*? Two thousand two hundred and twenty eight, by my count. Only 705 survived. The boats could hold 1,178 if all assigned spaces of capacity were utilized—more if they were crammed to overload, as I understand one was—five people more than its load rating.

And *Titanic* was built to accommodate up to about three thousand people—passengers and crew together. This left space for less than half the people on board had she been fully booked and staffed. Less than *half.*

Yet expert after expert testified that the ship actually carried *more* lifeboats than the British Board of Trade required for a ship of that size. More than 46,000 GRT—that's gross registered tons. This is the internal volume of the vessel, not the actual weight of the ship either empty or loaded. And based on this GRT is the calculation for lifeboat capacity. But that only went up to ships weighing ten thousand tons. The rules called for sixteen lifeboats with a capacity of 5,500 cubic feet. *Titanic* was more than four times that size; she should have carried a minimum of sixty-four lifeboats of that capacity.

Sixty-four.

But it was apparently felt that the addition of the four collapsible boats to complement the sixteen regular boats was enough, and Ismay and Franklin expected me to pat them on the back for their thoughtfulness and consideration for providing extra lifeboats on the *Olympic*-class ships!

The British government believed these new ships—not just White Star's ships, but the Cunard vessels that the government subsidized—were "unsinkable." Even though they've never come right out and said it, the implications are clear.

No lifeboat drill—how is anybody to know what to do without a drill to teach them? The officers and crew were lax in their duties due to this. And I'm told that many of the crew below decks resented the drills; the unions backed them so there was no enforcement of discipline to report for the drills, thus the drills were not conducted regularly. And when they were, they were done inefficiently. This was not the case just with *Titanic* but with many other ships; notorious was the fact that the resentment was strongest on White Star ships. In regard to *Titanic*, that ship never attempted a drill. I'm told that a perfect time for one would have been on Sunday morning; the captain preferred that church services be conducted instead.

All well and good, but why not both? The drill could be conducted either before or after the service. Or what about the day before? Or the Friday? Once the ship is clearly out to sea, I would think a boat drill—witnessed by the passengers, perhaps with some of the more hearty and adventurous souls taking part for the sheer lark of it—would be the order of the day.

But nothing. And I brook no excuse for the lack of this. And because of this, many passengers drowned who could have survived had the officers and the crew known their duty, known how to perform their duty, and impressed upon *all* the procedures and urgencies and used force, if necessary, to fill those boats to their full capacities.

As *was* their duty!

Mr. Lightoller stated in his testimony that he lowered the boats halfway full—all the officers did—because they didn't believe the boats were strong enough to load fully on the boat deck. His intent was to lower the boats, then have them rowed to open gangway doors and finish filling from there.

But the doors were never opened.

It wasn't until later—too late to do much good—that he learned from Mr. Andrews that the boats had been tested in Belfast with a full load of men and proven to be sturdy.

Back to the *Californian*. Was she the ship that lay dead in the water, her lights glowing frustratingly near as the *Titanic* was foundering? *I* believe she was. Captain Smith saw her. So did Fourth Officer Boxhall; he launched eight white rockets in the vain hope she'd spot them and come to the aid of *Titanic*. He even tried to contact her via Morse lamp.

To no avail.

In interviewing the crew of the *Californian,* I've concluded that she did indeed see the rockets and may have seen the Morse. Her watch informed her captain, but he didn't seem concerned. He adamantly insists that his men did not seem to believe there was anything out of the ordinary; in fact, he states they described the ship as a "tramp steamer." He knew *Titanic* was in the area; he learned that from his wireless officer a short time before. But he remained asleep, content to leave the operations of the ship—and the issue of the "tramp steamer"— to his officers. He never once felt concerned enough on the several times they'd awoken him to put on his coat and shoes and come up onto the bridge to see for himself.

And what *of* the wireless officer? *Titanic* had two, which allowed the office to be manned and operating constantly. *Californian* had one, and he turned his equipment off for the night approximately ten minutes before *Titanic* struck the berg. Nobody thought to wake him and see if he could learn of anything related to the rockets being fired.

All white rockets with starbursts. That's how the officers of the *Californian* described what they saw.

All white rockets with starbursts. That's what Fourth Officer Boxhall was firing to attract the unknown ship's attention.

All white rockets with starbursts. That's what *Titanic*'s survivors described.

Yourself among them.

At the same point in time.

I believe the *Californian* could have come to *Titanic*'s aid. I believe she was near enough to see—and near enough to help. Not more than ten miles away. Far closer than *Carpathia,* which was fifty-eight miles away. Steaming at better than full design speed, and she was *far* from new. Her well-worn engines ultimately steamed through the same ice floes that doomed *Titanic*. She too had only one wireless officer, but he was still awake, waiting for a response to a message sent to another ship. He just happened to catch a signal from *Titanic*, and he thought he would say hello. He became a hero in the process.

If *Carpathia* was silent? Other ships had responded and arrived on the scene shortly after *Carpathia*. The survivors would have been picked up, but there might not have been as many surviving. The people stranded on the overturned collapsible. Those on another that was swamped, and some had already perished on that one. Your own boat, leaking and riding low in the water.

Word would have eventually gone out. *Olympic* had twenty-four-hour wireless operation, she was steaming at full speed toward where *Titanic* foundered, and she would have alerted other ships as they came online.

Mr. Ismay made one very wise decision shortly after *Carpathia* had picked up the survivors. When Captain Haddock of *Olympic* offered to transfer the survivors to her from *Carpathia*, he shuddered and ordered Haddock to remain completely out of sight. He knew the sight of *Olympic*, which so closely resembled her sister, would be as a ghost to the survivors and cause extreme upset and duress. That was what Captain Rostron of *Carpathia* recommended, and Mr. Ismay quickly concurred.

This was an excellent decision on his part.

I must say, Mrs. McLean. You are quite brave to return home on *Titanic*'s sister. I can't say as if I could do such if it were me.

Reckless navigation through dangerous waters. No boat drill. Not enough boats. No set procedure for getting navigational information to the bridge. No control over the disposition of the messages that *do* get through. Bulkheads not high enough to make a compartment truly "watertight." Inadequate lookouts in dangerous conditions. *Carpathia* did not rely solely on the two men in the crow's nest on her foremast; *her* captain stationed men on the forepeak as additional eyes for the ship, and several others were on the bridge as well. If there was a berg, these extra eyes at various locations in the front of the ship would give him better warning. Experts explained to me with their charts exactly how—and I accept those explanations fully— two men alone, high up on the ship, would be disadvantaged where the visible horizon would mask, instead of reveal, a nearby object riding low, directly in the path of the ship. Eyes closer to the water could spot an object above the horizon much more reliably.

Precisely what doomed *Titanic*. The berg was sighted much too late; a reflection from the ship's lights made it visible. By then, it was too close to avoid.

There is no one reason why *Titanic* wrecked, Mrs. McLean. I wish there were. There are several reasons, which together resulted in the collision and sinking. And in the extreme loss of life.

But rest assured. The rules will be changed. Too late to save those 1,500 souls who perished that Monday morning. But not too late to prevent others.

We have learned. And we have more to learn.

My report to the Senate next week will outline that and will be the basis for laws to be enacted to enforce that. For *all* passenger ships sailing to or from American ports and carrying American passengers, for a start:

Lifeboats for all.

Twenty-four hour manned wireless.

The cessation of intercepting and interfering with wireless calls of distress and the resulting false reports.

Wireless communication regarding ship's navigation to take precedence over all other traffic.

Mandatory boat drills.

An ice patrol during the spring and summer months in the North Atlantic shipping lanes, and a change in those lanes if and as necessary to avoid ice drifting from the frozen north.

Better lookout procedures.

Others that we will evaluate and rule upon during the presentation of the report.

And now, Mrs. McLean, it is getting late. I wish to thank you for your offer to us to visit you and take your testimony and your recollections. I am truly sorry for your loss—more deeply sorry than I know how to express. I wish there was something I could personally do for you.

God bless you, Mrs. McLean.

Good evening.

Diary Entry — May 24, 1912

My dear diary, I can't believe I've neglected you all these weeks! I've missed hardly a day since you were begun back when I was a wisp of a child, and here I've gone over a month.

The last entry I made was on April 16 while on the rescue ship. Much has happened since then—but not much good for me.

I just concluded a visit by the American senator William Smith and his personal stenographer. It was the most soul-baring—and the most needed thing—I've done since arriving in New York. It did me good. I feel at peace with my loss now. I can go on.

But I will get into that in due time. First, to catch you up, we docked on the night of April 18. It was raining as the ship pulled into the harbor, and there were thousands of people, both at the wharf and on boats coming out to meet us. The clamor was unbelievable. People were shouting to us, offering money for our stories, and trying to get pictures of us. We had no idea the tumult that we'd be arriving under. I was still on the fantail, at the stern of the ship, rarely going inside to get warm. I'm afraid I must not have been thinking properly. My justification was that my husband was out in the cold; how unfair would it be for me to be inside where it was warm?

That was the state of mind I was in at that time.

Carpathia bypassed her own pier and steamed to the White Star Dock. *Titanic* would have been moored there had she not collided with the iceberg hours shy of four days previous. After *Titanic*'s lifeboats were lowered and rowed away, *Carpathia* tied up at her own dock. There were indignant shouts from the people waiting for *Carpathia* at her own dock and from many of those in the boats around us. By contrast, nary a sound was heard from *Carpathia*'s passengers or from the survivors of *Titanic*.

I must confess I was mildly disgusted at this behavior from those at the pier, but I tried to understand. The persons waiting for *Carpathia* at the Cunard pier were putting unreasonable and unfair stress on us who had just survived a catastrophe they'd not been able to imagine. Those people were not just relatives of *Titanic*'s survivors from whom I could forgive their indignity. Representatives from the press all wanted "exclusive" stories and were willing to pay hundreds of dollars. Their behavior distressed me.

I felt humbled by the passengers of *Carpathia*; my belief in human nature was anchored by their stoicism. Many of *Titanic*'s survivors, while understandably anxious to get off the ship and onto solid land, failed to realize the disruptions to the lives and activities of *Carpathia*'s own passengers—and their generosity. Their trip was canceled, and they were back in New York. They'd probably never have returned to them or be properly compensated for the belongings they so generously "loaned" us to aid and comfort and provide succor in our time of need.

And they *never* complained.

Apples to oranges. But still.

I had money—all the money Ian and I had in the world— but I was not about to ensconce myself in that mob. I left *Titanic* well and warmly dressed. I may have lived in those clothes for four days, but I was still reasonably presentable. I did take time to attend to my personal hygiene. And I stayed dry, seeking shelter from the rain. I was willing to endure cold for my husband. Cold *and* wet? Not this girl!

When I learned that the *Carpathia* passengers would be the first to leave the ship (with apologies and humble gratitude from the master of the vessel for their fortitude and patience), I slipped among them and got through the bustle, hoping I'd be mistaken for one of the ship's *own* passengers. I got away and found sanctuary.

I succeeded.

I was able to wend my way by cab into the heart of Manhattan, which is a principle island and comprises one of the five boroughs of New York City. I found myself deposited at the front steps of the Plaza Hotel, where I've been ever since. I paid for my lodging in advance weekly and ventured out rarely— once to purchase some new clothing, again to send a telegram home to Ireland asking for help in arranging transportation back, and another telegram to Ian's prospective employer (I found Ian's address book in an inner pocket of his greatcoat), informing him of Ian's loss.

On occasion, I would venture down to the dining room or a nearby restaurant just to get some air. I also managed to keep abreast of the news, and I followed the progress of the Senate inquiry religiously. When I learned that there had been ships chartered to go to the site of the sinking to retrieve what bodies they could find, I stayed focused on any information pertaining to the identities and dispositions of them. I learned that many would be brought back to Halifax, Nova Scotia (a seaport in Canada to the north), and I made arrangements to go there in hopes that Ian had been found so I could claim him and bring him home to our family.

He was not among them, and the glimmer of life I felt in me at the prospect of finding him (even if he was dead) faded at the realization that he was lost forever. I returned to the Plaza and sent a telegram to Washington, giving my name and location. I told them I was available should they wish to talk with me. I went on to state that I didn't know what I could add to the information they were already collecting, but if they were interested in *my* story, I was willing to tell it.

I received a telegram from an aide to Senator Smith that he would be in New York on the evening of May 23, and would be interested in interviewing me on the twenty-fourth if I was available and amenable. He was coming to tour *Olympic*, which was at the White Star Dock, on the twenty-fifth. It would be sailing back to England later that day.

I received the telegram on the morning of the twenty-first (ironically the same day my itinerary was confirmed for my return home). Coincidentally, I would be sailing on *Olympic* on her outbound voyage for England on the same day the senator would be on board. I cabled back that I would meet him at his convenience on the chosen date.

That date was today.

We had a very pleasant visit.

We started out with him questioning me as a witness. His questions were quick and thoughtful and pointed. He constantly hopped from subject to subject—though in reasonable order of the events of that night—and occasionally asked the same question more than once. However, it was clear to me that he was ensuring that he obtained as much information as he could. I answered to the best of my knowledge and recollection.

This was before lunch. We had our meal sent up to us and continued when we were finished.

It became a discussion, much different in feeling from the morning session. He asked me to tell him of my voyage—from start to finish. What did we think of the ship? Who did we meet? What did we do? I was asked to tell it in my own way and at my own pace. I started from the beginning and stopped at the moment *Carpathia* arrived. There was nothing more I could say.

I guess I surprised him. I asked him for the story of *Titanic* herself. Her owners. Her builders. Her crew. How was she built? *Why* was she built? What were the owners' expectations?

And why did she sink? Taking so many innocent lives with her.

He told me all he'd learned, but he stopped short of assigning blame. He said that it would be improper to tell me ahead of the rest of the world the full conclusions his board had reached.

Besides, he still had to review and incorporate my story (which his stenographer copied down diligently and I hope faithfully) into the official record as well as the observations he'd get on board *Olympic* and interviews with her master and other crew members set for tomorrow morning.

We concluded our visit and said our good-byes.

I feel as if a load has been lifted from me today. The crushing weight of Ian's loss, which I'd been trying to deny since it happened and unable to convince myself that I'd succeeded, was gone. I'd told my story and paid tribute to my life's love. He'd not be forgotten. He would be honored, albeit in such a small way.

It was the best I could do, and I know Ian would say it was more than enough.

Today has been such a long, trying day. I'm mentally exhausted though in body I'm as wide awake as I've ever been.

I'll certainly miss the American's preference for coffee when I'm back in Ulster Province. Tea just doesn't have the same stimulating effect on one's energy as coffee.

We should import more of it. I know we have it back home, but it's a luxury. Our traditional preference for tea is probably too strong to overcome.

I know! I'll bring some back with me. I know Poppa will love it!

Good-bye for now, my friend.

THE "DISPOSITION" OF THE DEPOSITION

Along with the deposition and the exchange between Mrs. McLean and Senator Smith, Mrs. Altford's granddaughter also provided additional information from within the pages of her grandmother's journal, which sheds some light on why Mrs. McLean's deposition was not included in the volumes of pages of testimony leading to the summation of the inquiry into the sinking of *Titanic*.

The entry was written in the late night hours of May 24, after the two had dined at a restaurant near their hotel, and comprises their discussion of the widow's answers and recollections of the events of April 14 and 15. Afterward, the senator retired to his room to read before sleeping.

His aide ensured the transcript was accurate and in order before she turned in. Her entry clarifies the reason why the testimony was not submitted to the panel for review and what the senator thought should be done with it. Unlike her shorthand notes for the deposition, Mrs. McLean's narrative, and the senator's summary, these ledger entries were written in full words and sentences and meant to be read by others in time. This entry is remarkably detailed and descriptive, which would be expected from a court stenographer whose memory must necessarily be sharp and accurate. The best stenographers had total auditory recall—much in the same sense that other people are described as having a photographic memory—and could describe with astonishing detail what they'd seen. Thus the same is true in this case: there can be no doubt that the words spoken over wine after dinner were written down exactly as spoken.

As with Mrs. Branigan's diary entries from 1903 until 1912, this single excerpt is reproduced verbatim.

SB.

Mrs. Altford's Diary—May 24, 1912

Senator Smith enjoyed a relaxing and informative day with Mrs. Ian McLean (Glynnis) today in her suite at the Park Plaza Hotel in New York City. She is the final witness among the passengers who Senator Smith intended to interview for the inquiry. Tomorrow, we'll be given a tour of the *Olympic* by her master, Captain Haddock. While there, we intend to visit areas of the ship similar to key locales on *Titanic* where startling events, as revealed in the testimonies, took place on the calamitous night. Her wireless officer would also be interviewed since he was involved in relaying the distress signals from *Titanic* to stations on the American and Canadian shores.

Following dinner, the senator—after we'd gone over my notes from today's interview—sat back and lit one of his cigars. "What is your opinion of Mrs. McLean?"

I thought for a minute before answering. I wanted my reply to be accurately conveyed.

"Very charming. The young girl is steady and quite mature for her age. She's held up well through this, and she's not seeking anything but to understand what happened and why."

The senator nodded. "My impression exactly. I like this girl very much. I think she's probably the only *real* person I've met in all this mess. The only *feeling* person. Oh, make no mistake, all the survivors I've talked with have suffered loss that night, and they're dealing with it in their own ways. But I'm amazed and somewhat appalled by some of those ways."

I asked him how so.

"Let me illustrate. Among the first-class passengers, I detect an extreme amount of indignity—maybe that's not the word I'm looking for, but bear with me. They feel more "inconvenienced" than anything else. Their ordered lives have been disrupted. There are more people clamoring for the loss of material goods than the loss of lives. They aren't as concerned about 1,500 people drowning in the cold Atlantic as they are about their jewels or wardrobes or consignments that were on board. And the entitlement attitude that far too many display. They're more concerned that Colonel John Jacob Astor was not allowed to board Boat 4 with his wife, while many in steerage weren't even allowed to the boat deck—or so it might seem. And denials from the crew that there were any locked gates in steerage, keeping the passengers down there, when reams of testimony reveal otherwise.

"And the steerage passengers—standing by idly, for the most part, waiting to be told what to do rather than following their human instincts for survival. Was that bred out of them? Were they passive because they didn't know—*couldn't* know— any better? I pity them, but I can't say as much that I feel sorry for them. Perhaps it's a cultural thing, but I worked my way up from a poor boy in a poor family to where I am today. That's the American way, and I believe that maybe England, Ireland, and Scandinavia don't know any better because their class systems don't allow for ambition. And they'd have to be ambitious to fight for rights they probably don't even know they have under God's great plan."

I listened to him as he went on. This was a speech meant just for me. I knew he'd never say it in the Senate; he'd not be allowed these types of thoughts or feelings, not with this type of clarity at any rate.

"However, there were quite a few who *did* rise above their stations and fight for themselves and their fellows below decks. If they manage not to be deported back to their homelands, I'm sure they'll be vital additions to the citizenry of this country.

"We have the crew. Many of them performed superbly, and I have to commend men like Lieutenant Lightoller and Fifth Officer Lowe—and others besides them—for their gallantry, bravery, and coolness under duress. Lightoller's loyalty to Mr. Ismay is to be commended, but I doubt he'll get any percentage from that. I believe his career is stalled since many feel he's covering up for a villain."

I interrupted him at that point. "Do *you* believe Mr. Ismay is a villain?"

The senator thought for a moment. "No. I don't. But I don't feel he's a man either. By that, I mean while I don't begrudge his survival, I do feel that his actions on board the ship during the voyage helped lead to the disaster. Talks of bringing the ship to New York late Tuesday night rather than on Wednesday morning, which was her scheduled arrival time. Conferring with the chief engineer about bringing *Titanic* to full speed through the North Atlantic in spite of the many berg warnings. He did a lot right while the boats were being loaded, but he has an arrogance about him. I still feel he hasn't told all he knows. His many attempts to get the ship's crew back home as soon as possible *sounds* charitable and probably are. But I wonder what his underlying motives were. Was he trying to deny the committee information that would allow us to determine what happened that night and what might be done to prevent it from happening again *and* take steps to protect lives should it be repeated?

"I don't know. But I know I found him somewhat hostile to the committee by the color of his arrogance at times, and arrogance ought to be the *last* attitude he should be displaying."

I nodded as the steward came by and refreshed our wine. When the steward left, the senator continued. "The bulk of the second-class passengers are just minor-league versions of first class, mostly. Not as self-righteous, but still indignant.

"I'm probably reading motivations and reactions into people that really aren't there, and I'm probably injecting a significant amount of my own personality into theirs. Please accept my acknowledgment that I'm most likely wrong about this evaluation, and I hope that I am."

I nodded. I did understand his sayings and feelings. Having been with Senator Smith his entire tenure in Washington, both House and Senate, I knew his words were often inadequate to express his feelings at times.

"Mrs. McLean presents a conundrum. She's the only person—the only witness—I've sat down and conversed with. Besides the testimony she gave, which was much like the others who met with us earlier, we talked openly. I've not done that with *anybody* in a case before. The young girl is intriguing. Sixteen years old—yet wise and deep as a woman of fifty. A six-day bride and now a grieving widow. But steady and mature, as you said. And with an inner strength that will see her through.

"She's not out for revenge or compensation. She only wants to know what happened that caused the loss. She doesn't want guarantees that it won't happen again; the fact that it happened at all is what cuts her, and she only wants to heal. The talk we had makes the whole episode on the ship seem real to me. Not the testimony—not hers, nor that of anybody else. Those were mere facts. You could read an encyclopedia and get that. No, it's her description of life on the ship—through *her* eyes—that makes it come to life. It makes all those people on board live again. This is the only time I've felt *true* sympathy and felt the pangs of loss and of sorrow. The *only* time."

The senator's voice had softened but retained its force as he spoke of Mrs. McLean. I must confess that I was often near tears as she recalled her few short days on the *Titanic* before cruel fate intervened. The young child left me believing that I, too, was on board the ship with the young newlyweds, that I shared their experiences, their joys, and discoveries as they lived them. And I felt the heartbreak and anguish as they parted at the rail: the sweet, pure young bride looking up at her adoring husband as her boat was lowered into the sea and rowed away, her last sight of him as he watched her boat grow smaller and dimmer as it left the glow of the liner's still bright lights, and how she watched mournfully as the ship stood on end and slipped beneath the surface and into the cold, dark depths of the unforgiving sea.

The senator quietly watched me as I mused over the afternoon's discussion between the senator and Mrs. McLean. I became aware of him studying the many feelings that must have been displayed on my features as I recalled them, and I quickly composed myself.

"I cannot use her deposition," he said simply.

"Excuse me?" I asked.

"I can't use it. I *won't* use it. She said nothing that I haven't already heard before; she's just another voice repeating the same lines, like actors auditioning for a play. But afterward—our conversation. What she spoke of as a passenger on the ship. Her observations, experiences, and feelings of the voyage itself. That is joyous and heartrending. Both at once and together.

"It doesn't belong in a dry document that's going to be read for the next couple of years while Congress decides on preventative steps and enacts legislation to make those steps into maritime law. Then it'll be put into storage, where it will gather dust and eventually crumble *into* dust as just another file that nobody will ever be interested in.

"Her story deserves better than that. It deserves to be read and cherished for the romance and the tragedy that it represents. It deserves to be understood and appreciated by all who hold life dear and realize how fragile our existence really is.

"Someday, when all this furor dies down—as all things of this sort do—we might want to reacquaint ourselves with Mrs. McLean and publish this as a memoir in honor of the husband she so dearly loved and so tragically lost. Not the deposition—that can be thrown away for all its value to the inquiry. There's nothing there that will alter the conclusion. Nothing contradicts or significantly adds to what we've already accumulated. But her *story.* I've heard that some of the survivors have begun to publish their accounts of the sinking. Colonel Gracie's is one I'd particularly like to read once the case is done and I can allow myself to read the papers again. And Miss Dorothy Gibson is quite the opportunist! An actress who survives the sinking goes on to star in a melodrama about it! I've heard it's very popular at the nickelodeons. I should see it myself after next week. It's probably a shame we never spoke with her.

"Mrs. McLean's story is human. It touched me, and not much does anymore—not with these types of emotions. All through the inquiry—the days we took testimony, the days we rested, and every single one of the nights—all I've felt was anger. Anger at the arrogance of the builders. Of the owners. Of the officers and the bridge command who knew what they were heading into and foolishly believed they were safe from harm. The ship meant to be its own lifeboat indeed! Not even God can sink this ship! What fools we mortals be!" The senator sighed and drank down the rest of his glass of wine.

I asked him what he wanted me to do with the testimony and my notes of his interview.

"Put them away where they'll be safe. In a few months—a year or two maybe—we can review them and decide what to do. They don't belong with the statements we've already gathered; as I've said, the testimony is redundant. We can return to the afternoon's conversation when the clamor has died down and things return to normal. Depending on what the other survivors tell the world in *their* memoirs, we can determine if Mrs. McLean's is unique in its honesty and candor. If she's interested, perhaps she'll allow us to give it to the world. It will, of course, be up to her. Don't bother to transcribe your notes at this time. It's a waste of time, and you'll be busy enough tomorrow. I'll let you know when I'm ready to have them.

"In the meantime, and speaking of tomorrow, we should get our sleep and be ready to tour *Olympic* and speak with Captain Haddock. I hope to learn a lot by the close of the day."

We stood up, and the senator paid our bill. We returned to our hotel, went in, and parted at my floor, which was one level below his, with an agreement to meet before seven o'clock to hail a cab to the White Star Docks.

Olympic and her captain would be waiting for us.

Diary Entry — June 10, 1912

I am home with my family in Ulster now. They are so kind to me, and they share my loss as deeply as I. We all loved Ian McLean, each in our own way. He was a devoted son and a dear sweet friend to many of those who he grew up with in our small village. Ian's parents visit often; Ian was their only child until our marriage, and now I am theirs, not in his place but still in their hearts.

And he was my husband. We were married two months and one day ago, by my count. April 9, 1912. The day I became a bride. A child bride, for I'm not yet seventeen. The day my childhood dream became a reality.

But no. *This* is the reality. My husband is gone from me— never more to hold me and to comfort me and to be strong for me and gentle to me. He is gone from me. Never to return. Never to share *our* dreams, *our* hopes.

To live *our* lives as we planned them.

Together.

And start *our* family.

Together.

I am alone now.

Though there is one glimmer of a future light, one spark of our dream.

I have confirmed that his seed within me has taken. A part of him will yet live on, entrusted to my care and devotion.

Still, for now, I *am* alone—in spite of all around me who love me and comfort me and take care of me. My Ian McLean was all and everything to me. All I cared for, all I dreamed about.

All I lived for.

You, my precious diary, are the keeper of my heart's desires. You, alone of all, know my innermost thoughts, hopes, and prayers.

Only you know how alone I feel and how bitterly I cry.

Alas, I must put you down now. For nine long years, you have borne my burden. You have shared my joys and my sorrows. You have been there as I grew—from a carefree child to a somber woman.

From a beaming bride.

To a grieving widow.

My heart, my soul, my love, and my life is resting on the deck of *Titanic*. I imagine him where I last saw him as the lifeboat was lowered to the cold, desolate sea. He was standing on the boat deck, his forearms crossed as he leaned against the railing with his thick hair mussed and a comforting smile on his face. His eyes looking directly into mine, never wavering, never showing the fear he must have felt inside. Staying strong for me, silently telling me by his stance and his expression that all will be well—even as he must have known the truth. He waved but never wavered; he spoke with his smile but never called out. He said all I needed to hear with just his confidence.

He sent me all his strength.

And all his love.

And I carry that with me now and forever.

I may heal someday, and I may dare to love again. My child will need a father. And I will need a provider. But my first love—my *true* love—will always be Ian McLean.

And so I will close you, my dearest friend. And I will preserve you and cherish you. For within your pages rests the story of my youthful happiness. Between your covers keeps the memory of the man I will always adore. My memory will fade as all memories do. I've but one picture of my beloved, and that is our wedding photo. It too must fade, but I know I can always open your pages and recall the happiness that once was ours: my husband's and mine. And I can relive the life we had—from childhood until fate forced us apart.

It would be sacrilege to share your pages with another in my future. I must keep Ian's life pure—as it was when he was on this earth and by my side.

So I close now. And I thank you, my dear diary. You will always be my best friend and confidant.

Keep my love alive for me.

Keep my love safe.

Glynnis

AFTERMATH

The story was never released; after several survivors of *Titanic*'s sinking published their versions of the experience, the senator decided not to allow Mrs. McLean's story to be lost in the crush. Before long, other areas of interest began to consume more and more of the senator's time, including his bid for reelection to a second six-year term in the Senate later that year. He won and served as efficiently as he did his first; his report on the *Titanic*'s sinking provided a significant boost in his qualifications.

On May 7, 1915, a German U-boat attacked and sank the *Lusitania* off the coast of Ireland, resulting in a tremendous loss of civilian life. Here in the States, the loss of nearly two hundred American lives on a British liner—a *civilian* liner—sunk by a German submarine led to rampant anti-German sentiment, and it wasn't long before subsequent events forced President Wilson to abandon the neutral stance America had publicly taken. America's involvement in what was called the "War to End All Wars" began, pushing aside the issue of *Titanic*'s sinking, where it was to remain for decades.

Mrs. Altford, furiously busy throughout the war years, forgot about Mrs. McLean's deposition and story. By the time Senator Smith retired from office in 1919, she'd left the senator's employ to become a wife and mother. Her papers and ledgers were consigned to the attic of her home in Dearborn, Michigan. Upon her death (with her husband) in an automobile accident in 1938, they became the property of her oldest child. He subsequently moved them into a shed at the rear of his own property with the intent of going through them and selling or giving them away. He planned on saving only the heirlooms to pass down to his own children. His two sisters had planned to do the same with their portion of the inheritance.

But due to the outbreak of World War II, he never accomplished this. Wounded in the D-Day Invasion of Normandy shortly before he would have been discharged from the army, he was physically unable and mentally uninterested in sorting through the contents of the back shed.

Upon the death of his wife and himself by 1957, the belongings passed to his only child and her husband. They finally went through the papers in the trunk and ultimately realized what they had in their possession, but they had no idea what to do with them. A friend from Los Angeles visited them in late 1960 and learned of the paper's existence. Unable to read shorthand himself, his guests translated and read excerpts from the papers to him. He was fascinated by what he heard. He told them he had a reporter friend in the newspaper business in Los Angeles. With their permission, he would pass the information on to his friend and give him their phone number to contact them directly.

It was fate that made me that friend and reporter. When I was contacted and made aware of this previously unseen information, I was ecstatic. As an amateur *Titanic* historian, my enthusiasm broke all boundaries. I spoke with my editor and received permission to fly to Dearborn to see this archive for myself. At that point, the owners of the papers had translated the originals from shorthand to transcript, and I spent a long, fascinating evening reading an incredible piece of history. Permission to follow up was granted from my employers at the *Herald-Examiner*, and thus began my long search for Mrs. Glynnis Smith-McLean-Branigan. Sixty-six years later, she was still very much alive and active in the small village southwest of Belfast where she had been born in 1895.

A wonderfully charming lady greeted me when I arrived at the quaint farmhouse she'd lived in all her life. I'd made the initial arrangements to meet with her through her husband; he'd had a difficult time persuading her to tell her story but was finally able to convince her to talk about her experience if only just once. She'd put the tragedy behind her upon her second marriage, and as the years went by, the events of that night fell further and further into the past. She'd preferred them to remain there.

The woman I met seemed to stand taller than her actual height (five foot one), such was her regal and confidant bearing as she stood in the doorway of her home alongside her husband as I strode up the well-worn path. Her crisp blue eyes met mine unwaveringly, and I could see the young teen as described by Mrs. Altford still embodied in the woman she'd become.

She graciously bid me enter, and introductions were passed as I stepped into the small room. It was immediately clear that many happy days of very happy lives had been spent there, though not without adversity, as I would eventually learn.

With me in the cozy little room that afternoon (besides Mrs. Branigan and her husband of forty-eight years) was her youngest son (Clement) and his wife (Erin). They offered me a chair at the dining table, and Mrs. Branigan sat directly across from me. The others took various seats in the room, positioning themselves where they could observe us both. We were together for less than two hours on this first visit, and few words were spoken in that time by anybody other than Mrs. Branigan and me.

I was permitted to take notes, and I was free to summarize my visit and conversation with her in this story. She would allow no pictures, however, so my description of her in the "teaser" article on April 10, 1962, would state quite simply:

> She'd aged very little visibly in the fifty years since *Titanic* sank. She hardly appeared to have suffered any tragedy in life, yet she'd lost her first husband in the sinking and the child she bore him was lost during World War II. Her life had otherwise been hard but not without its reward.

I was allowed to see the picture taken when she and Ian McLean were wed, and I could see the aura of two people deeply in love radiating across the years from that faded photo.

Prior to my visit, I had sent a copy of the deposition and Mrs. Altford's transcription of the conversation she'd had with Senator Smith—for her review before my departure from Los Angeles—so that she would be able to recall her experiences of the night and possibly share additional insights that would support and expand upon the newly discovered documents my paper was to publish. She remembered Mrs. Altford very clearly and with a warmth that could only come from deep fondness for the older woman she'd spent her final day in America with.

It was also hoped she'd share a bit of her life over the course of the years since her arrival back home in Ulster Province. She was more than kind enough to do this.

The widow McLean had known Edward Branigan nearly as long as she'd known Ian; he was her age, and the two were classmates throughout school together. In the summer of 1912, Mr. Branigan had become the young widow's "champion," ensuring that she not lock herself away in misery, if only for the sake of her unborn child. He was never "improper" in his attentions toward her.

Over time, they began to acknowledge feelings stronger than friendship for each other, and in the summer of 1914, they married, giving the young child a father. As before, Frieda Jorgesson was the maid of honor. The bond between the two women would be lifelong; they couldn't have been closer if they were sisters. A year later, Frieda married Mrs. Branigan's brother Peter, making the close friendship familial. I would meet Frieda Smith in the coming days.

Edward Branigan eventually managed to purchase the property adjoining the Smith homestead, and the two properties were combined. They shared all profits, losses, and expenses equally. Mrs. Branigan's three brothers drifted into careers far removed from that of farming, leaving their parents—with the assistance of the Branigan household—to operate the properties. They hired help as needed seasonally—and then year-round as they'd diversified their crops to maintain maximum land use throughout all seasons.

Edward Branigan enlisted in the British army at the start of World War I, fighting the Germans in France (though fortunately not in the trenches where mustard gas was dispersed). He returned home after the Armistice in November 1918 and was greeted with a daughter (Mary) who'd been born a few months earlier, conceived while on leave at Christmas.

The son Glynnis bore Ian had come into the world during the second week of January in 1913. She named him Thomas Ian in honor of both the *Titanic*'s beloved designer (Thomas Andrews) and the father he would never know. Frieda Jorgesson was his godmother. Thomas was the image of his father but had his mother's hair and eyes. He shared his father's love for all things mechanical. When he was just nine, he'd disassembled his stepfather's motor car in the dead of night without mishap (but with a severe spanking in the morning), somehow managing to find the proper tools to do the job and not damaging a single piece of the machine. (Mrs. Branigan's animosity toward the "infernal contraption," as she insistently called the automobile, was lifelong, but she did admire the coachwork on the models made by the Italians and imported throughout Great Britain before World War II.) Thomas was ordered to reassemble the vehicle as punishment, which he did successfully, to everybody's surprise and astonishment.

Clement was born in 1922 (the year Thomas disassembled the car), and the family of five settled into their lives as farmers.

Thomas excelled in his schooling and achieved the goal his natural father would have attained had he lived. He became a mechanical engineer, obtaining his degree and eventually going to work for de Havilland Aircraft Company, assisting in the design of the DH-88 *Comet* and its military successor: the *Mosquito*.

Thomas was killed in 1943 when the Germans bombed one of the de Havilland test centers where he was assisting in the development of the *Spider Crab* jet fighter, then being prototyped, which would see service after the war as the *Vampire*. He was thirty years old and had left a wife but no children.

Mary had married in 1938 and immigrated to America later that same year. As of 1962, the mother of three children with two grandchildren was working as a legal secretary in the Los Angeles suburb of Encino.

Clement and Erin have thus far been unable to have children and are still undecided about adopting.

None of the children knew about their mother having been a survivor of the *Titanic* sinking, and Thomas never knew that Edward was not his father. While Mrs. Branigan was proud to the depths of her being of her marriage to Ian—it was a period of her life that she still holds dear fifty years later—she never felt a need or reason to bring it up. I mentioned that I could see that pride, which caused her to reflect upon her life fifty years earlier.

Upon asking Mrs. Branigan if she would object to speaking about her late first husband, she asked me to sit where I was a moment and await her return. She left the room, taking Clement with her. Upon returning, the two of them were carrying dozens of personal diaries of different sizes, thicknesses, and colors. They were placed on the table, and I was invited to pick one up and view it.

Nine years of the young Glynnis Smith, chronicled daily, from her eighth birthday (the date she received her first diary) to two months after the sinking, when she closed that chapter of her life—forever she thought then. Her need to record was forever silenced by the sinking.

It included the only known recorded impression of the sinking and rescue written by any survivor while still aboard the *Carpathia*. It was meticulously detailed and a rare historical chronicle all by itself!

Mrs. Branigan had charted her growth from a young girl to a bride to a widow. Her growing love for her first husband was within those pages, and her emptiness and despair was there as well. Likewise, the ordinary life of an Irish farm girl was detailed as the foundation in each daily entry (and she rarely missed a day, excepting on the *Carpathia*, where only one entry was made, and then only two entries afterward), and the documents were charming in their innocence.

She could obviously read the longing in my eyes. I knew the worth of what was laid before me, and she knew I knew. No fool, she smiled craftily and gave me the jackpot. Her request was included in the April 10 teaser:

'You may read these, and we can decide together which entries you will be allowed to quote in your article. You cannot photograph them. You can copy the approved entries into your notebook (in truth, I dictated them into a recorder) and reproduce them in your paper, but you are not permitted to change a single word, not even for spelling. I want the flavor of a young girl growing older to remain, with the simplicity and any grammatical errors intact. The girl is a child; please recall and please respect. Also, I want the impressions of a maiden in love to come through in her own words and feelings exactly as they were set down here. I will allow this as a tribute to my beloved first love since these will help clarify the material you already have.

'Those are my terms for allowing you to visit me and to publish the private conversation I had with Senator Smith those many years ago. That private conversation is owned by me, as your lawyers will inform you if you ask them, and I *can* deny you the right to publish them as an invasion of my privacy.

'Publish the approved excerpts of my diaries for my husband's memory. I ask nothing else—not money, not acclaim.

'They never found his body; he lies with *Titanic*. In these journals, however, I've tried to find his *soul*. Perhaps I've succeeded. Perhaps not. It's for your readers to decide and for them alone. But I ask only that they accompany the deposition in the same publication.

'*Then* you have your story.'

And now, on the fiftieth anniversary commemorating the loss of the RMS *Titanic* and the 1,500 souls who went with her, her story is now ours.

CONCLUSION

Samuel Bellingham extended his stay in Ireland for two weeks and painstakingly transcribed the diary entries that saw publication in the April 15 Sunday supplement. And as they worked together, sixty-six-year-old Glynnis Branigan once again became sixteen-year-old Glynnis Smith, a young Irish lass who'd found her love and her future in the strong arms of the handsome, intelligent, and gentle Ian McLean.

For this republication of the story behind the lost deposition, there can be no better way to recall the emotional tragedy of that night than to update for the public what has since occurred to become part of the history behind this bittersweet and courageous story because so much has happened in the fifty years since its release.

On September 1, 1985, an expedition led by Dr. Robert Ballard of the Woods Hole Oceanographic Institute in Massachusetts found and photographed the wreckage of *Titanic*. A year later, they went down to her grave in manned submersibles to extensively survey the site. Their discovery, relayed and accompanied by photographs in *National Geographic* and several publications since, raised more questions than they answered in regard to what caused the ship to sink on that tragic night in 1912. They confirmed that the ship broke into two main sections at the surface, but no sign of the three-hundred-foot-long gash could be found. Photographs and video from the bottom of the Atlantic showed her bow section still appearing regal and sturdy, sitting upright in the ooze. A "bow wave" of silt at her prow gave the illusion of motion; it was as if she were still sailing proudly to some distant shore. Ultrasonic examinations of the hull behind the bow wave of silt revealed what had been hypothesized all along: that the hull plates were bent, rivets popped sporadically along the three-hundred-foot-long gash area, and the opening to the sea was between twelve and thirteen square feet.

This was followed by additional expeditions—some to document, others to salvage. No bodies were discovered outright, but indications of where many came to rest was revealed by matching pairs of footwear, the tanned and treated materials impervious to deep-sea organisms that had already claimed wood, fabric, and other organics as well as the very steel of *Titanic*.

Pictures and videos obtained from these (and other) dives appeared on the market along with books and documentaries derived from them, all relating the story of *Titanic* and her demise and all reexamining the evidence of her fate. Many dives were intended to obtain salvage, and in 1987, one atrociously produced and televised documentary—hosted by the late Telly Savalas (former star of TV's "Kojak")—did more to disgust and infuriate the few remaining survivors and the general public than it did to tell any semblance of a story.

Then in 1997 came the film *Titanic*, incorporating a fictional story of an illicit shipboard romance with the factual story of the voyage, including details of what was learned of the ship's demise based on explorations of the wreck over the previous decade. The film was well and extensively researched and well and extensively received (and in 2012 was rereleased in 3-D) and included footage from several dives by director James Cameron, using special camera sleds of his own design, which allowed footage to be obtained from deeper within the ship than any previous robotic vehicles had obtained in the previous twelve years of exploring the wreckage.

The public's appetite could not be sated. Books, documentaries, and photo albums were snapped up as quickly as they could be published. Conspiracy theories abounded, including one that claimed that *Titanic* and *Olympic* were swapped just before the former's maiden voyage so the ill-fated *Olympic* (victim of several mishaps in her first year of service) could be sunk and claimed on *Titanic's* insurance, implying that it was actually *Olympic* that sank in 1912 while *Titanic* sailed on as her own sister! This was far-fetched and proven false by the few indisputable pieces of forensic evidence obtained through salvage. Each ship had its own identifying numbers on key onboard components. Those viewed on—and in some cases brought up from—the ocean floor positively identified the wreckage as that of *Titanic*.

Olympic meanwhile sailed on for another twenty-three years, including as a meritorious troop transport in World War I, before being retired and scrapped in 1935.

Britannic never saw a paying passenger. Because of World War I, construction was halted shortly after her launch. Eventually she was completed as a hospital ship, her never-installed luxury appointments put in storage until the end of the war, when she would finally be commissioned as a luxury liner, taking her place alongside *Olympic*. But it was not to be. In late 1916, she struck a German mine in the Aegean Sea and sank in four hundred feet of water. She never carried a single civilian passenger.

And what of Glynnis Branigan?

Mrs. Branigan passed away in 1998, just shy of her 103rd birthday, living long enough to see the film *Titanic*. In spite of her panic forty years earlier when she attempted to see *A Night to Remember*, she viewed the newer film in its entirety. She'd remained friends with Sam Bellingham and said, "The primary events are true as I recall them. True enough that I felt I was on the ship again and Ian was by my side. It was time to face it, and I'm glad I saw it."

She died in her sleep six months later. Her husband preceded her by eight years.

Frieda Smith passed away from a stroke in 1965. She outlived her husband Peter by six months. Mrs. Branigan was at her side.

Edward and Glynnis Branigan's children have all passed away. The Branigans are survived by Mary's three children and two children adopted by Clement and Erin—as well as many grandchildren and great-grandchildren.

Sam Bellingham is still alive and remained with the *Los Angeles Herald-Examiner* until it closed in 1989. From there, he became a contributor to various small-town newspapers until he retired in 2003. He lives in Ojai, California, with his wife and two dogs.

And the story of that night?

That story will never pass away.